ZARA DUSK

Vestige

First edition

This book was professionally typeset on Reedsy.
Find out more at reedsy.com

Contents

Scarla

I try to inject sexy into my walk to get past the guards, but my damn ox-hide boots are working against me.

Clomp... hip sway... clomp. It'll have to do.

I need to get out of this cave. The dank air makes it feel like my lungs are lined with mud, and I long for the fresh taste of outside.

Two men are on duty at the cave's mouth, as usual. One tall and well-built, the other short and slight. Thick coats over rough-spun gray pants with swords slung at their hips.

As I approach, their features emerge from the dim, flickering firelight.

I recognize the taller guard. Hair and eyes like coal, and a crooked nose that could be a lump of the stuff painted white.

"Hi, Tone," I say brightly. It's a relief to see a familiar face on duty, and my smile is genuine.

When he sees me, Tone straightens and throws back his shoulders. "Hi, Scarla. I was hoping you'd come by."

This time, I inject extra flirt into my smile to make sure he lets me pass. "I imagine you don't get a lot of visitors." I reach out a hand and touch Tone's arm, feeling the rough material of his coat and his thick arm underneath.

Tone shivers, and I wonder if it's because his body is

responding to me or because he thinks I'm a witch.

Some folks believe I'm a witch.

I'm not.

The second guard is short and young like he just got out of creche. Baby. Dark hair, pasty skin, same as most people around here. But his skin is so pale I wonder if he's ever been outside. I've never seen him before and hope he won't give me any trouble.

After about two seconds, I can see Baby is trying to play the big man. He appraises me openly, his gaze traveling down my fitted pants and back up, lingering on the place where my light blue shirt pulls against my chest. I spent so long dyeing this damn shirt with macerated berries that I'm loathe to upgrade it, but maybe I need to.

"Hi, Goldilocks," Baby says, aiming for cool and missing.

I'm used to being noticed for my hair, but it gets old. I sigh. "My hair isn't blond."

Baby nods, and I can see the idea of a witticism cross his face. "Well, hi there, Copperlocks." He snorts at his own joke and elbows Tone, who shuffles awkwardly and avoids answering.

I hold Baby's gaze. "Not a thing." I blink slowly and watch him wither under my stare. Long experience has taught me that I need to get the upper hand with these guards on their very first shift. After all, I need to be able to come and go as I please. "Well, good chat. I'll see you boys later."

I go into saunter mode and swing my hips—boots or no boots—but Baby blocks my way with his cute little arm. "It's not dawn yet."

There's fire in the new guard, yet. Good on him. I snap my gaze to him, but the worried look on his face softens my tone. "I know, babe. Thanks for your concern, but I'll be fine.

Honestly."

I try to push past, and his thin arm presses into my ribcage but doesn't yield. "I—I can't let you go out, miss. It's still an hour until dawn. You'll freeze to death."

Well, he's changed his tune. He's gone from sexualizing me to calling me miss. Both awful options. But I need to play nice so he'll let me pass. "No, I won't freeze. Pinky promise. Just let me through."

Baby doesn't move an inch, except his pupils, tap dancing in his eyes. "I... Wh—why are you insisting on going out there?"

Good question. Why is everybody else in the Undercity happy to live their lives in the dark when I can't go even a day underground?

I sigh. "Oppositional defiance. Habit of a lifetime, I'm afraid."

The new guy doesn't know how to respond to that, but Tone chuckles. "You got that right, Scarla."

My lips tick upward. "I know, right?" I cock my head toward Baby. "Can you tell him please, Tone?"

I wouldn't say Tone is a friend of mine, exactly, but we've known each other for years, and he's aware of my quirks. He grows a grin. "Scarla here can go out at any time of day or night, Bron. Hot or cold out, she's fine. Honest. We can let her through."

Baby Bron's eyes narrow in skepticism. "Nope. Nobody survives outside except during dusk and dawn." His voice strengthens as he finds firmer ground for his objections. "And nobody goes out while I'm on guard. Orders is orders."

I lean toward Bron and ruffle his hair. "Good boy. I can see you're a man of principles." He's slightly shorter than me, so it's easy to reach his dull, greasy head. His hair is slick, and I

3

resist the temptation to wipe my fingers on my shirt.

My touch takes Bron by surprise, and his arm softens against my ribs. I take the opportunity to push past. "Later, boys."

I shoulder aside the thick, ox-hide hangings that are the final thermal barrier between the Undercity and the outside temperature. Bron's protests are silenced when the curtain swings back into place.

Cold assaults me, frosting my breath and raising bumps on my skin. It won't kill me—that's why people call me a witch—but that doesn't mean I don't feel it.

I exit the cave's mouth and, despite the cold, throw back my arms and raise my face to the stars. Deep, long breaths fill my lungs with sweet, crisp air. I could stand here all night just breathing. Every exhale takes away another layer of grimy funk from my insides.

Once I've had my fill, I trudge through the snow to where a little path winds up the mountain, then I clamber up into the foothills, thanking the Maker for blessing me with long legs. My knee grazes against a boulder, but it doesn't draw blood—these limbs of mine are covered in rhinoceros skin.

Up here, a rock is shaped perfectly for my butt. I dig aside the snow and sit on my throne. Nobody exists in the world except me. This is my favorite place.

I'm on top of the Undercity, I guess, which burrows into the earth beneath me. From here, I can see all of Malanox. I can see across the hovels of Lowtown, over the stone structures of Hightown, clinging to the river's edge, and all the way to Malanox Castle.

The further you get from the Undercity, the richer you are.

The world is blanketed in snow and reflects cold moonlight from every surface. The castle is a dark growth, black against

4

the deep gray sky. Tension creeps along my muscles as I stare at it, imagining the soaring stone walls. Just thinking about the Margrave who lives there makes my hands curl into fists—all that wealth, all that power, and nothing better to do with his time than slice off the heads of townsfolk he doesn't like.

If I ever meet him, I'll punch him in the ear.

As usual, my thoughts turn to my sister, Leesa. This is the only time of day I allow myself to mourn her. A strand of copper hair drifts across my face, and for a moment, I hear Leesa's soft voice in the breeze. I can almost see her toothy smile and her black hair, so much darker than mine, so shiny it's almost blue.

I don't really, of course. She's worms by now, rotting into the soft earth with just frost beetles for company. My heart clenches, turns as cold as the rock beneath my butt, and a tear freezes on my cheek.

Snow covers the ground, but it will be gone before long. The sun is a fierce master, and she will melt that white blanket within minutes of showing her face, evaporating the moisture right out of the ground, ready for tomorrow night's snowfall.

As a hint of gray lightens the sky to the east, I crack away my tear. The time for crying is over.

I push to standing, and my hands come away wet, the snow already turning to slush.

Below me, the hardiest Undercity-siders emerge from the cave and begin to set up the dawn market. They are brown and gray smudges against the red earth, peeking through the white snow. There's so little color in the world—that's why I take the time to grind up blyberries to dye my shirts blue, even if the result is patchy.

5

A trickle of water catches my attention. It's my own personal snowmelt, the moat for my throne. My shoulders relax, and I slurp from the cold rock, filling my dry throat, then catch some drops in my canteen. I'll have to line up at an Undercity catchment or slog the half-mile to the river later, but this fulfills my need for now.

I dab some melted snow over my face and into my armpits, shivering. This is the most privacy I ever get, so I unlace my not-sexy boots, wriggle out of my pants and drape them over my rock to keep them off the wet ground. I dip my fingers into the stream and clean properly between my legs and around my toes. Then I get dressed again.

My feet need to dry before I pull on my boots, so I watch a few minutes longer as the mountain's shadow slides down the castle's towers and the sky turns pink. Soon the road from town brings customers rushing to the market.

Leesa used to love this time of day.

I square my shoulders against the world. Dad says Leesa died from her illness. Everybody thinks that.

Except me.

There was more to her passing than simple poor health. I'm a doctor, for Gods' sake—well, kind of—and I know more about death than most folks in the Undercity. Leesa's death was unnatural, and somebody has to pay.

A faint mossy aroma tinges the air. Time to descend from my throne. Time to put aside mourning and focus on the future.

Time for revenge.

Scarla

Revenge is a dish best served at ground level.

I descend from my throne, taking it easy, feeling for footholds before committing.

I make it down the mountain with zero scratches, so that's a win. I always like to start a day of retribution without injuries.

The problem with avenging my sister's murder is that I have no idea where to start. Just the name Zaden, which she whispered on her death bed.

Hell, I don't even know if that's a name. Maybe it's a town on the other side of Aubia. It could be a village across the desert to the north, or a city over the mountains in the far east. Or it could be a guy in the next sleeping hub.

The dawn market is bustling. Sounds of haggling over coal and mountain-seed bread ride on the warming air. Pride buzzes through me as I watch Lydia, a mom with three kids who shares my sleeping hub, get the better of a Hightown lady wearing a puffy-sleeved dress and with more money than brain cells.

Three copper pieces for a coarse bran muffin? You've got to be kidding me.

Even rich dudes can be dumb.

My sister's voice filters through my mind—it happens less

7

and less the longer she's been gone, so I welcome it. She's right too, but not snarky enough.

Rich dudes are especially dumb.

Dawn is too busy to be my favorite time of the day, but it's the most comfortable, even for me. All too fleeting, though. I take a swig from my canteen. My palms are already sweating in the mounting heat.

I amble around the market. I've got nowhere to be until the burn starts—which won't be long. Already, some Hightown folks are whipping their horses into a trot, and the Lowtown workers wheel their barrows along the city road. The days get hot enough to boil the saliva right out of your mouth, and nobody wants to be caught outside in the full sun.

Somebody jolts my arm roughly, and I whip around. "Watch it."

Sadie. The bitch bumped me deliberately because she hates me—and I'm happy to return the favor. She's a head shorter than me, but she's mean. She reminds me of a giant octopus with those big gooey brown eyes and wild tentacle hair. She wears the same coarse, dull clothing as everybody else.

"Leave it alone, Sadie." Frankly, my mind is turned to avenging my sister's murder, and Sadie might be a hound of hell, but she's not on my list of suspects.

She cocks her hip and her tentacle hair waves in the breeze. "Don't tell me what to do, Scarla. Even a South dog like you should know better."

She's from North Undercity and thinks me being from the other side is a good reason for us to hate each other. I kind of agree.

I growl. "At least a dog has brains. You're just a walking husk filled with chicken shit." The words are out of my mouth before I've properly assessed the situation—three chunky men with scowls circle Sadie protectively.

Oh well, might as well go all in.

"And these three idiots probably fall over when they're trying to take a piss." I wink at the nearest idiot, a tall bloke whose long legs poke out the bottom of his gray pants. "Can't do too many things at once, am I right, Frank?"

Frank moves a hand to his dagger hilt. He's removed his shirt, which is tied around his waist, and is showing a lot of pale flesh. I wait for Sadie to stop him, but she doesn't. The sound of metal scraping out of leather turns my arms to gooseflesh, and the nearest stall owners turn to watch us.

I can't drag my eyes away from the mottled blade. It's only four or five inches long, but it's coated in rust—basically a tetanus stabber. I'll have a lovely selection of ways to die if that thing pierces my flesh.

"Whatsa matter, Scarla? You scared? Better run and find your big sister. Oh, I forgot." Sadie smiles slowly. "Your sister's dead. Gone to hang out with your mom in hell."

The three bodyguards laugh at their boss's wit. Their chuckles fuel my rage.

The world shimmers, and I launch myself at that thin neck holding up Sadie's octopus face. My fingers find the knot inside her throat and press until she gurgles, spit forming in the corner of her mouth. She can't talk now, and that's all I focus on. Maybe I'll never let go so she can't open her Maker-be-damned gob and spit her trash words.

One of Sadie's cronies digs bony fingers into my shoulders and yanks me off her. Petie Mackintosh. He pins me against his sweaty bare chest, pressing my lungs so tight I can barely breathe. Which works out okay because his stench of onion and coal dust is so foul I don't really want to.

It's satisfying watching my nemesis. Sadie's face is as red as the Dead Desert soil. Still, it's a step up from the blue while I was strangling her.

"You bloody bitch." She splutters and spits, all saliva and steam.

I wriggle in Petie's grip until I can breathe enough to choke out some words. "Tell... your thugs... to shower more."

I haven't got the upper hand here, clearly. No moves, no backup, just words.

Usually, that's enough. Fingers crossed today is no different.

Around us, the crowds thin. Produce is bundled away and taken back into the caves for storage in the under-warehouse—close to the surface with easy access to the dawn and dusk markets.

Petie's arms are hot and already slick with sweat. He growls and, at a nod from Sadie, releases me. Sweet relief.

Sadie's smaller pet, Ralph, leers at me. His oily bangs flop over his brow, and his gaze lingers over my breasts, making my skin crawl. "You're too pretty to be alone. I can protect you, flower."

My insides churn, and I don't even try to hide the disgust from my face. "You couldn't protect a mountain lion in a field of lambs."

Ralph squints at me, and I'm pretty sure he doesn't understand the insult. Maybe he's just trying to get those oily strands of hair out of his eyes.

Sadie's voice cuts like steel. "Leave it, Ralph. She's an Undercity skank."

That barb doesn't even prick. The corners of my mouth twitch. "We're from the same place, Sadie."

A look passes between us that whispers of a truce. Deep down, Sadie and I are identical. Same lousy upbringing, same lousy routines, same lousy lives.

"You're a skank, Scarla."

Same lousy insults.

Suddenly I'm too tired to bother with the menace. Beads of sweat form on Sadie's brow; one runs down her cheek like a teardrop. Her wild, wavy hair is wilting like it's giving up the fight. She needs a good nap.

Her three keepers are getting antsy, too, shuffling in the pressing heat. Ralph keeps pushing the hair out of his eyes, and Frank is hopping from foot to foot, eager to get away. Petie's chest sweat could drown a rat.

The sun is well up, and most sensible people are inside by now.

Plus, we all know that if this confrontation goes on long enough, I'll win. They'll have to give in to the blistering sun and scuttle underground for relief, and I'll take victory by default, the same way I always do.

Same as the cold, the heat doesn't affect me like other folks. Sure, I can sweat as grossly as the next girl, but the sun doesn't blister my skin or boil my blood. It's been that way as long as I can remember—everybody else shelters indoors or underground for twenty-three hours a day, but I'm immune.

I once asked my mom why.

"Because you're an angel, Scarla," she joked.

Better than being a witch, I suppose.

Scarla

I'm pretty sure heaven is a blast of cold air after a hot morning.

I'm the last one inside the cave, and the burst of coolness is delicious. Tastier than honeyed wine.

Tone and Bron are still on duty in the cave mouth. Their overcoats are in a pile behind them, and their coarse gray shirts match their pants. It's cool enough that they're outside the first ox-hide hangings, but they'll move inside later.

I wave. "Hiya, mouthguard."

Bron contorts his baby face, clearly torn between rejecting the insult and amazement that I'm still alive.

"We're the Undercity Guard, Scarla," Tone reprimands. His coal-black eyes swallow the light.

I grin. "Just teasing. Seen any ice gangs today?"

The mouthguard exists to prevent desperate gangs of men strapped with ice packs from raiding the Undercity.

Tone straightens his back and looks earnest. "Not yet, Scarla. But you never know. The biggest danger is mountain lions, of course."

I hold back my snort. Nobody's seen a lion in years. My nod is as solemn as I can manage. "Yes, of course."

"So..." Tone shifts his weight and goes for a relaxed look. "What's up, Scarla?"

A smile plays on my mouth. "The sun, Tone."

"Good one." He waves me through. "You working in the underwing today?"

I swan past, then call over my shoulder. I'm already running late for my shift, and that scuffle with Sadie didn't help. "Yep."

He calls after me. "Look after my grandma, will you? Give her a kiss from me."

Here, where the walls are close, our voices echo loudly. I spin around to face Tone. "Your grandma? Who's that?"

"Giselle Perkins."

Fra Perkins is Tone's grandmother?

I swallow my surprise. "Sure. I'll give her an extra pillow."

My feet carry me further into the gloom, and I'm glad the darkness gobbles my features. Fra Perkins won't last much longer, and there's nothing I can do about it, so I do the wussy thing and shut up.

Hey, it's not my job to tell her family she's about to pop her clogs.

So why do I feel guilty?

I push through the first set of heavy ox-hide hangings, and the temperature drops again. Voices echo from the tunnel to my right—some folks must still be sorting goods in the warehouse area.

Otherwise, this part of the city is empty. My footsteps resound on the rocky ground. A hundred feet further along, another hanging of hides marks the entry to the main cavern. It's swinging; somebody else has just been through.

I shoulder charge the heavy curtain, and the world on the other side feels cool but damp. Like the air is moldy.

Despite the sun, I prefer being outside. If I could live out there, the first thing I'd do is get myself a dog. A beetle-

13

chasing, kid-repelling, bed-sharing mutt. The only animals allowed in the Undercity are chickens and goats, and they make shitty pets.

School is in session, and the chanting of children floats across the main cavern. The little ones are learning their letters, and the sing-song chorus informs me that C is for Coal.

On my right, somebody has lit a fire in the old folks' nook, and its flames lick the rock walls. I want to veer over and join in on a game of cards with the oldies—I kick ass at Aces Over Nox—but I stride straight for my destination because I'm already running late.

At least I won't surprise anyone by being on time. Wouldn't want to cause a heart attack.

I glance at South Gate, wondering if Dad is awake. We sleep in one of South Undercity's few night hubs, which means we're supposed to catch zees during the day and tend to the city at night. He's probably already dreaming of watching sunrises with Mom.

Nobody polices it, though. As long as you don't cook or chat during the day, nobody cares if your eyes are closed. Anyway, the upside-down sleep routine suits me just fine, even if I often get out of sync with it. It keeps me from clashing with idiots like Sadie—although it's also hard to catch up with friends.

A bunch of people crowds around the snowmelt catches. There are two out here in the main cavern and extra ones in North Undercity and South Undercity. It looks like a bumper melt overnight—they're letting people fill canteens to take away.

Behind the lower snowmelt catch, I duck down the narrow passageway that slopes down to the underfactory and the underwing. The air is shifting like somebody has just been this way.

"Sorry I'm late," I yell, swinging into the hospital wing.

There's not a lot of proper medicine going on like they practice up in Hightown; no syringes or pills or lotions. We just keep people cool if they're hot, and vice versa.

I have a knack for it. My mom was the same. I used to sleep in a cot in the corner while she applied her hands to feverish bodies and sucked out any illness's heat. Of course, she died when I was young, so I don't remember much about her.

There's no reason for the knack, as far as I can tell. No skill or learning, nothing like that, and I have no idea how I do it. Just the luck of the draw, I guess.

It's also the reason folks ignore my witchiness—because it comes in handy and might just save their lives one day. Theirs, or someone they love.

Fra Wang frowns—but then again, she usually does. She's short and thin with a nasty scowl but a kind heart. The matron is good at her job—bossing her staff around—so she doesn't need to be pleasant. She's kind of a role model of mine.

Fra Wang's gray hair is pulled back into two severe braids that tickle the tops of her shoulders. The only nod to her status is the white apron over her coarse shirt and pants.

She thrusts a damp cloth into my hands. "You wouldn't be you if you were early."

"I'm glad you agree." I cock my hip.

"Well, I agree you're always late."

"Good thing I'm your best doctor."

Fra Wang splutters. "Doctor! That's awful high and mighty of you, missy."

Smiling, I pretend she's paying me a compliment. "Why,

thank you."

Before she can set me straight, I head into the underwing proper. I grab an extra pillow from a shelf and beeline for Fra Perkins. She's in a natural rock nook by herself—a private room, I suppose.

When I round the corner, I stop in my tracks.

A hooded figure is curled over her bed. A man—definitely a man. He's huge. Masculinity pulsates from him in waves. I can practically see the muscles rippling through the layers of his black cloak. The cloak sweeps the floor, and its hood hides the man's face. Firelight glints off the silver scabbard hanging from his waist.

His large hands look soft, but his intent is clear.

"Get away from her," I yell.

He unfurls and stares at me. At his full height, he's taller than any man I've ever seen. Down here in the Undercity, I have to duck my head where most women—and plenty of men—don't. But this dude has a good foot on me.

He's broad, too, surging with strength. Just looking at him, my insides coil and tense, and a tingle rips through my middle.

But I'm drawn to him. I want to run my fingers over his cloak to feel its softness—I've never touched such delicate material.

Or such a hard man.

It takes all my energy to remain rooted to the spot and ignore the urge to approach him. I rip my gaze from his body.

A haze obscures his face; my gaze slips off his features like an ice slick, so I can't identify him. A memory floats past me, too tenuous for me to catch and examine, of seeing this man earlier, on some other day, maybe many times. But before I can grasp the thought, it disappears.

All I can see are his eyes. They glow with murderous intent, big and piercing green. Those eyes skewer me to the spot, seeing right through me, seething with menace. If I stay where I am, those green pits will devour me.

I open my mouth, but I can barely breathe, let alone speak. My nerves are on fire. Every exhale burns.

This monster of a man has me under his power; I can't move, I can't breathe, I certainly can't look away. Some evil prevents me from even making out his face—other than those eyes.

He is shrouded in darkness.

But somehow, I can hear him inside my skull, and he is laughing.

Scarla

The freaky man without a face left after I confronted him.

I try to imagine it was because I scared him—but that seems as likely as me growing wings and flying away. Every time I close my eyes, those awful green eyes flash against my eyelids.

The rest of my shift in the underwing passes slowly. I'm itching to talk to Leo about what happened. He's been my best friend forever, and I rely on him to shake stupid ideas out of my head—which is a service I really need now. Magic and devilry haunt my thoughts, and I could do with having some sense knocked into me.

The matron rouses me from my thoughts. "What are you doing, girl? Pa Lostum is cold. Go and see to him. Quickly now."

Pa Lostum is another old man on the verge of death. This job would be depressing if it wasn't so damn rewarding.

I weave around the grogum stalk mattresses to where he lies, mumbling away to spirits only he can see.

Flickering torchlight from a wall sconce makes his wrinkles dance with every breath he takes. His face is folded upon itself, a large man who lost his flesh and is now just excess lengths of skin over bone. I happen to know that his body is the same beneath the blanket.

"Hello, Pa Lostum. It's Scarla. I've come to warm you up."

I watch to see a reaction, but the wrinkled lips just keep moving to their own incoherent tune.

"Can I lay my hands on you?"

I always like to ask first, but I'm not expecting a sensible answer. Still, seems polite to request consent before throwing myself at the defenseless fellow.

I pull down his thick blanket and lay my palms on his concave chest. Icicles penetrate my hands, and I suck out the coldness as best as I can, feeling the heat pour from my fingers.

Finally, he stops shaking. His ribs rise and fall evenly, but he's only taking small sips of air. At least he's more comfortable now.

I pull the thick blanket back over him and fetch a heated brick to tuck in with him.

My shift's over, thank the Maker. I'm tired enough to sleep through a dust storm. Before I go, I sneak a peek at Fra Perkins, dreading that I'll find her dead.

Don't even look, I tell myself. I don't want to put myself into the position where I have to lie to Tone Perkins—or even worse, tell him the truth. Best to remain ignorant. But that freaky monster man with those green eyes—those terrifying eyes—won't leave my thoughts. So I go.

Fra Perkins is alive. She's flirting with the Grim Reaper, for sure, but she hasn't committed yet.

Her white hair is loose on the pillow, brittle and thin, but her expression is serene. She always struck me as a wise woman, and it seems she is planning to carry that enlightenment to the end.

Happiness surges through me. I weave through the under-wing, smiling. Nobody died today, and I eased some suffering.

A good shift.

"Later, Matron." I slap Fra Wang on the ass as I walk past.

She growls—really loudly for such a tiny lady. "You have no respect for your elders."

I stop and spin around, not about to let that slander go. "You're amazing at your job, Fra. A great healer."

Her frown eases. "Well, thank you."

"And you are particularly skillful at bossing people around."

She hesitates. "I see. That's good to hear. I guess."

I nod seriously. "I respect the hell out of you, Fra." I wink. "And your ass."

Before she can slap me, I duck out into the corridor. It's quiet, as usual, but when I get to the main cavern, it buzzes with activity.

The lower snowmelt catch is busy with folks drinking their fill—it must be almost dusk. I search for Leo among the line of waiting people, looking for that familiar splash of red hair among the dim and the dark.

Between us, I reckon we have all the hair color in the whole Undercity. Pity his red clashes so awfully with my copper.

Anxiety pulses through me; I need to see him. I need to dissect what happened and talk about those piercing green eyes. The eyes that seemed to see right through me, all the way to my soul.

A hand grabs my shoulder, making me jump.

It's Leo. I pull him into a hug. He smells of grain, and my cheek rests against his shoulder like it belongs there. I take a moment to smile into his shirt. The rough fabric holds my face in place.

When did Leo get taller than me? I was always the tall one growing up, and now he's all muscles and height.

He mumbles into my hair, holding me tight. "There's my favorite fighter!"

"Huh?"

"The Sadie strangler."

I detach myself and shuffle my feet. His narrow lips are quirked in a grin, and the smattering of freckles across his nose is jittering. "Oh. You heard about that?"

Leo guffaws. "The way I heard it, you almost choked her to death and took down three of her goons too."

I bark out a laugh. "I wish."

"So what happened?"

"Well... I did strangle her."

"Holy crap!"

"Yeah. And Frank drew a dagger on me."

Leo grabs my shoulders and spins me around, looking for damage.

I shrug out of his grip. "Babe, I would've mentioned it if I was bleeding to death."

"No, you wouldn't. You're stupidly stoic." Redness creeps into Leo's face for some reason. He glances over at the well like he's avoiding my gaze.

I nod solemnly. "Yeah. Like that time I bruised my knee over in North Undercity and only cried for three days."

A grin spreads across his face, erasing that weird awkwardness in his features. "Scarla, you were a kid. We must have been, like, six or seven. I haven't seen you cry since. Except when..."

I thrust my hands into my pockets and speak fast to cut him off. I don't want to talk about Leesa. Or Mom.

"We should do that again. Sneak into North Undercity, sweet talk our way into the sleeping hubs.

21

"Yeah. You remember that old lady who took us under her wing and fed us pancakes?" He laughs. "I still wonder how she made that syrup. It can't have just been blyberries. It was so good."

Reminiscing puts a smile on my face, but this isn't what I need to discuss with him.

"Look, I need to tell you something."

A strange expression flits across Leo's face—like a hopeful lamb that expects milk. I shake my head. I don't want to think about his feelings now—he's been acting strangely for months. Since he got back from his big adventure across the Desert, actually. The elusive city of Desert's Maw changed him, and I worry he wants more from me than I can give him.

He smiles. "First, you need to tell me how you escaped from Sadie and Frank."

"Don't forget Petie and Repulsive Ralph."

He folds his arms and settles in. "I'm listening."

People stream toward the cave mouth, buzzing and stomping. Dusk must be imminent. "No story, I'm afraid. I just waited them out. It got hot, and they went inside. No biggie."

Leo used to think it was awesome that I could go outside at all times of the day and night—now it seems to bother him. I don't know when it happened. It's not like a switch flicked one day, and he stopped talking about my *super skills*. It's unspoken between us, but his manner changes as soon as I say the words.

"Look, I've gotta go." He ticks his head toward the stream of people passing by. "Dusk."

I nod. "Yeah. Are you harvesting grogum?"

"Yep. Same old."

The main cavern is louder now—folks are emptying the

north and south undercities and heading outside for the brief window that they can.

Suddenly I don't want him to leave. "Can you skip this shift?"

Softness enters his gaze, and I wish I could take back my words. He pulls me close into a loose hug, but the muscles in his arms are rock hard with tension. "Do you want me to?"

Shame creeps through me. I'm toying with him. He's my best friend, but he's changing... traveling down a path of emotions that I can't follow.

I pull away and lower my head, trying to shake it off, pretending the moment never happened. "Oh no, it's okay, go for it. I just wanted to chat about something."

He stiffens and slaps a false smile on his face. "Good. Because they need me out there. It's a big harvest night."

"Great."

I want to scream in frustration. This isn't going at all like I planned—I need to talk to him about that creepy man in the Undercity, but our conversation keeps slipping out of control.

What I really need is to have my friend back.

Leo turns and walks off, raising an arm in farewell, then slips into the river of people.

Scarla

Well, I'm a bitch.

Guilt swarms through me at how I treated Leo, mixing freely with the freaked-outness that lingers from my encounter with that monster lurking around Fra Perkins.

At least the cavern quietens down as the stragglers leave.

There's nothing calm about it, though. At least not for me. The more I think about Leo and that cloaked monster, the more fraught I become. My nerves won't settle. I could go outside for a walk—maybe watch the harvest come in for an hour or so before getting the place to myself.

But I'm tired. Dead tired. More fatigued than Perkins or Lostum or any old-bones person ever was. I could sleep for years.

I lug my heavy limbs through South Gate and along the winding corridors to my sleeping hub. Mine is one of the closest to the gate, so I don't have to travel far. The torch flickering in the wall bracket casts jumping shadows across the round walls, and the air smells even danker in here.

My sleeping hub holds forty or fifty families, all cloistered close around the central bonfire. Since it's a night hub, they've all just awoken. Bustle, hustle, fuss. Not the best place to nap.

I'm so out of sync with this hub—but it works for Dad, and

he's got nobody else, so I stick with him.

It's not like I've got anyone else anyway.

Dad's already gone for the night. I settle into the corner, shifting on the mattress until I can't feel any stalks poking through. The blanket's up around my chin, but it's still cold.

The cold isn't the problem, though; it's the noisy, bustling families. I toss and turn, then give up. I'm too tired to sleep through this crap.

Anger creases my face into a frown, which I know isn't fair. I scowl at baby Annie since she won't be able to tattle on me. She just stares back at me with large, blinking eyes. Stomping, I retreat back into the blessed dark of the corridor.

There's only one other place I can think of to sleep.

Leo's hub.

It's a few rows south of mine, deeper into the labyrinth of the Undercity, but I've traveled the route a million times and could do it in a handstand with my eyes closed. There are patches of the corridor without wall lamps, which is fine. I know this place.

With every step, I go more slowly. Guilt gnaws at me. What will Leo think when he climbs into bed, finding me already in it?

Still, I don't exactly have a choice.

I need to make some more friends.

I sneak into his hub furtively, although I'm recognized and welcome here. Parents murmur to their children, telling stories of fairies and angels and princesses. I lay down my head and tune in to a tale about a warrior prince who married an angel and bore children with powerful skills, then I drift gratefully off to sleep.

* * *

When Leo's warm body slides onto the mattress beside me, I stir awake. He kisses my cheek, his breath hot against my skin, and mumbles, "Goodnight."

"Hey," I say sleepily. "How was the harvest?"

"Good. Go to sleep."

"I am asleep."

"Then stop talking."

Warmth radiates from him, and I feel cozy and happy. "I hope you don't mind me sleeping here?"

He rests a hand on my back, warm and comforting. "Course not."

Drowsily, I listen to him slipping out of his trousers and shirt. He pulls on a fresh shirt, probably because I'm sharing his bed. Usually, he sleeps naked.

The rhythm of his movements feels comfortable, ordinary, and our relationship feels normal again. Contentment suffuses my body and loosens my tongue. "I saw a strange man at the underwing today."

"Oh?"

I listen for any strain in his voice at the mention of another man but detect none. "He was looking at Fra Perkins."

"He was?" Leo's voice tightens in interest—or maybe he's just being polite. "Who was it? Is she all right?"

Somebody on the next mattress rolls over, and I realize we're talking too loudly. I turn to face Leo. He rests on an elbow, looking at me intently. In the darkness, I can't make out his red hair—he is shades of gray and a slash of a mouth, but his familiar grainy scent is comforting.

"He was leaning over her, but I don't think he did anything.

26

He was just watching her. It was really creepy."

"Huh." He's whispering, and it's dark, so I can't be sure—but he seems intrigued. "Fra Perkins, did you say?"

"Yep."

Those green eyes flash into my mind, and my pulse spikes. Maybe I'm coming down with a fever—or perhaps it's fear.

On instinct, I reach out and touch Leo's face. I want to check he's really there. His skin is hard and warm, and his touch calms me. My hand brushes his lips, and his breath catches.

I pull away. I want to tell him about the green eyes and the face that my gaze kept slipping off, and the evil laughing inside my skull that was probably my imagination.

But I've ruined it again—by touching his face, his lips, his heart, and making him squirm.

"Go to sleep, Scarla." He puts his head on the pillow, just inches from mine, but rolls away, leaving me alone in his bed.

* * *

My internal alarm clock wakes me before dawn. Leesa's friend Raylee, who lives topside, once told me that the lightening sky wakens folks in Lowtown. Down here, we rely on our bodies.

Other people are up too, of course. This is a day hub, so everybody is up and at it before dawn. Parents help their kids dress for school, finding shorts and tying shoelaces. The Bailey's baby has clearly 'performed' because a whiff of dirty diaper wafts by. I didn't hear it if it cried in the night, so I'm grateful for that.

Leo is still asleep—his face is sweet and vulnerable like this. His mouth is relaxed and slightly open, and his tongue floats with every exhale. Those freckles over his nose are super cute.

27

He'd hate me thinking that he reminds me of a cute kid, so I'll keep that notion to myself.

I don't want to disturb him, so I'll sneak away and have breakfast in the nearest kitchen hub. I wriggle into my pants and pull my long shirt on over my bra. Limbs and bare backs litter the space—we're used to nudity around here. We keep our private parts covered and our eyes down, but there's no escaping a little bit of skin.

I pick up my boots, and something tugs my hem.

"Morning, strangler."

Man, I hope that nickname doesn't stick. "Heya."

He squints at me. "Where are you sneaking off to?"

I snort. "Hardly sneaking. I just didn't want to disturb you. It's an act of extreme kindness, in fact. You can call me Saint Scarla."

Leo rises to his elbows. "Saint Strangler. I like it."

My eyes roll of their own accord.

A smirk crosses Leo's face. He runs a hand through his red hair. "I can see you hate the Strangler moniker."

"Yes."

"So it stays." He winks at me, and I groan. As loud as I can. A kid from the closest family looks at me like I'm his entertainment for the day. I scowl at him, and he snaps his head away.

Leo gets up, and I look away while he pulls on his pants. "I'm starving. Let's go eat."

I grin. "It's like you're reading my mind."

The nearest kitchen hub is inside a small cavern with two entrances and a tiny snowmelt catch in the center, bringing a whiff of freshness to the air. It's early, so the water is still frozen. Snow falls in from a tiny crack that reaches all the way from the surface and pools into a stone bucket.

When we reach the kitchen, I freeze. Somebody is already here—a woman, dark hair, dark eyes, familiar, but I can't quite place her name. Irritation itches my skin. The whole reason I come here is to avoid the crowds in the main cavern.

I step into the hub and address the woman at the stove. "Are you going to be long? We'd like the hub to ourselves."

I'm just asking a simple question, but the woman gets pissed off, her shoulders up around her ears and an angry scowl on her face. "How dare y—"

Leo cuts her off before she can develop steam. "Sorry, Penny. Scarla is exhausted from a long stint in the underwing. She gets a bit too direct when she's tired. You know what it's like. Hey, didn't Scarla look after your aunt there last year? The Sighing Sickness, wasn't it?"

The lady—Penny, I guess—shifts her attention from me to Leo, and her face softens as he talks. "We'd be delighted if you'd join us for breakfast, Penny. I'll even cook."

"Leo, I—"

He cuts me off, which isn't cool, but Penny seems to be putty in his hands.

She smiles at him. "I'm just finishing up, actually, Leo. It's all yours."

Leo continues charming the woman, and I set about lighting a fire to melt some of the snow. Finally, she leaves us alone.

"She's a bit old for you, don't you think?"

"Common courtesy does wonders. You should try it some-time." Leo looks around the available ingredients, twisting his lips. "Should we go out to the main cavern for a proper meal? There's not much here."

"You fancy some chef-cooked eggs?" Trained cooks serve

meals out in the main cavern, but it's too busy for my taste.

"Yep."

I've already set the wood for the fire, and I like the solitude here. This kitchen hub is so tiny that most people give it a wide berth.

"But you just got rid of that lady. Let's stay here. I'll make you porridge."

Leo rubs his belly. "Mmm, heated bran mush, my favorite."

I whack him in the chest—he deserves it for teasing. "Just siddown and shut up."

"Yes, boss."

I collect the supplies from the shelving and add snow. "I went to see Raylee a couple of days ago."

Raylee was Leesa's best friend, and I'm sure there must be some useful information lodged in her brain if only she'd try harder to find it. I visit her often—too often, really. At least once a week. Just to find out if she's remembered anything else about Leesa's death, anything my sister might have mentioned that could be important.

Leo looks up sharply. "Learn anything new?"

"No." I stir the porridge, waiting for the grains to soften into something edible.

"You know Leesa was sick." Leo speaks like he's gentling a madwoman. Raylee is sick of my visits, and Leo knows it. He scrapes out a stool and sits down.

"Yeah, but she only got sick after she went to Hightown. I'm sure it was somebody she saw up there that made her sick." Leo sighs, and my shackles raise in response. "Out of everybody, I'd expect you to believe me."

"I do... I want to. I just... She was sick. I think you need to accept that and move on."

Flecks of porridge leap out of the pot because I'm stirring too fast. "She got sick after she went to see somebody called Zaden."

"Yeah. Okay. I know."

"And Petie mentioned a strange bloke visiting her in the underwing before she...."

"Before she died. Yeah. But you know Petie. He's an idiot and a liar. Sadie probably put him up to it to annoy you."

I throw down the wooden spoon. "The strange man visited her, and she died. He obviously killed her."

Leo's eyes gaze into mine, pleading. He clearly thinks I'm insane.

"Let it go, Scar."

But I can't. I can't let it go. A stranger visited my sister at the moment of her death.

I just wonder if he had piercing green eyes.

Scarla

Elegance isn't my strong suit.

I slop porridge into two bowls with a big spoon and pull out a stool beside Leo. It's my day off, so I'm at leisure to sit and chat over breakfast.

Leo demands a blow-by-blow description of my encounter with Sadie yesterday, so, of course, I oblige. I make sure to sharpen the dagger and speed up my own movements in the retelling. A slight exaggeration never hurt anyone.

We both tactfully avoid discussing the fight's ending—the part where they went inside and I stayed out in the broiling sun. It's that unspoken agreement between us not to speak of my skills.

When did we get so mature?

As usual, our conversation turns to his grand adventure across the desert to the northern towns and cities. Desert's Maw is the city just over the desert, but the terrain between here and there makes it almost impossible to reach. Very few people ever make it.

"How did you even get across the desert? Where did you rest during the day?"

As always, he doesn't give me a straight answer. "I've told you a million times."

"No, you haven't. You just say you took a ground fox and found hidey holes to sleep in." I take the last spoonful of creamy mush, rolling the oats around my mouth. The grainy porridge smells like Leo.

"Exactly!" Leo takes my empty bowl and wipes the smears of porridge off with sand.

I wipe my mouth with my hand. "Leo Billson Farmer. Stop talking in riddles and tell me where you slept. Where did you stay the very first day after you left here? I watched you walk north at dawn and disappear into the shimmering heat. I thought I'd never see you again."

Leo puts down the bowls and pulls me into a hug. I'm still perched on my stool, so my face squishes against his chest. My lips shove right into his rough gray shirt.

"Shh, I obviously came back, right?"

He knows me better than I know myself—and he's circumventing the volcano before it even erupts.

It works, too. I chuckle into his shirt, enjoying the feel of his arms around me. "I guess so." I pull back and look at his face. "But you're way more annoying now."

He snorts a laugh and picks up the bowls again, wiping the sand away with a rag. "Maybe I shouldn't have returned."

I smile, but then I detect a serious note in his tone and on his face. "What? No. I missed you so much while you were away."

The bowls clatter on the shelf as Leo returns them, knocking down a mug. Neither of us moves to right it.

I'm concerned that I've said the wrong thing. I worry about that all the time since he came back from Desert's Maw—it never used to be like that.

Finally, he looks up and smiles. "That's because you don't

33

have any other friends."

I whack him in the chest. "I don't need friends. I'm a lone wolf."

"Just be careful you don't end up lonely."

The words sit in the air like dust motes. Neither of us makes an effort to wipe them away. I'm glad nobody else is here to overhear us.

I bite my lip. "Cool chat." I head for the doorway with Leo on my heels, but I hold out my hand to stop him.

"Shh!"

"Wha—"

"Shh! I heard something." I'm whispering now, and my mood must be contagious because Leo stays quiet for once.

Footsteps approach along the corridor. That in itself isn't unusual—this is a small hub, but it's not deep in the labyrinth—but something else has my hair standing on end. I swear I heard that name.

It's a woman's voice that I don't recognize. High-pitched and nasal; makes me want to strangle her. That kind of reaction to people may be a factor in why I don't make friends easily.

"The password is Zaden," the woman says to her friend.

Leo tenses beside me. He heard it too.

Another woman giggles. "That's so cool. And where's it at?"

"In the North Undercity pleasure hub."

Leo takes a sharp breath. He and I used to joke about the pleasure hubs when we were kids, but when we became teenagers, it became awkward, and we started pretending they didn't exist. Now we're in our twenties and still acting like teens, I guess.

"Today?"

The nasal woman says, "Yep. Two hours before dusk."

The voices recede along the corridor, discussing how they'll find it and how they'll get in. Leo relaxes beside me, and I grab his shirt. "Zaden!"

"Yeah, I heard." He looks mildly terrified of my reaction.

"They said 'Zaden'!"

"Yeah, I know. I'm right here."

I release his shirt and cross the kitchen hub, thinking hard. Then I travel back, pacing a groove into the floor. "Two hours before dusk in the pleasure hub."

"Eww." He twists his mouth.

"Come on, it can't be that bad! It might even be fun."

His eyes boggle out of his head. "You can't mean you're planning on going?"

Of course I am.

I frown at him like he's an idiot. Which he is.

He frowns back. "Trust me. You won't like it."

Fire rises in me at those words. "You don't know the first thing about what I like."

"Scarla... it's an erotic den." He slants his head.

I resume pacing. "I know what it is. And I'm telling you I might like it."

An answering heat lights up his eyes. "You...?"

My arms fold themselves across my chest. "I'm going, whether you like it or not."

"Well, for the record, I don't."

"Fine."

"Fine."

Leo and I sure know how to bicker. Sometimes I worry that we never left the teenage stage of conflict resolution—state

35

your case, put the other person down, state your case again but louder this time.

I can't be bothered setting things right. Fire embers explode in my belly, and my legs won't stay still.

Tonight, I'm going to find out about Zaden.

* * *

Pleasure hub, here I come.

I check the sun clock five times over the next few hours. Finally, I figure it's time to put my plan into action.

I mean, I don't actually have a plan, but it's time I got one.

I'll be fine. I've sneaked into North Undercity a bunch of times.

But not in the last fifteen years.

Still, how hard can it be?

I fill a handful of canteens with water from the upper snowmelt catch in the main cavern, keeping half an eye on North Gate. There's a guard—just like we have on South Gate—but he doesn't seem to be doing much. People walk past with a smile or a nod, or they just ignore him altogether.

I can do that. I've been ignoring people all my life.

I drape the canteens ostentatiously around me so the guard can't miss them—I'll look like I'm fetching water for some-body. Time for action. My best stride carries me to the gate. Now isn't the time for my fake-sexy walk.

I wave like he's my best buddy and shout, "Hey, babe!"

I've definitely overbaked the cake. But somehow, through a miracle of the pleasure Gods, the guard lets me through. I jangle through North Undercity, weighed down with damn heavy water. Stupid—I didn't need to fill them; the guard wasn't about to check their level.

These winding tunnels look identical to the ones in my city, but they criss-cross in the wrong places and bend at unlikely spots, and ramps lead to upper levels where I'm expecting a descent. I could get lost here within the blink of an eye, I reckon. Even worse, the pleasure hubs will be deep in the city, well away from the family sleeping hubs.

From my forays here as a kid, I know the basic layout is the same as ours. Family hubs, kitchens, dumps, and the occasional recreation hub.

As I walk deeper into the city, fear throbs into my body, step by sneaky step. It would be awkward as hell, but I kinda wish Leo had come with me. I might be walking in the wrong direction and get hopelessly lost, and at least if he were here, we'd be lost together.

I can't handle it anymore—I need to ask for directions. An old lady wanders around the next junction carrying a beige woven bag with a stick of bread poking out. I can just imagine our conversation.

Excuse me, Fra, can you tell me the way to the pleasure hub?
Pardon, dear?
The palace of erotica? The rooms of sin?

That's a hard pass—I'll wait for someone else. With every step, my tension mounts. Minutes tick by, and I could be headed in the wrong direction. This is the only chance I've ever had of finding out about this Zaden person, and I might be about to blow it. My shoulders creep up around my ears, and my fingernails press moons into my palms.

At the next junction, I almost smack into a man walking the cross path. He's broader than me but shorter, and I nearly gave him a good shoulder to the face.

"Hey!"

"Sorry!" My lips are already moving, so I might as well go for it. "Do you know where the pleasure hub is?"

A smirk creeps across the man's face. His dark gray eyes turn all knowledgeable and sneery. He's about my age, maybe slightly younger, so I shouldn't be too embarrassed. I mean, everyone has sex, right? Even I have rumbled with a couple of boys in the past.

He looks me up and down slowly, soaking in my body with his gaze.

My arms fold across my chest. "Look, if you don't know, I'll just keep going."

I move on, but he grabs my arms. "Don't be like that, berry. I know where it is. Follow me."

Suddenly I don't want to. This whole endeavor feels seedy as hell, and I didn't like the look in this bloke's eyes.

"No, actually, I...." I pull away from his grip.

He looks at me for a second, then shrugs. "Suit yourself."

I watch him walk off for all of two seconds before I sprint after him. "Changed my mind. Take me."

He keeps walking but nods his head. He glances at my clothes and says. "You can't wear that."

Scarla

"Like hell I can't!"

If this dude expects me to put on a sexy outfit to enter the pleasure hub, he's got another thing coming. How dare he tell me I can't wear my regular clothes.

An army of words forms on the tip of my tongue, but he cuts it dead. "Suit yourself."

This guy doesn't care if I join him or not. He's not trying to fool me into taking my clothes off—he's simply passing on information.

I trot a few steps to catch up with him.

"So, what do people wear to these places?"

He looks me over, his gray eyes assessing, then shrugs. "Not that."

"Yeah, I get that much. So..." My cheeks explode in flames. I haven't even set foot in the pleasure hub, and I'm already embarrassed right down to my toenails. "Where can I get a more appropriate... outfit?"

The guy snorts, clearly holding in a laugh.

My discomfort teeters back toward anger, and my fists coil again. But I can't take it out on him—he's helping me out, for heaven's sake.

"They have a wardrobe. You can choose something from

there."

Our footsteps echo off the tunnel walls. Lamps are few and far between down here, and the air is musty. Still, I'm not afraid. Crime is almost unheard of in the undercities—it's outside in the light of day that you've gotta be careful.

Still, I'm starting to wonder if this guy is yanking my chain. Surely nothing can be this deep except unexplored passages and rockfalls.

Finally, a drumbeat throbs in the distance. It crescendos as we approach, and other instruments join in—it sounds like an eight-stringed guitar and a flute. The music is slow and dangerous, like a devil flirting with my soul.

A guy and a girl with matching smarmy smiles watch us approach. He has a buzz cut so short I could use it as a sponge. Maybe his chunky legs would make good tea towels. The girl is almost as muscled—her tank top exposes corded arms that could punch right through a Lowtown hut.

My fearless leader runs a light hand down my cheek, making me shiver. His gray gaze undresses me, lingering on my breasts. "Maybe I'll see you in there, virgin."

"I'm not a virgin!" My outburst makes all three of them smile. Clearly, I'm not winning any cool points.

My "friend" passes by the door bitches, slapping the bloke on the ass as he goes. I move to follow him, but the girl bars my way with a muscled arm.

"No way, virgin."

A spluttering noise erupts from me. "I'm not a bloody v...." That is so not the point. I pull myself together. "Why not?"

"You're not invited."

"I am!"

Best to lie, I reckon. I rustle up so much indignation that I almost believe myself.

A couple of women rock up behind me. Long coats cover their bodies, so I can't get a preview of what to expect inside, clothing-wise. One of the ladies has red lipstick so bright it could attract flies in a snowstorm. She smiles coquettishly. "Hi, Georgie. Heya, Boon."

The ladies are waved through. They push past ox-hide hangings and into the hub proper, leaving breadcrumbs of loud music as the skins swing back into place.

Fine. I'll copy them.

I thrust out my chest and cock my hip, feeling thoroughly ridiculous. "Hi, Georgie. Hi Boon." Nope, nothing but blank stares. I focus on the woman. "Look, Georgie, is it? Some people told me about tonight, said I should check it out. They said I'd really *enjoy* myself if you know what I mean?"

I toss a wink at the male door bitch—Boon, I guess—and he smiles back, which is encouraging.

But Georgie isn't having a bar of it.

"You don't know the password."

I try for an annoyed look. "The password is Zaden."

Georgie lowers her arm, and Boon takes over the interrogation.

"First time here?"

"Well... yes."

He ticks his head. "Over there. You gotta wear something else."

"I know." I smile charmingly, hoping it doesn't come across as constipated.

A small rock chamber off to the side has a small selection of outfits I can choose from. None of them are exactly modest; if I sewed them all together, I could make a decent hat.

I take one off a shelf. A deep red bra attached to a teeny red skirt by straps and buckles.

Pass.

The next is a tight black minidress with a cut-out right above the chest.

Pass.

My final option seems to be a bright yellow mask with long tassels hanging off that would form a very transparent curtain from neck to knee.

Hard pass.

Instead, I unbutton my shirt halfway and roll up the hems of my trousers. I poke my head out, hoping to sneak through, but Georgie and Boon are watching. Boon laughs, and Georgie frowns and points back into the changeroom.

Fine. I always wanted to wear a stupid black minidress with boob exposure.

Hoo-bloody-ray.

I shuffle out like a hunchback. Boon pulls my shoulders back and whispers, "You gotta look the part, sweetie."

I guess he's giving advice, but it feels like criticism.

Still, he's right.

I straighten up and push aside the heavy curtain. It's not what I expect. The music is loud enough to break bones, and the skin display is endless, but there's no orgy.

People lounge around a central platform, which is elevated like a stage. On the lower level, tables and soft benches are mostly occupied by near-naked people. That yellow mask outfit wouldn't be out of place.

Will there be a performance?

In an attempt to look like I belong, I move away from the entrance. A table up back serves stewed wine, which is precisely what I need right now. I weave through the crowd, accidentally touching four or five bodies as I make my way through.

The hole in my dress exposes the top of my breasts, and I'm acutely aware of the stares I'm receiving.

Frankly, I'm giving a few stares too.

One woman with small breasts has nipple rings, which seem to be the only things holding up her orange apron-like dress. At least it wouldn't weigh much because it only reaches below her butt and is nearly transparent.

Where did she find that shimmering material?

"Hi, sexy," a woman purrs in my ear, and I feel a soft hand on the small of my back. This one wears tiny red shorts and a matching red bra, and I have no idea how she poured her curves into that outfit. Despite myself, there's heat pooling in my panties, and I'm considering the woman in red.

But I'm not that way inclined. I think.

In any case, I'm here for answers. I keep my momentum going, and I make it to the bar. It's just a trestle table covered with a softly woven purple cloth and a serving man wearing a wicked smile.

He's not wearing much else—just tiny, form-fitting shorts. Honestly, they must run classes on how to get into these outfits.

The barman's chest is sculpted to perfection, and I could lick berry wine off those arms for days. I shake my head to focus.

"Who's Zaden?" I yell at the bartender. He doesn't look impressed by my seductive words.

"Is that supposed to be dirty talk?"

"Er... no." I decide to change tack. "Can I have a drink?"

Adonis slides a mug across the bench. I had no idea the community pool of resources included providing alcohol to pleasure hubs.

"Is this from the community fund?" I gesture at my mug.

The bartender leans on the table and winks. Sexy as fuck, but not very informative.

I don't think I'm nailing this seductive chat thing.

I gulp my wine fast, surveying the room for clues. But my gaze is stuck on that lady in red, who is running her fingers down another woman's arm, this one wearing a white catsuit that just exposes her breasts.

"Another wine, please, Adonis."

He licks his lips, and I try to keep my eyes off his perfect pecs. Not that he minds my stare.

I drown myself in the second glass. The room is less intimidating the more I drink. And it makes more sense, too.

Why shouldn't mature adults take their pleasure as they like? As long as everybody consents—and the enthusiasm here is undeniable—then there's no problem.

I take another sip, barely tasting the berry notes.

When I turn back to the barman, he's staring at me. He leans in and beckons me close. "You wanted to know about Zaden?"

"Yes." The heat in my skin turns to ice. "Who is he?"

The guy nods toward the stage. "Take a look."

I spin around, expecting to lay eyes on the man who killed my sister. But I just see a couple standing stock still on the raised platform. The woman wears a small purple corset that showcases her full breasts and a tiny triangle of purple at the top of her shapely legs. She is barefoot, her feet slightly parted, staring down the crowd like a dare.

I travel the curve of her waist and breasts with my gaze and imagine myself in her place, bared and vulnerable before a roomful of people. I take a deep breath, and my tight dress presses against my breasts, tantalizing my nipples.

The man on stage wears tight purple shorts that cling to an impressive erection, but he is otherwise clad only in oiled muscles. Corded legs are planted apart, drawing the eye upward to his straining cock and sculpted chest. I imagine myself running a flat palm across his belly and up his arm to his shoulder, feeling the firm muscles under his oiled skin.

A warm breeze brushes the exposed skin at the top of my breasts and my thighs, and my breathing comes faster. This is starting to feel more like a pleasure hub, and I'm starting to think I like it.

A second man, wearing a full button-up shirt and trousers, emerges from behind a curtain to my right. He is way over-dressed. Georgie and Boon ought to have a word with him.

But the overdressed man has something remarkable—he carries a black feather, as dark as sin.

The crowd swivels and gasps.

I feel it too—that feather beckons me, pulling my nipples into points and clenching my core. My response is beyond my control. The tight, black dress chafes against my skin, and I suddenly wish I were wearing the yellow tasseled mask. Or nothing at all.

Warmth floods my core, and my body bends toward the feather.

The well-dressed man carries the feather lightly, but I feel its weight right down to my soul. My gaze travels its path, unable to look elsewhere, as it weaves through the room of skin and musk to the stage.

The fully-dressed man climbs the steps to the stage, with

every lustful eye in the room on him. He runs the plume lightly along the woman's arm on stage, from fingertips to shoulder. She trembles, and her breasts swell and jiggle. A collective sigh runs around the onlookers. I want to be the woman on stage, with all the eyes on my body. I want to feel the feather's touch against my soft skin. I need to.

Next, the feather brushes across the man's bare chest, circling his nipples. He quivers and groans, jerking like he's in pain. He looks to be on the verge of falling over—perhaps into a chasm he'll never emerge from—but he stumbles and keeps his feet. The crowd moans. Wetness forms between my legs. I would give away my precious ox-hide boots for the chance to feel that feather on my flesh.

The barman leans over the desk and speaks into my ear. His voice is sexy as hell, and I want to leap over the table and press myself against him and inhale his words. My body is alive with need. I skirt the table to be nearer to him, eyes glued to the stage, my skin hot with desire to be pressed, touched, ravaged.

Until I register what he said. "Zaden."

I tear my eyes from the scene on the stage. "What?"

"It's Zaden's feather. Plucked from the angel himself."

An angel? What the fuck?

I gape my mouth like a fish. "Bu... But..."

The barman's voice is breathy. "They say if you fuck an angel, you never recover. You fall so deeply in love with them that your life is theirs. It'd be worth it."

The couple on stage is no longer standing. They are wrapped around one another, desperately pressed skin against skin like they want to become one, and the feather still teases them with the lightest of touches.

"B... But angels aren't real." Despite my shock, I'm pressed

46

against the barman, feeling his hardness pressing against my panties, trying to relieve my aching need for touch.

He moves his lips to mine and repeats his mantra. "Zaden."

The word shakes me from my trance, and I push away from his muscled chest, mumbling an apology.

Angels are real. My own reaction to the feather is proof of its power, as are the thrashing limbs and frenzied desire all around me.

Angels are real, and an angel killed my sister.

Getting revenge just got harder.

Scarla

Bodies writhe around me, hands on breast, on ass, on cock.

Energy thrums across my skin and through my blood as I wind through the pulsating crowd and burst out of the hide hangings. My ears ring with the sudden silence.

I duck into the changeroom and wriggle out of my ridiculous dress. I pull on my sensible shirt and trousers, letting my hands linger longer than strictly necessary over my breasts—hearing the name of my sister's murderer is a mood-killer, but my body is still catching up. A few deep breaths should sort me out and shake the pleasure hub from my skin.

Georgie and Boon smirk as I rush past them—probably imagining that I'm running from the erotica. But I'm not. It's the knowledge that an angel killed my sister that courses through my mind on repeat.

Finding my way back is more manageable than coming in; I head uphill and toward the light spilling from the busier tunnels. The air is less damp up here, and voices from nearby hubs keep me company.

By the time I'm in North Undercity proper, I'm jogging. I take the last few turns from memory, then I breeze right past the guard on the North Gate and into the main cavern.

Halfway across, I stop dead. I left the water canteens in

North Undercity. Man, I'm gonna get in trouble for that from the people I borrowed them from.

Especially since I didn't ask permission first.

Doesn't matter. Well, it does, but I'll go back for them later. I'm practically best friends with the gate dude.

I run all the way to my sleeping hub, hoping Dad will be awake. It's almost dusk, after all. My skin is cold, despite my sprint, and my brain buzzes with my discovery. Voices and the shuffling of mattresses drift around the corner, giving me hope. The hub is alive with activity, and I spot my dad over in our spot.

"Dad!"

His beard is bushy and slashed with gray, and his shoulder-length hair is wild and copper-colored, like mine. It's a mystery where Leesa's blue-black tresses came from. Dad's the hairy-mountain-lion version of me—bigger, broader, taller. He even has my big brown eyes, but his are still puffy with sleep.

Even so, he puts energy into his greeting. "Heya, berry. I haven't seen you in a couple of days. Come 'ere." He pulls me into a bear hug, which I swear almost breaks my spine.

I wriggle free. "Dad, we've got to talk."

"We are talking."

"No, I mean talk talk."

"Shoot." He folds his blanket and places it on his pillow.

His calmness is infuriating. I hop from foot to foot. "Not here, Dad. Let's find somewhere private."

"No can do, Scar. Those blyberries won't pick themselves."

I tug on his arm. "This is serious. It won't take long."

It's unusual for me to interrupt his work, so he doesn't just dismiss me outright, thank the Maker. "Okay, but it'll have to be quick."

"Sure thing."

I only have to mention that angels are real and, oh, the reason I know that is because I just got seduced by an angel feather, and, oh yeah, I'm pretty sure an angel killed Leesa.

Should be quick and easy.

Dad grabs his satchel and follows me. I lead him around the next sleeping hub and down a tiny tunnel that narrows to shoulder width. We have to duck under a plunging rock outcrop and waddle a few steps before we can straighten out. It's a dead-end, so no through traffic.

"Jeez, you're serious about wanting some privacy, hey?"

A high-pitched giggle comes out of my mouth before I can stop it. I'm nervous, I guess. The tunnel widens out slightly—enough to stand side by side.

Now that I've got him, I don't know what to say.

Dad places a warm hand on my arm, his brows knitted. "Is it about Leo? You need to be careful with him. Did he tell you he's working with the Council, and he—"

"It's not about Leo." I don't want to talk about my best friend and how awfully I'm treating him. Besides, my mind is firmly on Leesa, but I can't broach that topic again—my obsession drives everyone around me crazy. Instead, I say, "Angels are real."

There is no wall lamp here, and only stray photons make it this far along our narrow tunnel. So Dad's expression is unreadable, but I'm pretty sure he's not grinning with joy.

"Are you telling or asking?"

I'm bursting with energy, and it takes every ounce of my effort not to bounce off the walls and scream. "I'm telling. Those fairytale creatures with big wings that only idiots

50

believe in... they're real."

"I see."

"You don't see. They're physical entities. With actual feathers you can touch."

"Not usually."

"Well, I've seen o... Hang on. What do you mean 'not usually'?" Heat rises through me; if I had the space to put my hands on my hips, I bloody well would.

Dad sighs. He's lost so much—a wife and a daughter—that I try not to get angry with him. But sometimes, he makes it hard.

"Oh, baby girl, I know angels exist."

"I... You... What?"

His dim outline looks around. "Are you sure we can't talk about this somewhere else? This isn't very comfortable."

That anger that I try to repress pushes against my barricades. Heat burns in my armpits and on the back of my neck. My words sound like steel. "Did you also know that an angel killed my sister?"

Dad puts a hand on my cheek. I usually love random moments of affection between us—they don't come often—but today, his fingers feel cold and hard.

He says, "I've heard the name Zaden—"

"No kidding. I might have mentioned it once or twice."

"—and that he or she is involved in the celestial sphere."

"Bloody hells below."

"And I've given it a lot of thought—"

"Glad to hear it." I hope my sarcasm isn't lost on him.

"—But I've come to the conclusion that he wasn't involved in their deaths."

I almost choke at that. "Their deaths? You think he killed

51

Mom too?"

Dad breathes loudly, and some part of me worries that he might have a heart attack or faint, but the rest of me is laser-focused on what he's telling me.

"No, I'm saying I *don't* think he—or she—killed either of them."

My heart pounds out of my chest. "Can you hear my heart?"

"No, berry."

"Fine. Whatever. Can you admit that this angel person—"

"Not a person."

"—Right, this angel thing might have been involved in Leesa's death."

Dad exhales all over me—his breath is heating this space up. My sweaty armpits might be contributing too.

"She was sick, Scarla. She got sicker and sicker. There's no reason to think anybody else contributed—"

"I just want to hear you say it's possible."

A pause lengthens between us, and all I hear is my breath pounding out.

When he finally speaks, Dad's voice is soft. "Fine. I'll admit Zaden might have been involved. But not murder. And anyway..."

I wriggle my shoulders. My energy is gone, and I lean into my dad's chest for a moment. I want to fall asleep against him.

"Yes?"

"Anyway, Zaden is an angel."

Dad's heart pounds away under his shirt, more frantic than he's making out. His blyberry scent is sweet and calming, but I sense a hard truth incoming.

I pull away and strain through the darkness to see his features. "So what?"

52

His face is a blob of dark gray against a blurry gray background. Even his words are gray. "So he's unbeatable."

Scarla

Dad leaves me standing alone.

He squeezes my shoulders, then hurries off for his dusk shift. I follow, but more slowly, and end up in the main cavern. It's buzzing. This is one of the busiest times in the Undercity—both the day and night hubs are awake and active, and people are coming and going through the cave mouth.

I pick my way to the back of the cavern, past the upper snowmelt catch, and plonk myself down in the dining area. The hard stone bench chills my butt. This is where Leo wanted to come for breakfast—qualified cooks make decent meals and serve them to whoever comes. They're folks who are either talented chefs or too scared to go outside and farm or go deeper and mine.

Everybody does their bit around here.

"You're late for the main meal, love. But I could rustle up some leftovers." A haggard lady with dropping jowls looks at me—her teeth are yellow, but her smile is warm.

I'm ravenous. "Yes, please. Whatever you've got is fine."

She nods and wanders off to the kitchen behind the snowmelt well. I watch her for a few minutes, stoking her fire and chatting with the other cooks. Between clangs and chuckles, the cluck of chickens reaches me. The chooks live right behind the central kitchen.

Dad's words echo through my skull. *He's unbeatable.* Well, I don't buy it—everybody has a weakness. Even angels. It's just that nobody has discovered it yet.

I need to process this information about angels and the effects of their feathers—whoa, boy!—and what my dad does and doesn't know. But my mind slips around the topics like balls of ice, too slippery to grip.

Instead, I find myself staring at the kitchen and marveling at its design. There's a hole over the snowmelt catch that goes all the way to the surface. Obviously. That's how the snow gets in. So during the day, it acts as a chimney for the kitchen.

And those chickens have it best of all—a well-regulated temperature near the bustle of the kitchens. They're too sensitive to survive outside... a bit like us humans. And the cooks have ready access to eggs—and the occasional chicken dinner.

The russet-haired lady brings me a plate of eggy bran seasoned with rock salt. Somehow the chefs make things tastier than I ever can, even with the same ingredients.

"Thanks."

"Welcome." She wanders off.

I tuck in. Yum. This is one of my favorite spots to sit—and not only because kind people bring me food. From here, I have a good view down the couple of hundred feet of the main cavern to the hanging ox hides at the other end. I can see people coming and going through the gates to North and South Undercity, plus I'm near the two snowmelt catches where all the action happens.

I scoop a spoonful of creamy egg rice into my mouth. Delicious. Oh crap, maybe it only tastes so good because I saw that angel feather... perhaps it heightened all of my senses.

My nipples peak. I can definitely see why people keep going to those pleasure hubs.

Sadie comes to the snowmelt and helps herself to a drink of water, and my shoulders tense as I watch her. Her wild hair waves in every direction as she slurps. I statue, hoping that will make me invisible.

It doesn't.

"Well, well, well. If it isn't sad, lonely, no-friends, no-family Scarla."

Dammit, she really knows how to hit my buttons. Anger wells in my chest. "Careful, Sadie. You forgot your backup today. You got nobody to pull me off your octopus neck."

I turn all tough-mouthed, but we both know I can't do anything with all these witnesses.

She laughs. "You're full of crap, Healer. And your dad better watch himself."

The atoms in my chest bounce harder. "What's my dad got to do with anything."

"Oh, he didn't tell you? Guess he thinks you can't handle it. Oops." She puts her stupid hand up to her mouth in mock horror.

"He tells me everyth—"

"Whatever. Just tell him to back off. And get your boyfriend to back out of my business too."

Sadie must be talking about Leo, but she stalks off before I can win the argument, which is infuriating. I want to tell her Leo isn't my boyfriend. And ask what the hell she's talking about him being in her business. And I'm gagging to defend my dad.

But mostly, I want to slap her stupid face

I grip the table so I won't pounce on her receding back. I'm happy to dismiss anything she has to say about my family, but I hate that she says it. Surely Dad's not involved in any business dealings with Sadie? I shudder at the thought.

The pounding of feet behind me makes me swivel in my seat. A line of blackened adults—mostly men—emerges from the coal mine tunnel. Unless you're a coal miner, you're not supposed to venture down that tunnel, so I've never been far along it. Apparently, it opens out to a labyrinth of mines. It's the lifeblood of the undercities, really. The reason we can stay warm overnight, the reason there's always a fire burning in every sleeping hub, and the reason we can purchase things from Lowtown and Hightown.

Even the rich need coal.

For the first time in a long time, I peer into the faces of the miners. They look happy enough. Their shifts are short, and they are well respected. Somebody claps one of them on the back, releasing a puff of black dust.

"Thanks, buddy."

Grins all around. It's a choice, of course—another career option for people who don't want to work outside.

"Are you finished, love?" My favorite chef is back.

"Yes, thanks. It was delicious." I'm still annoyed about Sadie, so maybe I'm overcompensating with kindness.

The cook looks at me through narrowed eyes, her jowls wobbling slightly like she can't tell if I'm taking the piss. "Okay," she says noncommittally, then takes my plate.

Across from me, on the cavern's southern side, is the lower snowmelt catch and the tunnel leading to the factories and the underwing. On a whim, I wander across and follow my feet down the corridor and into the well-lit underwing.

57

Fra Wang is here, of course. Her twin gray braids are pulled so tight they're practically peeling back the skin of her face.

"Hi, Lee. Do you ever go home?"

She bounces her gaze to my feet and back to my head. "My name is Fra Wang."

"I know that, Lee." I'm in the mood for a fight, and I seem to be picking an easy target. I can be a real bitch.

Anyway, Fra Wang is above all that. She deals out crap; she doesn't take it. "What are you doing here? It isn't your shift."

"Nice to see you too." I walk past her. "Just thought I'd check in and...."

Honestly, I don't know why I'm here either. I could happily wander off somewhere for a good sleep—or follow Sadie outside for a good argument—but instead, I've turned up at work.

Fra Wang doesn't seem to hear me anyway—she's too busy muttering to herself. "Either she's late, or she comes at completely the wrong time...."

In the underwing, the scent of the sick is as evident as the midday sun. It's real hard to get air to circulate down here. We do weekly fanning, where all of us workers get sheets of metal—or sometimes just thick cardboard—and wave our arms about like crazy, trying to push the sick air out into the main cavern where it can whisk up the snowmelt chimney.

That's the idea, at least, but it never seems to make much difference.

The place is half full. Half empty for the optimists. Some mattresses are piled up against a wall, leaving a patch of lovely free space on the floor. Still, it's a poor place for a dancefloor, so I keep my jive to myself. I weave around the occupied cots and poke my nose in to visit Fra Perkins, Tone's grandma.

Tension floods from my body when I see her chest rising and falling, albeit slowly. Her brittle white hair is still laid out across her pillow like a halo, and her face as knowing as an angel. A good angel, clearly.

I fluff her pillows and speak softly to her, though I doubt she can hear me. Next, I fetch a heat brick and tuck it in beside her. When I can't think of anything else to do, I sit beside her and lay my hands across her forehead and her chest.

She doesn't feel feverish or particularly cold, so I don't know if I'm helping. But surely, a human touch is worth something.

Matron pokes her head around the corner. "You've done what you can. Clear out now, Scarla. There's somebody come to visit with Fra Perkins, and he wants privacy."

I guess it's Tone or his family. I tuck the blanket under Fra Perkins' chin, then, on some impulse I can't explain, I lay a kiss on her forehead. She was always kind to me.

A scraping from behind me grabs my attention.

"Okay, okay. I'm leaving," I grumble.

Standing in the doorway is a large figure. But it isn't Tone or anybody else from the Undercity.

It's the cloaked figure, and his eyes burn green.

Scarla

The monster crosses to the bed in one stride. Beneath his cloak, I catch of glimpse of black cargo pants with pockets and zips covering thick, muscular legs.

He leans over Fra Perkins, paying no heed to me.

I gather my shards of fear and sharpen them into anger. "What the hell are you doing?"

The hooded figure looks at me, studying me for a moment. My gaze slips off his features, and I wrestle to find something on his face to lock onto so I can see him properly, but I can't. All I have is that sense of masculinity and raw power.

After a few moments, he returns his attention to the Fra. She is still breathing, and although I can't see the man's expression, his intent is clear as day. He wants her to die.

Me? I want to find out who the fuck this is. "Are you Zaden?"

His head snaps up, and I freeze.

There's a monster standing two feet away, and I've just gotten his attention.

Way to go, Scarla.

"Who are you?" I didn't see his mouth move—didn't see his mouth at all—but I can hear his words. Or maybe they're resonating inside my skull.

"I asked you first."

60

Great. Now I'm acting like we're kids in crèche.

He ignores me, which I can't say shocks me. He doesn't seem like the sort of bloke who values etiquette and polite conversation. Next, he swooshes out of the room like a giant bat, leaving me staring at the space he used to occupy.

My ears pound with blood, and I can't think straight. I rest a hand on Fra Perkins. She's burning up—he's done something to her, and it's going to kill her. I'm torn by indecision—Fra Perkins needs help, but I might never get this chance again.

"Maker be damned!" I run out of the underwing, yelling to the matron as I go. "Fra Perkins needs a snowpack." In the main cavern, I catch a glimpse of the man's cloak up the far end, almost at the exit. I sprint after him, managing to bump into at least three pissed-off people on the way through the crowded space. The inner hides are still swinging when I reach them. I catch them on an outswing and barge into the cavernous foyer, with the under-warehouse stretching off to my left. I dash to the outer hides and barge through.

"The man in the hood—which way did he go?" I demand of the mouthguards.

Two sentries from North Undercity are on duty, so I don't know them well, but they're familiar. They aren't too impressed by me, clearly.

"Don't I get a please?" the smaller guy says. I bet he never said that to a man who asked him a question.

The guard with the big nose just shrugs. "Didn't see no one."

"Come on." I jump from foot to foot and squint into the distance. "You can't have missed him. Tall, broad, big black cape, looks like an evil mastermind."

"Nope."

These must be the thickest guards in Malanox.

"Thank you so much for your help," I say sweetly, dripping with sarcasm.

They both grin. Yep, thick as ox hide.

The fresh air greets me with a gentle breeze and lungs full of sweetness. I savor the clean breath against my cheeks, even as I sprint toward Lowtown. Of course, people are near the cave since it's dusk and the temperature is moderate, but I'm sure he's headed to town.

He came into the Undercity to kill Fra Perkins and would have done so if I hadn't disturbed him. Guilt slaps my hand at remembering how I left her in a fever when I'm the most qualified person to bring it down.

But I need revenge for Leesa. If she was killed by Zaden, and if that cloaked figure is Zaden, I need to find out for sure. So I can kill him back.

When I reach Lowtown, I have to slow to a jog. Small dwellings rise from the dirt, each with a large hole dug beneath it—personal caves for just one or two families. Lucky buggers.

By the time I reach the first snowmelt barrel—one of four drinking wells in Lowtown—I have to slow to a walk. The people here are outside, too, tending their crops and herds and fetching water to last them overnight.

Winding around the first snowmelt wells, I see Raylee. Her eyes cloud with concern when she spots me, but she needn't bother—I'm not looking for her. I wave merrily, as though this is a running game, not a race for information, and she raises an eyebrow in return, then ducks her head.

Jeez. Nice to see you too, Raylee.

Up ahead, I glimpse a dark figure disappearing into the paved streets of Hightown. My breath is ragged, but I give an extra burst of speed to catch up.

Hightown lies inside the river's curve, so the rich people have ready access to fresh, cool water. Of course, the top layer turns steamy in the middle of the day, but it's always cold down deep. They say it springs from inside the castle, which is why it doesn't boil dry completely. If you follow the river south, way past the factories, it eventually evaporates into nothing.

I'm panting so hard that I've got to rest before I burst. I lean against a Hightown house. This is no Lowtown hut—it's constructed from thick stone, and I'd bet my left eye it has quality insulation. Maybe even a heat battery—although I'm not convinced they actually exist. Enchanted stone that captures sunshine during the day and releases it at night. Sounds bunkum.

But yesterday, I didn't believe in angels.

My target walks into view, thank goodness. I pull myself together and follow him. He starts strutting, the asshole, like he owns the whole world. A woman smiles at him and bobs a little curtsy. A little girl wearing thick boots and a silk dress runs up and murmurs to the man, then he holds out his hand for her to kiss. And she does.

What is going on?

The Hightown people are idiots. "*Even rich dudes can be dumb.*" Spot on, Leesa. Turns out they also love murderous monsters. I shrink into the shadows and sneak closer to him.

A young couple descends from a horse-drawn carriage. She wears an orange silk dress with puffy sleeves and zero points for practicality, and he wears trousers that trail past the ends of his heels, wearing holes in them with every step. I've never seen a more ridiculously rich pair of twits.

Curiosity prickles my scalp. Will my monster finally meet someone he has to be polite to, forced by their clear social superiority?

I have to lean against the nearest building for support when I see it: *they* bow to *him*. The man holds out his hand to shake, but my monster ignores him; the woman practically drops to her knees and sucks him off. They are both in awe of him.

What in actual hell is going on?

We're traveling deeper into Hightown here, reaching the deepest part of the river's curve, and we're almost out of land. He'll have to enter his house soon. Then I'll have him. I'll sneak back later and force the truth out of him.

I keep expecting him to turn into a doorway, but he keeps walking west. Strutting west, really. When he should be slinking to the bottom of a pit.

Finally, we reach the bridge that crosses the river, connecting the very tip of Hightown—where the richest of the rich live—to the other side.

The other side, beyond the castle, is a forest with a plethora of beasts that remains unhunted because it belongs to the Margrave. He sits in his enormous castle and ignores the people who need his help because he simply doesn't care.

He's also on my list of people to deal with.

My monster is actually heading to the bridge—he's going to talk with the guards. I've never seen anybody do that. Heart pounding, I risk darting across the street and hiding in the deep shadows by the river. I need to hear what he says.

But he doesn't say a thing. He doesn't even acknowledge the guards.

In fact, the only person to utter a sentence is one of the sentries, and he isn't challenging my monster or, better yet, punching him. "Evening, Margrave," the guard says.

Scarla

My monster strides across the bridge like he owns it.

Which, of course, he does. My hands curl into fists, and I shove one into my mouth to stifle the building scream. When he's out of sight, I jump up and dart across the road into the deep shadows by the stone houses.

I sink onto my haunches. The world is spinning around me, hazy and obscure. My brain is feeding me a bunch of information, and I can't make sense of any of it.

The man in the cloak is the Margrave. The Margrave is the man in the cloak. The ruler of Malanox, the king of the region, creeps into the Undercity and kills poor people.

No, that's not right. I don't know that for sure. I certainly can't be sure that he's Zaden—in fact, the more I think about it, the less it makes sense. The Margrave definitely isn't an angel. Therefore the Margrave isn't Zaden. Therefore Zaden didn't kill my sister.

But the only thing in this whole mess that I know for sure is that Zaden is "involved with" my sister's death.

Argh. I hate you, logic.

I push myself to standing, scraping up along the cold stone wall. Night has fallen. Moonlight shimmers off the river. From here, I can see the castle on the other side, although it's several hundred feet from the bridge. Penngrove Forest, the Margraves' personal hunting ground, waves in the distance.

I turn my attention to home. My footsteps echo loudly off the paving stones. Chill seeps through my long-sleeved shirt and pants, making my tiny hairs stand to attention. There's no denying it's cold out.

Nobody else would deny it, which is why nobody else is out here. The nannies of Hightown have ushered their charges indoors, and the men and women have retired to their warm houses. By the time I reach Lowtown, it's snowing, and the world is quiet. This is my favorite time of day. I have the universe to myself—it's just me and the snowflakes dancing together through life. There are no gangs to worry about, no chores to do, no bullies to beat up; it's just me and the weather.

By the time I reach the mouth of the Undercity, the snow makes it hard to walk. My feet drag through molasses with every step.

The mouthguards are the same two thickos on duty when I left. Might as well pump them for information.

"Hi there." I turn on my sweetest smile and hope it doesn't make them want to puke. "Could you boys do me a favor?"

Is that even how real people speak?

They don't seem to recognize me. Big Nose smiles, friendly enough. "Maybe. Whaddya want?"

"I was wondering how often the Margrave comes here?"

The smaller guard grins at me, sticks his hands in the pocket of his rough gray pants. "Not real smart, are you? But if you promise to keep your mouth shut, I'll take you on a date."

My smile drops. "Just answer the question."

The small idiot elbows the big-nosed idiot in the ribs. "She wants to know how often the Margrave comes 'ere."

Both of them giggle, working themselves into a full laughing fit. "Oh, he's always poppin' down 'ere for tea, isn't he!"

"Yes. And twice on Sundays."

"He usually drops into my hub to ask after my old mom."

"Brings me a present, most days."

This is the best thing that's happened to these bozos all day. "Forget it," I say.

Big Nose says in his poshest voice, "Would you like us to tell him you're askin' after him?"

"Good one, Lan. Yeah, we'll let him know. Maybe he'll invite us all up to the castle for solstice." The smaller idiot doubles over laughing.

Fine. I guess they haven't seen the Margrave arrive. Which is weird because I saw him come right through here. At least I saw him in the cave, then saw him out here. Maybe there's a secret entrance I don't know about? My heart quickens.

"Thanks. You've been super helpful, guys." I'm not even joking; I'm considering the possibility of a hidden passageway.

I push the heavy thermal hangings aside, and the temperature jumps up into a more comfortable range. I cover the hundred feet to the next hide hangings at a jog, then push through into relative warmth.

Not many people come and go at this time of night, so my arrival turns a few heads. The mood I'm in, I could flip all those idiots the bird or scream at them, so I keep my head forward and avoid catching anyone's gaze. I don't want to get distracted.

Too bad. A hand grabs my shoulder, and I spin around. "What?"

"Calm down, Scarla, it's just me." Leo stands with a goofy grin, his freckles dancing, but at least he snatches his hand

68

away. "I just want to hear how it went in the...." He leans in close. "The pleasure hub."

"Oh. I—"

"Scratch that. I *need* to hear how it went. Did you go? Did you get in? What was it like? Did you... you know?" A knife enters his tone at the last words.

"Yes. Yes. Yes. No."

"Huh?"

My hands fly to my hips. Impatience is bursting to get out... but actually, it might be useful to discuss this with someone. "Come here."

I drag him to the crèche—a mini cave-within-a-cave north of the main entrance. It's conveniently located so parents can drop off their kids on their way out, and also nicely contained with just a narrow opening so their charges can't escape. Hopefully, there won't be too many folks in here now.

There's a couple of babies and an old lady wearing a red apron who looks at them like she hates them—but at least they're occupying her attention. I drag Leo to the farthest corner and sit him down on a grogum stalk beanbag.

"Do I have to sit?"

"Yes. Shut up."

He folds his arms across his chest. His sleeves are short, and I see a sprinkling of red freckles down his forearms. "Fine. Go on then. I'm listening."

"Zaden is an angel."

Leo throws back his head and guffaws—he snorts so hard that mucus runs out his nose. Maybe I should have led up to this revelation more slowly.

A baby starts wailing at the noise, and the old lady snarls at us before attending to it. Good—now she won't be able to hear us.

"No such thing as ange—"

"Remember that part where I told you to shut up?"

He mimes sewing his lips together.

"Okay. I didn't believe it either, but there was an angel feather in the pleasure hub, and it... *did things*... to the other people there." No need to mention the extreme reaction I'd felt myself. "They said it came from Zaden. Then I saw another dude hovering creepily over Fra Perkins—"

"You think it was Zaden?" Leo's fists curl into the softness of the beanbag, and I'm not sure what he's reacting to—the existence of angels or the man-monster in the underwing. Or me visiting the pleasure hub.

"I don't think so, actually. I followed him, and he went all the way back to... guess."

Leo smirks. "What? So now I'm allowed to talk?"

I aim a soft kick at his leg, which he catches, then releases. "Guess," I repeat.

"He went to... a big fancy house in Hightown."

"Nope."

"A hut in Lowtown?"

I cross my arms. This is quite enjoyable. "Nope."

"Okay. The creepy dude disappeared into the night, headed toward the desert, absorbed into the darkness of the falling snow."

I smile. "He went into the castle."

Finally, I've shocked my best buddy into silence. He blinks at me, those pale eyelashes fluttering. "No way."

"Yes way."

"Who was it? A servant, or something?"

"Guess."

Leo leaps up in a smooth movement and grabs my shoulders. He's so close I can feel his breath on my lips. "Just tell me." But he's obviously already guessed.

"Fine." I shake him off and step away. "It was the Margrave."

Scarla

Leo's amazement is like a tonic to my soul. I don't know why I love it so much—probably because it justifies my own reaction. Makes me feel less alone. Maybe there's something in all that crap about having friends and sharing burdens... or maybe I just like manipulating peoples' emotions.

Anyway. There's one last thing I need to do before I curl up for the night.

"You gonna sleep with me tonight?" Leo asks, super casual.

"You wish," I joke before I can stop myself. I rush on to cover my embarrassment. My sleeping hub will be jumping with activity at this time of night, and I won't be able to keep my eyes open much longer. "Actually, yes. If that's okay."

He shrugs like it's no big thing. "Sure."

We exit the crèche together, and he heads toward South Gate. I peel away. "Be there soon."

He raises an eyebrow but doesn't question me. He knows he won't get a straight answer. It doesn't speak well to my personality, but I smile at his frustration... there's something undeniably addictive about being mysterious. I could easily tell him where I'm going, but that would ruin my fun.

Plus, I feel like I've already overshared with him tonight, which is a terrible idea given his recent weird behavior toward me... I should be keeping more distance from him. Which is hard when I sleep beside him.

I sigh.

It's only the night shifters awake at the moment, so the main cavern is quiet. The catches have started dripping with incoming snow, which always adds eerie punctuation to the evenings. Drip, drip, drip.

I scoop up a few mouthfuls of water as I pass, then I head to my destination. The underwing.

Matron is napping on a stool near the entrance, one gray braid flicked forward over her shoulder. My footsteps startle her awake.

"Whassais?" She clears her head, then wipes her hands on her apron and regains her customary calm. "Back again so soon, miss? I just can't keep track of you. Might as well rip your roster up and throw it in the bonfire."

"Yeah, thanks. That'd be great."

I'm joking—kind of—but I don't think she can tell. She bustles about noisily, huffing and puffing and muttering under her breath.

"I need to ask you something, Fra." I lay on the politeness to butter her up.

She tips her head forward, putting on her stern expression. "Yes?"

"That man who was here earlier, wearing the hood?"

Her face remains blank. I give her a few seconds to think it through, pawing with impatience.

"I didn't see anybody like that."

A wail dies in my throat. "Yes you did! The man wearing the hood and the long black cloak. He looked like an overgrown bat."

73

Fra Wang is getting worked up. She's even pushed herself off her stool so she can remonstrate with me properly... but she's still tiny and hard to be scared of. "You come in here in the middle of the night, wake me from my slumber, and then talk nonsense about strange men wearing cloaks. Well, listen here, girlie, you may be good at cooling a fever and heating a cold body, but—"

I need to cut her off before she gets too carried away and bans me from working here. "I was visiting with Fra Perkins. I was treating her really rather wonderfully...." I hope I'm not overdoing the self-praise here. "And you came in and said somebody wanted to see her, and they wanted some privacy."

A battle wages inside the matron's head—I can see it in her eyes. Her brows are pulled together, and her head is cocked. "Yes. I did say that, didn't I?"

"You did. Because a man in a black cloak wanted to visit with her in private."

I let the silence extend again, though I want nothing more than to pummel her with my fists and force her to remember. What did my monster do to these people to make them forget? Did that mean there wasn't a secret entrance to the undercities at all? Perhaps he'd just waltzed past the mouthguards and magicked them into forgetting.

This is driving me crazy. More likely, he bribed the mouth-guards... but that would make them excellent actors, and they didn't have the smarts for that.

The matron's brow finally clears. "I must have been mistaken. There was no visitor. I can't imagine why I told you there was. Sorry, dear." She pats me on the arm, and it's all I can do not to grab her fingers and break them. My violent urges are out of control tonight.

I smile tightly. "No problem. I'll just go and check on her."

"Actually, somebody asked me about Giselle," the matron says, and I freeze in my steps. "They wanted to know when she's likely to die. I said she had another few weeks left. But... I can't for the life of me remember who was asking. Was it that friend of yours?"

A thousand copper pieces say it was the Margrave. My feet trip over themselves to get to Fra Perkins—I need to see for myself that she's all right. I round the corner to her private area, and seeing her chest rise and fall draws the tension right out of my limbs.

"Fra. You're all right."

She doesn't hear me, of course. I check her for fever, but her temperature is normal. Her white hair frames her face perfectly, and her expression radiates serenity. I can't help but relax. Even so, I sit beside her and place my hand over her tiny, frail one.

Her chest rises and falls lightly as though she doesn't want to take more than her fair share of oxygen.

"Saving it for the rest of us, hey?"

Her only response is another light sip of air, barely enough to keep a fairy alive.

"Be right back." I duck off to find a stool, then drag it back to her bedside.

Perched there, I keep my focus on her chest, willing it to keep oscillating. It is mesmerizing. My own head droops, and I startle awake to find her staring at me.

"Fra Perkins!"

"Shh." She's hushing me for the sake of the other patients, I think—the ones she's leaving all that oxygen for.

I smile and rub the back of her hand. Her skin is papery

and dry as though it hasn't seen water in decades... I must remember to bring her some aloe oil tomorrow.

Her gaze is locked on me, and it's intense. There's no color in her hair or skin, but her eyes are as blue as the midday sky. Somehow I muster the courage to stare back. Her pupils are enormous, surely big enough to drown in, and I almost do. Black pools in deep blue oceans that reflect infinity right back at me.

"I..."

There's nothing for me to say. I feel as though I'm looking at the Maker—and maybe I am. Dark terrors ravage her gaze, but I don't flinch.

She parts her dry lips, and I hold a flask of water to them.

She sips. "Thanks, girl. You're an angel."

My mouth twists—today seems to have a crazy theme, which I never would have guessed when I peeled my eyelids apart this morning.

If it weren't for the drops of water lingering on her lips, I could think I imagined the whole encounter, our brief conversation. Her face is already placid again, her eyes closed.

But her chest is no longer moving. I don't need to check her pulse—the absence of life is evident.

A great wave of sadness engulfs me, pulling me into a pit of quicksand I may never escape.

The feeling that invades me is unlike anything I've experienced before. It isn't just the grief of loss—I've had my share of that. It's closer to a physical entity, a ghostly being that slips down my throat and into my very core, pervading every atom of my being.

The world blurs... every pinprick of light becomes a smudge that my brain cannot distinguish from its neighbor. I open my mouth to rail against the injustice of the Fra's death, to shout bloody murder to the angels and Gods, but nothing escapes me.

Instead, that sense of being invaded is even stronger, ramming its physicality down my throat until I gag.

I didn't even know Fra Perkins. Not really. But her passing has affected me viscerally. My soul is shaking. The world morphs into blackness, and the last thing I feel is my cheek thumping against the dead woman's ribs.

Scarla

The matron's fussing wakes me.

"What're you doing there, Scarla? You turn up in the middle of the night with nothing to show for yourself except a cloak full of snow, then you lie down and nap on the patients. Now up, and away with you."

The underwing looks different this morning. The colors are off. Like an artist came through in the night and brushed a glaze over the beds and walls.

"She's not a patient," I say, and I can't be bothered explaining more. She's dead. She's not coming back. She doesn't need our care and attention now.

Fra Wang rarely listens to me, and she keeps muttering and fussing. "Hop out of the way, missy. Not a patient indeed! What will be next? This isn't a cave? Goodness gracious."

I step back but don't trust myself to move farther. The world is tipsy and odd, like it's been submerged in a dream.

The matron's competent enough to tell when somebody's dead, so she figures it out pretty quickly. "Goodness. Fra Perkins has left us."

I nod. The event's magnitude defies description—I couldn't put words to her passing if I tried. The feeling of something thrusting itself down my throat still lingers.

"Yeah," I say, but that doesn't begin to cover it.

The matron leaps into action. She barks instructions at me, but I don't respond, so she gives up and orders Melandra around instead.

"Fetch a red sheet to cover the body. Bring an Undercity elder to bless her passing. Notify the family. Clean the poor woman's face properly first."

The commands fly like arrows, and I'm glad they're no longer aimed at me because I'm barely capable of understanding them, let alone carrying them out.

I'm too preoccupied with the strangeness of the cave this morning. The walls glow faintly red, and I have the odd sensation that I can see the seams of coal running deep below the visible surface.

Fra Wang and Melandra rush about me while I sit like a lump on my stool. Their faces are shades of gray and brown and are difficult to distinguish from the cave walls; I have to squint to read their expressions or even to identify them at all.

I grab Fra Perkins's hand and hold it to my lips. "What have you done to me?" I whisper into her papery palm. Studying her face gives me no clues; she is a wrinkled husk with slack skin. She doesn't look in the least unusual—for an old dead lady.

But something transferred from her into me when she died.

I shake my head. "I'm just tired." Saying it aloud makes it seem normal and true. Too many strange tales have met my ears over the last twenty-four hours, and I'm imagining intrigue and magic where there is none.

There's no indication of how long I've been asleep. My body clock is off-kilter, and I can't tell if it's morning or night, but I do know I'm exhausted and long for a soft mattress.

"I'm going," I mumble.

The matron mutters something back, but I can't hear her. Pretty sure it isn't complimentary. Before I can round the corner of the private nook into the underwing proper, a group of people blocks my way.

One of them looks like Tone Perkins, but it's hard to be sure in this unusual light. Everyone blends into the background. I nod at maybe-Tone-Perkins, and he nods back. This must be the family.

I edge around the cave walls, making way for the grieving group and trying to reach the private room's exit—there are way too many people in here, and I don't want to be among their number anyway.

Suddenly a glowing figure appears in the doorway. A man. He shines with a white light tinged with purple, as though he's been swimming in starlight. So bright. So very bright against the dull room and the dull people.

I squeeze my eyes tight against the sudden glow and hope that when I open them, the world will have returned to its usual palette of browns and creams.

No. The man still pulses with energy, tall and majestic, a man apart from others. Is this a second mysterious figure in the Undercity, or the same as last time? I try to reconcile the dark, hooded figure with the shining one before me and fail.

Among Undercity folks, I'm known as cool, calm, and collected... and I'm freaking out... So why isn't everybody else screaming?

I squint at the nearest person—a man about my dad's age with a head like an egg and a flat face. Probably Fra Perkins' son, maybe Tone's father? He glances at the newcomer, then away, like it ain't no big thang—like a descendant of the sun god didn't just walk in the room.

When the sun god speaks, his voice rumbles like water crashing into a canyon and echoes in the small space.

"Leave me."

He's got to be kidding, right? As if we'll just leap to follow his orders, glowing skin or not. But everybody else shuffles out, bumping into each other like they're blind. And their gaze is unfocused like they've all inherited old Pa Lennard's lazy eye.

Not me. I'm leaning against the wall, and I put one foot on it behind me to add to the cool, relaxed effect I'm going for. My arms are crossed over my chest for extra points.

The tall man snaps his head toward me, and anger flares from him like a flame.

His eyes narrow when he sees me, scanning my whole body. "You," he growls.

My lips are as dry as the Dead Desert. I lick them, hoping I'll manage a sensible response.

A couple of beats pass. "Me," I say. Okay, not sensible then. "Hang on. What do you mean? Do you know me?" At least I'm stringing sentences together, which is a start.

It dawns on me that disobeying this sun god's command to leave him alone was a terrible idea. It's not like Fra Perkins needs my protection anymore.

I start toward the door, hoping my legs and arms are moving naturally and not as woodenly as they feel. "Well, no need to answer my question. I'm not sure you were planning to anyway. But, I've got to go, things to do, places to be, mattresses to sleep on."

It would probably be better if I wasn't stringing sentences together because I wouldn't utter such ludicrous ones.

"I know you," he says, and I stop in my tracks. "I've seen you." His gaze rides the length of my body. "Every man in the Undercity has seen you."

There's something vulgar about the way he says it, like every word is licking me.

"Well, I *do* live here."

Okay, so the words I'm spewing forth are stupid, but the thoughts in my head are clearer. What does he mean he's seen me here before? I would definitely have noticed him if he'd been within a hundred feet of me. He's tall and as bright as the sun. A silver scabbard hangs from his waist. A flicker of recognition tickles my memory, a sense that maybe I have met this man before, but I shake it aside.

"You haven't seen me," I say. "I would have noticed if an oversized glow worm paid me a visit."

His head cocks.

By concentrating on him, I can dim his glow a little. His features emerge from behind the blinding glare. A broad forehead with a long nose, full lips, and a jaw chiseled from marble. Typical man-god. Those eyes, though, are not regular—they hold a black fire that rages at me, and I step backward to escape, but I bump into the curved wall. I try to melt into it.

He steps closer, and I cringe against the cold stone.

"You were here when she died." His voice pins me to the wall, and my breath catches in my lungs.

"Yes. How did you know?"

"I know everything."

I push off the wall, emboldened by his lie. Beneath the glow, he's just an idiot man like all the others. "Bullshit."

His scent is perfumed—forest lilies, maybe—and I realize

82

he must be rich. Laughter echoes through my mind, and I freeze. I swear my pulse actually stops for a moment while I figure it out. The laugh might be happening now, or it might just be a memory; I can't tell for sure.

But one thing I know for certain.

The man I'm staring at and whose aroma I'm breathing in—the sun god—is my monster.

The Margrave.

Why the fuck is he so shiny?

Scarla

"Let's talk outside." The Margrave clenches my upper arm in an iron grip and marches me toward the door.

I wriggle free, spitting with anger. "Let go of me. And use your Maker-be-damned manners!"

That must be the first sentence I've ever uttered about etiquette. But then again, I've never encountered anyone so rude or entitled.

At least he releases my arm. His irises dance with black flames, and his jaw is clenched. I have the feeling he could end my life with a word, and he's clearly pissed off with me—so why doesn't he smite me, or whatever it is that angels do?

He's definitely an angel. The glow, the green eyes dancing with black. And it must have been him I saw earlier over Fra Perkins' bed. I don't understand why he isn't trying to hide himself this time—his magic was clearly cloaked the last time he visited the Undercity, so why expose it now?

I need answers. I might not ask that question about why he hasn't killed me yet—I don't want to give him any ideas—but I do want to know what the hell he's doing here and why he's revealing his true identity now.

Still, I can't give into his rude demands. I've asked him to use his manners, so I can't go anywhere with him until he does.

His mouth barely moves as he speaks through a clenched jaw. "Let's talk outside. Please." His tone is terrifying... it would turn a skitter beetle into stone.

"Fine." I flounce past him to demonstrate my total lack of terror. At least, I walk past and bounce on my toes, hoping it passes as a flounce. These ox-hide boots make it hard.

The family is waiting outside in the main section of the underwing, standing between mattresses mutely. They watch the Margrave's movement like adoring servants, and I want to puke.

But on closer inspection, I see their eyes are cloudy.

The Margrave waves his arm. "You may go back in."

After we pass, I spin around to see the family filing back into the room as though nothing happened.

"What kind of crazy voodoo did you do on them? How does it work?"

We exit to the corridor and then out into the main cavern. I expect mayhem when we appear—a shining God in the dim cave—but the few people around ignore us altogether.

"That's not the right question," the Margrave growls.

Heat builds inside me. How dare he treat me like a crèche child? I inject all the sarcasm I can into my tone. "Oh, please, Margrave. Tell me what the right question is."

His head snaps to me when I use his title. The black flame in his eyes has died, replaced with that intense green I saw on our first meeting. "The question is, why doesn't my... voodoo... work on you?"

Heat tingles along my skin. Good. I'm glad he can't make himself invisible to me, although it does raise another question I need answered myself: why can't he? The first time

85

I saw him, leaning over Fra Perkins, my gaze couldn't settle on him, and now it can. What has changed? I thought it was him doing something different—like cloaking his magic last time—but apparently not.

We march the length of the cavern, and I try to figure out the time of day based on the activity levels—my internal clock is usually excellent, but it's been warped since I woke up. Nobody's serving in the central kitchen, and the snowmelt catches are quiet. After a moment, I hear the drip, drip, and figure it must be snowfall. But the odd coloring in the cave makes it hard to tell.

An old lady in the retired folks' section dozes beside a fire, but her eyes flick open at the sound of our footsteps. Her gaze seems to catch us for a moment before it slides right off and she looks away.

The Margrave marches through the first temperature lock and lets the heavy curtain of ox hides smack my face.

"Such a gentleman," I mutter. Since when have I been so obsessed with manners? Since this entitled prat started ordering me about, I guess.

He stops and looks at me expectantly.

"What?" I demand.

"Go get a cloak." He nods toward the alcove where we keep the boots and outer wear.

I let him wait for my reply for a moment. "No."

His eyes flash black. "It's the middle of the night."

"So?"

He presses his lips into a thin line. Clearly, he thinks I'm the biggest fool in Malanox. He slows his speech down to make sure I understand. "It will be cold outside."

Most folks in the Undercity know about my insensitivity to

temperature, and I'd forgotten how fun it was to meet some-one who doesn't. The whole scene unfolds in my imagination: me stepping outside in my cave clothes, his jaw-dropping open in surprise, and him prostrating himself on the ground and worshipping me.

Okay, it might not go exactly like that.

He's still staring at me expectantly… but this time looking for any drool running down my chin. "Get boots too."

There's no point showing him my hand. I might as well keep my best skill hidden. He's my enemy, after all—he may have killed my sister, and he definitely tried to kill Fra Perkins.

Annoyance filters through me that he could think I'm stupid—or suicidal—enough to not know about putting on warm clothes when it's freezing outside. I take a deep breath and run with his misinformation. Better him to believe I'm dangerously idiotic than to know my top skill.

"Fine." I march toward the alcove where the communal outerwear is stored. I select a coat of about the right size that doesn't look too heavy. I pull the hood over my head and stuff my hair down inside. I ignore his command to switch boots—mine are my most treasured possession, and I won't swap them for some Undercity clodhoppers.

Luckily he doesn't check my feet. "Outside."

"You know, we could just talk here."

He ticks his head toward the guards at the cave entrance. "Too many ears."

Fine. He probably thinks he'll have the upper hand as soon as we set foot outside and that I'll be shivering too hard to think straight. Bring it on.

"Are we using a secret tunnel?"

His stare could wither dawn flowers. "No."

I said that on purpose because I want him to think I'm stupid, I tell myself... but I'm not very convincing. I actually am a bit stupid.

We cover the distance to the second curtain of hides in silence. One of the mouthguards is inside the curtain, leaving the other guy outside. They take turns in the warmth.

"Hi Luke," I say brightly. I want to say something memorable, then come back later and see if he recalls it.

"My name isn't Luke," he says flatly. "It's Rojo."

"I crossed the Dead Desert this morning," I tell him. "And killed a man."

Horror creases Rojo's face.

"Bye!" I chirp.

If he doesn't remember that conversation, I'll know there's magic involved.

The outside guard just waves us through.

I expect the Margrave to stop so we can talk, but he just keeps marching. Snow falls softly, dancing on the light breeze on its way to the hard, frozen ground. The water in my eyeballs stiffens, and I have to blink frequently to keep it from turning to ice.

"Keep up," the Margrave orders, and my instinct is to do the opposite—but I want answers, so I pick up my pace. Maybe he's trying to kill me—most folks can't survive longer than a minute or two out here, even layered to the moon in furs.

A carriage with a pair of harnessed horses emerges from the gloom as we approach. It's black with ornate golden lettering on the sides.

He opens the door and ushers me in. "We'll be warmer in here."

A longstanding dream of mine is to step inside a carriage

and feel like a Hightown lady. This could be the only chance I get. Besides, I still have the upper hand—I can jump down and escape into the night whenever I like, which he doesn't know.

I smile sweetly, pleased with my own sarcasm even though I know he won't understand it. "Of course, sir."

Once inside, I relax into the soft bench seat facing forward. I fumble for the curtain that I know must be there covering the window, so I can open it and let some moonlight in.

There is no curtain.

The carriage lurches to the side when the Margrave steps in. At least I can see now, by the light of his glowing skin. He thumps his fist twice on the carriage roof, and we immediately lurch into motion.

Alarms sound in my brain. My pulse leaps. "Where are we going?"

His shining lips twist into a self-satisfied smirk. "Home." I recognize his glow now—it is pure evil.

I reach for the door latch. My heart beats like a rabbit's, and I just want to get out of here—I don't care about answers. I just want to feel safe. Sweat beads on my forehead, and the Margrave's malicious intent surrounds me like glue. I can barely breathe.

"You're not going anywhere, mortal," he says flatly, as though my terror bores him. "You can't escape. You don't leave until I say you do."

"But why?" The words flee me like a cry.

He closes his eyes as though I'm no more of a threat to him than a frost beetle.

"You don't need to know," he says softly, and anger licks my chest from within.

One day he'll regret his treatment of me. I'll revenge myself and my sister and every other innocent whose life he's destroyed.

And while he weeps, I'll laugh.

Scarla

The carriage jostles and bumps me, smacking my ass with its bench seats, which don't feel so plush anymore. At intervals, the wall whacks into my shoulder to keep me alert. I can't see the road because there are no windows, but it's obvious where we're going.

To Malanox Castle.

The Margrave—who is definitely an angel and probably Zaden—is kidnapping me.

"Are we in a hurry?" I ask. The words sound more plaintive and less kick-ass than I'd planned, so I'm glad when he doesn't bother to answer. Then annoyed at his arrogance. "Are you too far above me to even speak?"

His eyes are closed, and his head rests against the seat. "Yes." How he can relax in this bumping cage, I have no idea. But I take the opportunity to study him.

First, I squint, then I can just manage to make out features from his bright glow. His long black cloak is draped across him, obscuring his body. But I can tell it's big, powerful. His face is hard, with a square jaw and solid cheekbones. Even in repose, his broad forehead looks pissed.

The only thing that looks soft is his lips, but I imagine they'd be cold to the touch. I revise my opinion that he's carved from marble—he looks like ice. The faint purple-white glow adds to the effect. I imagine running a finger down his cheek, tracing the line of his jaw, and touching those full lips.

A shiver runs through me. It's definitely icy in here.

This may be the most vulnerable I'll ever find him. I consider launching myself at his throat and hanging on until he stops breathing or peels my fingers off him. But I don't know for sure the role he played in my sister's death, and I have many unanswered questions that only he can resolve.

Plus, he'd probably smash my skull against the shiny floor.

I'll wait. I'll extract the information I need from him. And then, if necessary, I'll kill him. I've seen enough death to be unafraid of it.

A thud reverberates through the front wall, jolting me out of my reverie. I hope it's the driver communicating with the Margrave and not a crazed Lowtowner banging a severed head on the roof... I must stop listening to horror tales around the bonfire.

Keeping his eyes closed, the Margrave raises a fist and thumps the ceiling in reply. The carriage slows to a stop, low voices filter from outside, and we jolt into motion. I guess we've come to the bridge across the river and have just passed the guard post.

"What is your name?"

I give him a few moments to answer, but he doesn't. His eyelids don't even flicker.

"Where are we going?"

I figure I might as well play up the dumb-woman act so he underestimates me, but I wasn't counting on him continuing to outright ignore me.

I huff. "Good, thanks. How are you?" I might as well have

my half of the conversation and pretend he's civil enough to join in. It keeps me entertained, if nothing else.

I'm still staring at his face when his eyes flash open. Their green pierces my soul, even more intense against his dark hair and cloak. Somehow they glow even brighter than his overall shine. "Don't you ever shut up?" he growls.

Irritation skitters through me. "I was under the impression we'd just popped out of the Undercity so you could answer some of my questions. But so far, you've just bundled me into a carriage and fallen asleep. You make a terrible date."

Still reclined, he raises one eyebrow, then lets his line of sight drop to my breasts.

"A date?" he asks.

I guffaw at his open assessment of me, wondering how I ever could have been intimidated by him. "You're no better than the idiot men in the Undercity, with their wandering eyes. Keep it in your pants, buddy."

His carved face doesn't budge, but he flexes his shoulder muscles ever so slightly... a tiny movement that would have escaped me entirely if it hadn't revealed a flash of feathers.

My lips fall open. The throb of raw sexuality hits me off guard, and my nipples tighten into buds. I arch my back slightly, demanding him to touch me and hoping like hell he hasn't noticed my arousal.

A smirk twitches his lips. "Tempted, mortal?."

I dig my fingernails into my thighs to tear my attention away from his aphrodisiac wings. Even though he's already hidden them again and only showed me the briefest flash, their intoxicating effect lingers.

Back in the pleasure hub, a single angel feather had entranced a whole room and had made my panties soaking wet...

now, I'm facing an entire blade full of feathers, and my core aches.

I manage to spit out a lie. "Never."

I need to fight it. I concentrate on the moons of pain from my fingernails carving into my legs. Finally, the urgency of my desire passes, and my pulse returns to a sensible rate. Still, I have to revise my opinion of him.

"I take it back," I tell him. "You're worse than the dickheads in the Undercity. Not only do you leer at women, but you also resort to cheap parlor tricks to get them into bed. And you have the arrogance to assume I'll just fall at your feet."

Finally, I've aroused an emotion in him other than apathy and boredom. His jaw clenches, and his fists curl around his cloak. That black flame dances in his eyes again. He looks dangerous.

The carriage jerks to a stop, and the door is opened from the outside. I see a flash of red-and-gold livery.

"Milord, I—"

"Not now," the Margrave growls, and fear lances across the footman's face.

The uniformed man quickly shuts the carriage door.

His blast of rage turns to me, and I force my back to stiffen. He has the power to murder me right here and now, and there's nothing I could do to stop him. Certainly, begging and shrinking into the corner won't help. So I hold myself firm and wait for the worst.

"How dare you speak to me that way?" Gone is the danger-ous quiet, now his voice is tinged with fury.

"Who me?" My voice holds firm, and I shriek a silent hallelujah. "Oh, I thought you weren't talking to me. Sorry, can you repeat the question?"

I squeeze the seat cushion, and my thumbs feel as though they might snap. But I have to keep my composure.

The Margrave glares at me unendingly, and I try my best to match his stare, but he doesn't seem to need to blink. Soon my eyes are watering, and I feel ridiculous.

"It's like having a staring contest with a statue," I say.

His eyes narrow, then he unlatches the door—how did he do that from the inside?—and exits, leaving me to scramble out behind him and follow in his wake.

"Maker-be-damned humans," he mutters, then he slaps a footman across the face, hard. "Don't interrupt me again." Blood spatters the cobblestones and my pulse skyrockets. What an asshole.

The castle looms before me, dark and forbidding in the moonlight. I crane my neck upward and follow the line of the nearest turret that soars into the night. Four towers mark the four corners of the castle, protruding from its rectangular form like the sentinels they are.

Massive wooden doors stand closed and forbidding. I can't imagine where they sourced all that wood from—probably the ancient forests that used to cover the land and have now dwindled into the few sacred hectares of Penngrove Forest.

A red-and-gold footman clears his throat, and I realize I've stopped in my tracks, staring. I keep moving and glance at the man's face, which is smeared with blood. "Are you all right?"

The man ignores me and stares straight ahead. I said it loud enough for the Margrave to hear, hoping to guilt him into an apology. My mom always told me that a person's quality is measured by how they treat those less fortunate than themselves, so I'm about to find out the Margrave's true worth.

Not that I doubted it—it's zero. He lets people live in squalor in the Undercity and Lowtown while he flounces about in silken luxury in the castle.

The massive castle doors swing open, revealing a short passageway to the interior—the walls are at least two meters thick, probably full of ox-hide insulation. I take my first step inside Malanox Castle.

The foyer would barely fit inside the main cavern of the Undercity. It extends almost the castle's width, and the double-height ceiling soars above me, disappearing into the darkness. Torchlight flickers from evenly spaced sconces around the room, but most of them are empty and dull.

A big stone room doesn't impress me—it's just like living underground—but the intricate carpets covering the flag-stones do, and I've never seen anything as fine as that grand marble staircase that curves and splits.

Most remarkable of all is the warmth, with just that wooden door separating us from the outside and no visible fires. It's super toasty in here. I can't even begin to imagine how they heat a vast castle like this... it must use heat sinks, meters of ox-hide insulation, and probably sorcered stones.

Two days ago, I didn't even believe in old wives' tales of magic and sorcery, but now I've been kidnapped by an angel and am contemplating which spell might keep his castle cozy.

Man, I need a good night's sleep to process all this.

"Where's my room? I imagine I'll take the eastern wing, and you take the western?"

The Margrave's cloak flows around his muscles like water over rocks. He deigns to throw a glance my way but doesn't reply. Obviously. Instead, he strides off along a torch-lit corridor in a very unwelcoming don't-follow-me kind of way.

A servant appears beside me out of the darkness.

"Jesus! Where'd you come from?"

"Sorry, milady."

"Oh, God, stop. That's even worse. Don't call me that. My name is Scarla. What's yours?"

She ducks her head. She's dressed plainly in coarse-woven layers of brown and blue, and she smells like hay. I instantly like her.

She bobs a curtsy. "You can call me servant. Or girl, if you prefer." A large freckle over her upper lip dances whenever she talks.

"I do not bloody prefer. What's your name?"

She pauses. Maybe she's waiting to see if I'm joking or if I'll slap her molars out. Finally, she raises her head. "Molly."

"Hi, Molly. I'm a prisoner, you know. You don't need to treat me well. But, obviously, I'd rather you did." Crap, I'm an idiot. Why did I tell her to treat me like trash?

"Milord told me to show you to a guest room."

"Not a cell? Well, that's a good start, I guess."

Finally, Molly cracks a smile. "Yes. Follow me."

She leads me up the grand, curving staircase with its marble treads to a carpeted floor that gives way beneath every step like soft dirt. Tiredness creeps over me as I follow Molly along a series of dimly lit corridors to the room where I'll spend the first night of my incarceration.

And the last, if I have anything to do about it.

Scarla

Time to see my prison cell.

Despite the high ceilings, the door into the bedroom is small, only reaching halfway up the wall but still plenty tall enough to walk through. The room itself, however, is large enough to sleep five families. A four-poster bed sits on a raised platform, tapestries hang from the walls, and a nightstand holds a bamboo water jug. An open doorway leads to a small washroom with an empty stone tub

"You'll sleep here," she tells me.

"Alone?"

"Of course."

It would be weird to gush over my prison cell, but it's hard not to be impressed and excited—I have my very own window. I cross over to take a closer look. Because the walls are so thick, the window is in a small alcove with a bench covered in furs and cushions. As far as I can tell, it isn't a bed, but it looks more comfortable than any place I've ever slept.

"Who sleeps here?" I ask.

"Nobody."

It must be a sofa—a soft place just for sitting like the Hightowners have. I kneel on the sofa and rest my elbows on the windowsill. The river curves into the distance, and the town flickers sleepily at my feet. The mountain that holds my precious Undercity looks so far away, and my heart lurches.

"Is there anything else I can get you tonight?"

I cross my arms. "Just a warm drink, then a ride home, thanks."

Molly's lips don't even twitch. I'll have to try harder to get another smile from her. "I'm not authorized to order the carriage, milady."

"Scarla."

"Sorry, Scarla." To her credit, she barely stumbles over my name, but it must be foreign to her to use a guest's first name. She's probably used to serving visiting lords and angels. I hate being miladied, and I'm glad she catches on quick.

She turns to leave, and I stop her with a word. "I suppose you're going to lock my door?"

She nods. "Yes, Scarla."

That, obviously, will make my escape more difficult. But I sense that Molly is like a frozen lake, and if I can just thaw her out a little, then cracks will appear.

Shame I'm entirely lacking in charm and social skills. Still, I whack on a smile and hope for the best. "And, what would happen if you didn't lock me in?"

She pauses a beat, then stares at the stone floor. "I would be killed." She speaks matter-of-factly as though discussing the color of the rug.

"Oh. And... what if you just forgot to lock me in? Or if I managed to overpower you and escape before you could lock me in?"

She micro-steps away and glances up at me. "The Margrave would have me killed."

Concern lances her body, breaking through her calm exterior, and I raise my hands, placating. "Okay, never mind, I was just asking. I won't fight you. I promise."

And I *do* promise—for now. But at some stage, I'll need access to the castle to find out what happened to my sister, so I might have to break that oath. But not yet. Not tonight.

Fatigue overcomes me, and I perch on the sofa's edge.

Molly reaches the door and, after she closes it, the click of the lock turning sounds like my impending doom.

I pull off my clothes, dropping my patchy blue shirt and rough brown pants onto the rug. Smiling, I slide into the clean sheets. No stalks poke out of this mattress—perhaps it isn't even made of grogum. Despite being a prisoner, I bet I'll have the best night's sleep ever. Still, the room is enormous and silent, and I imagine it will take me ages to get to sleep without another soul within earshot. No mumbling, no shuffling, no snoring.

But before long, my eyes close, and the world turns black.

I awaken with an adrenaline spike, which is an awful way to greet the world. It feels like I'm stuck in a dust storm with no way out. Knowledge of my captivity comes flooding back, and I have no idea what to expect of the day.

Maybe the Margrave was just letting me nap before sitting me down and answering all my questions. Or maybe he'll smite me after breakfast. Who knows? Angels, am I right?

I slide out of bed and onto the plush rug, which feels like fresh grass. I wiggle my toes to enjoy the sensation properly, then take myself on a small tour of my domain. Bed on a pedestal, bedside table with a water jug, plus a bunch of tapestries.

An adjacent room has an large stone tub for bathing, but it's empty. I've never been fully submerged in water, and I wonder if I'd be brave enough to get in. It's a moot point because there isn't enough water—just a few cupfuls in the jug. Maybe I should stand in the tub and pour it over my head?

No, I pour myself a cup instead and drain it. How luxurious to have water at my bedside.

I dress in my stinky clothes and check the bedroom door. Still locked. I cross to the sofa in the wall and try the window. Luckily, it unlatches. I fling it open and breathe in the fresh air of dawn.

With no way out—and no idea how this castle's schedule operates—all I can do is sit on the sofa and stew in captivity. I watch the city at my feet awaken and stir, small ant people scurrying about. In the distance, activity blurs the mountain's foot, but I can't make out individuals.

Leo must be awake, probably finishing off his porridge and heading out to the grogum fields. I picture his red head among the beige crops. A pang of loneliness lurches through me.

The world is still lit differently from whatever Fra Perkins did to me—instead of the layers of gray and yellow that dawn usually brings, there is brown upon brown with the occasional misplaced streak of green or orange like a child has painted outside the lines. I practice squinting and dimming the world, trying to make it morph into something more familiar.

Finally, the lock clicks, and my bedroom door swings open. The Margrave strides in, wearing black pants and a cream shirt, no cloak. I wasn't expecting him to swan into my room, and it's all I can do not to adjust my shirt and flick my hair. He's terrifying but alluring too.

He looks me up and down. "You are disheveled."

Suddenly, his allure evaporates like snow at midday. I cross my arms and feign indifference. "And you're rude. What a lovely start to the morning. Is there anything else you wanted to get off your chest?"

"I didn't know clothing was in short supply in the Under-city."

I straighten in my seat. "It isn't."

He cocks his head. "I'll have some clothing sent up."

"And I'll ignore it. Will that be all? Or have you come to apologize and send me home?"

The arrogant man doesn't appear to even hear me. He's taking in the state of the room—the state of me—with a shrewd eye, and I'm aware that angels must have heightened senses. He can probably hear my thumping heart. Maybe he can smell the blood rushing to the capillaries in my cheeks.

He turns his attention to me, and I grab hold of the seat cushion to avoid fidgeting. "How old are you?"

My mouth drops open. He certainly keeps me guessing where the conversation will go next. "I, er..."

"It isn't a difficult question. Is it?" Interest glimmers in his eyes, like he's trying to figure out just how dumb mortals are.

"No, it isn't difficult," I snap, annoyed that I'm even replying, that I'm playing his game. I take a deep breath and steer the chat elsewhere. "Why? Are you planning on buying me a gift?"

His green stare pins me to the seat. "I am doing some calculations."

Again with the non-sequitur. This male keeps me on my toes, that's for sure. I can't see any harm in answering the question. Maybe it's a test. Perhaps he's assessing my honesty or something. It might make him more likely to answer my questions too. "I'm twenty-five."

He nods, spins on his heel, and moves to leave.

"Wait." He spares me a glance. "I have a question too. What's your name?"

The Margrave narrows his eyes but says nothing. He swishes out the door, leaving me staring at the empty space.

At least the door is open now.

Scarla

I sidle toward the open door, sensing freedom.

But in an instant, Molly fills the doorway, like she was just waiting for her master to leave. She carries a tray, her calloused hands grasping the sides firmly. Her clothes are the same as yesterday—or an identical brown and blue set. It's a deeper shade of blue than my blyberry-stained shirt, and I wonder how she got that hue.

Molly looks at me warily, and I attempt to look approachable... and try not to threaten her with violence again.

"I've been instructed to show you around the castle."

"Great." I step toward her.

"After you breakfast." She places the tray on the side table and stares at me as I pour fresh milk and creamy eggs down my gullet. Being watched is extremely off-putting—I don't know how Hightown folks bear having servants.

I gobble so fast I nearly choke. But I'm eager for my tour of the castle. Mostly so I can plan my escape but also—and I hate to admit this to myself—the little girl inside me wants to see the pretty things.

Molly crosses to the window and shutters it. Disappointment flows through me. It seems such a waste to have the luxury of sleeping aboveground then just ignore the outside world, but I can't admit my temperature imperviousness—that's the only ace I hold.

Finally, we're out of my room. Molly shows me the castle, and I file away every turn and door in my memory. Living underground has honed my spatial awareness, and I find navigating through dark corridors easy. The stone glows dimly in places, and I figure that must be the sorcered stone.

The castle is roughly square with three floors, plus a tall, round tower at each corner. The first floor is where the servants live and work and is "not for the likes of me," as Molly tells me.

"There's no underground?"

Molly shakes her head. "Not for livin'." What on earth does she mean not for living? Is there a graveyard down there? Suddenly I'm shivering. "You okay, Scarla?"

"Yes, yes, keep going."

The truth is, reality has just hit me like an ice storm. The Margrave probably killed my sister... and chances are he'll kill me too. I suppress my chills and try to pay attention to Molly.

She points out furnishings and locations with a real sense of pragmatism, and I sense she is a realist. Not offended by the wealth around her, nor intimidated by it, just accepting of it and her position relative to it.

"Do you like it here, Molly?"

She shrugs. "I live here," she says, as though that answers the question.

We continue with the tour. The second floor is where the guest rooms are, including my bedroom, halfway along the eastern wall. Like mine, all the doors look undersized compared to the high ceilings.

"Let me guess," I say. "The Margrave has the third floor all to himself."

Molly looks at me askance—clearly, I'm adding to my she's-an-idiot reputation without even trying. "No. The Margrave has the northwest tower."

I nod, trying to take it all in. "And the other towers?"

"The guards and whatnot," she says, as though that explains it. Then she bustles me to the central staircase. "These are the only stairs that go underground."

She marches down them insouciantly, but a feeling of dread seeps through me as I follow.

That's not for living, she said.

So what is it for?

My arms bristle, and my fingers curl into fists. I listen for sounds of an ambush—or a fight—but all I can hear is the echoing thud of Molly's footsteps against the cool stone. The air grows damper as we descend, and that familiar odor of must and rock fills my nostrils.

Molly's voice booms through this space, startling me. "You have permission to bathe here." She watches me carefully, monitoring my reaction, as though she's just offered me a bite of poison oak and wants to see if I'll take it.

But I don't see any immediate danger. I relax my guard and look around. We are standing beneath the castle in a natural cavern of rock. A cool pool bubbles up from beneath the stone and idles away in a stream before ducking beneath the castle wall.

"Magnificent."

Molly nods. "Yes. This is the river's source. It rises from Mother Earth and flows out of the castle to feed the town."

"That's why the castle was built here," I say with new understanding.

"Yes. It keeps us cool during the day."

I dip a foot in the gently flowing stream and retract it immediately. Freezing. I try again, ready this time, and wiggle my toes. The water is cool and refreshing, like the first breeze of dusk.

In the Undercity, we clean our bodies in the washing hubs, where snowmelt catches are diverted into long troughs. There's plenty of water, as long as you wash overnight, but it's a cold and unpleasant task. We just do the important bits.

Grime coats me, and I feel stinky. I want to wash away the last 24 hours. I peel off my clothes, not caring that Molly is watching. Naked bodies are nothing to be ashamed of in the Undercity, where dozens of families share a sleeping space.

I scoop some water into my armpit and shiver. It's delightfully cool. I splash water all over myself and rub my breasts and belly, then work my way down my legs to my feet, scrubbing at all the grime.

"Would you like some soap, Scarla?"

"Yes! I'd kill for some."

To her credit, Molly doesn't flinch, even when I practically wrestle her to the ground as she proffers a small, gray bar.

I run the soap along my limbs and wash away the dirt. Wiggling down the stone incline, I ease myself further into the stream. Imagine if I leaped in completely. I long to do exactly that. Without a second's thought, I push myself into the cool liquid, and my pulse accelerates. I've never been fully surrounded by water before, and it is thrilling and exhilarating and terrifying.

My laughter echoes off the chamber walls. Every inch of my skin from the neck down is submersed. I wonder what would happen if I put my head under... would I be able to breathe?

Would I die instantly? Following an instinct, I lie back into the water until the tip of my nose joins me in the underwater world.

The buoyancy is fantastic. This must be how it feels to fly.

"Join me, Molly!"

She shakes her head and backs away. Not afraid, but with a sense that the pool isn't her place.

"I'll bring you fresh clothes." She rests a foot on the steps, and I get the sense she's retreating from temptation. I wonder whether she is forbidden from swimming here. "And the Margrave would like you to join him for dinner."

"Am I free to do as I please until then?"

I'd expected to be locked back in my room, so I'm delighted when she nods. "Yes. During the day, you may roam in the castle. Just do not go anywhere off-limits."

"How will I know where is off-limits?"

She climbs the steps and says softly, "You'll know."

I close my eyes and duck under the water's surface, holding my breath to explore the underwater world.

Scarla

I'm clean enough to eat off.

Energized too. Wandering around the castle unattended only fuels my determination—never has it been more apparent to me that the Margrave feasts while the peasants starve.

Lush tapestries hang from most rooms, and iron brackets for torches line every corridor. I come across a statue of a family of oxen carved from wood—not from reams of grogum stalk wound together or even the scarcer bamboo, but from proper hardwood that must have come from a distant forest. The carving alone must have taken hundreds of hours, not to mention the outrageously expensive material it's forged from.

The statue's beauty entrances me... then enrages me. How dare the Margrave own such an outlandish piece?

Anger simmering in my chest, I explore the rest of the castle, memorizing its twists and turns, taking in all those short doors and thick walls—even the internal ones are a good meter thick. The central staircase is the only one that leads down to the underground stream, but the other levels in the castle can also be accessed by stairwells in the four towers.

Except for the northwestern tower, which is guarded at all times. The dude on duty looks friendly enough—a round face and a round nose—so I try batting my eyelids at him.

"Hi there, soldier. Can I take a peek at the stairwell? Pretty please?"

The flattering tone doesn't suit me, and the dude looks like he wants to laugh. "No," he says gruffly.

So I try threatening him instead. "You don't want to cross me, buddy," I say, in my most fierce tone.

The damn metal-chest doesn't even cower. I guess my reputation doesn't precede me here. Which is a pity because it's all I've got. The reality of me fighting isn't nearly as impressive as my notoriety.

My belly rumbles, and I follow my nose to the first floor. The kitchen isn't hard to locate—it has to be by an outer wall so the smoke can escape and to catch snow for water, so I run the perimeter.

My belly grumbles even louder when I detect a strong, greasy funk with a roasty undertone. The kitchen takes up the entire western wall of the first floor, directly under the dining room. My shoulders relax when I enter the cooking space... this feels more like home. Dank lighting, stuffy air, and bad smells. Home, sweet home.

A dozen kitchen staff bustle about busily, tending to fires, stirring pots, and chopping unidentifiable vegetables. They don't wear the Margrave's red-and-gold livery, so I guess they don't serve upstairs. Their coarse brown and blue clothing is a close match for Molly's.

Shame. That means Molly probably didn't dye her own dress, so I can't shake her down for secrets.

I grab a roll from a pile of steamy, doughy goodness. Nothing better than freshly baked bread—and this stuff doesn't even have crunchy husks in it. I take a large bite and groan. I've never tasted anything so good. Maybe I can handle living with a despotic murderer if I get to eat like this.

"What are you doing, undergirl?" A hand smacks mine, and my roll flies across the kitchen and onto the floor.

I spin around, spittle flying. "How dare you!"

A thin man with the clean-shaven face of a Hightowner scowls at me. He's curled and hunched over with a narrow jaw, pinched lips, and beady eyes. Perhaps he's a master-servant, or maybe he's a visiting lord; I really can't deduce it from his outfit and demeanor.

The only thing I know for sure is that he's a pig.

Flecks fly from my mouth, and I make no attempt to stop them. "What a waste of good food! Why would you throw a perfect roll onto the floor." I pull myself to my full height, which doesn't reach his even with his stoop, and inject all the authority into my voice that I can muster. "Do not ever touch me again, or I'll rip your head off. And don't you dare call me undergirl."

The air seems to be sucked out of the kitchen—I swear, every servant gasps at once.

The man's eyes narrow so tight I wonder if he can still see. Then they widen all at once, and he leans in, whispering, his rancid spit lashing my cheek. "I make threats, undergirl. I don't take them."

Rage fills me. I open my mouth to retort, but he whirls around so fast I can barely follow his movements and slams my head onto the counter. A knife appears in his other hand, and he holds it before my eyes, tilting it so the kitchen fire reflects off its sharp edge.

"You will call me Lord Xerxes. And I will call you whatever I please. Do I make myself clear?"

He presses his weight against my skull, and the pressure

inside my cranium builds. I try to nod but can't move my head at all. This has gone south real fast. My gaze flies around the room, but I can't see any way out of this.

The sharp blade presses against my neck, cold and deadly. A shiver rolls from my neck to my toes, making me spasm. Fear sits heavy in my gut.

He leans in to whisper, and his foul breath reeks. "Do. You. Understand?"

"Yeeeah," I manage to squeak out.

He releases me with a flourish, grinning through rotten yellow teeth. "Good. I like quick learners."

My fists are curled, and I want to slam them into his smug face, but the fear inside me is stronger. It loosens my muscles and makes jelly of my fingers.

He strides off, bristling with importance, and I add another name to the list of people on whom I'll take vengeance. Lord Xerxes the Fuckwit. He joins Zaden and the Margrave.

I lock eyes with a cook whose long hair is tied back, and he nods at the platter of rolls, then at me. I force my head not to swivel like a hunted deer, searching for my enemy; instead, I calmly reach out and take one.

"Thanks," I mutter. "I'm used to the community fund."

Maybe the long-haired cook doesn't know what I'm talking about—the fact that everything in the Undercity belongs to everyone and is free for the taking—but he nods and returns to his work, avoiding my gaze any longer. I guess being on the wrong side of Lord Xerxes makes me poison around here.

My prison is a beautiful cage—all the trimmings of luxury but none of the freedom. Time to test the bounds of my captivity. Heading to the castle's front gate—those massive wooden doors—I push my tongue through the soft bread, marveling at how it dissolves. It's demolished by the time I get to the fancy foyer.

The trio of guards on the front gate pays me no attention when I saunter up, and my hopes rise.

But the lance that blocks my path soon dashes those pesky hopes.

I shrug. "Worth a try." One guard snickers, and I memorize his features as a potential ally. Brown hair, flat nose, dull eyes. "Scarla." I thrust a hand toward the flat-faced guard, and his smile evaporates. He stares at my palm like it's a book and he can't read. "You're just gonna leave me hanging?"

His lips twitch, and I figure that's as chummy as Flat-Nose and I are going to get today. "Nice meeting you," I say, then wander away, looking for a back exit. Corridors lead off either end of the foyer, but they are guarded and, surprise, surprise, I'm not granted access.

This place sucks. The afternoon passes fast and with growing frustration. I can't see a way to escape this damn castle.

By the time my belly gurgles again, Molly finds me. She's red and huffing. "I've been looking for you everywhere, Scarla. The Margra—"

"Hi, Molly," I say brightly, trying to atone for my earlier rudeness. That part when I threatened to have her murdered by attempting to escape. She's the closest thing I have to a friend here, so I pump her for information. "I need you to tell me something. Who's Lord Xerxes?"

Molly looks up sharply, her intelligent eyes assessing me. She shakes her head, mute. She struck me as a strong, sensible woman, so this reaction to a simple question is worrying. Clearly, I'm treading in dangerous territory.

"I won't tell anyone." I try my gentlest tone of voice, but I'm not sure I have one.

Molly sighs. "I suppose you'll find out anyway, and better you learn the truth before you get yourself in real trouble." She leans close. "He... he's the Margrave's second in command. He's theoretically a lord, but he lives here. I—I'm not sure where his county is."

That makes it so much worse. Not only is that pathetic excuse for a human living under the Margrave's roof, but he's his right-hand man. My grip on poor Molly's arm tightens, and she flinches.

"The... "

"Spit it out."

"The Margrave wants you to join him for dinner. Hurry. Please."

The nerve of that man. Xerxes' sneer fills my mind, and heat lashes my body. "What if I don't go?" Molly's face whitens, and I rush on so she doesn't have to answer. "Don't worry. I'll go."

"You'll find a change of clothes in your room. Follow me, and I'll take you there."

"I know the way to my room. And I know where the dining room is. And I definitely don't plan to change into a slinky gown for the Margrave's pleasure."

She looks me up and down, taking in my grimy pants and shirt. "Are you sure?"

"Yes." I turn and stride away before she can stop me to say her parents will be tortured if I don't go to dinner naked or something.

My internal clock and growling belly tell me it must be almost dusk. The corridors flash past, and I realize I'm jogging, my feet echoing off the stone floor. Fear builds in my gut, mixing with dread and hatred. Everything I've seen today makes me detest the Margrave, and it's growing to a crescendo.

I wonder if I'll be able to restrain my hand over dinner... with all those shiny forks and knives within reach.

Scarla

The dining hall could seat a hundred people and still have space for a dance floor.

It occupies the entire western wall of the second floor, above the kitchen. In the entry vestibule, low ceilings and dank air make it feel like home—and not in a good way.

But when I walk through to the main hall, my mouth drops. Vaulted double-height ceilings soar above me, plastered in ornate paintings. Large windows let in unfiltered light from outside—there must be sorcery in those openings because the temperature here is perfect.

Red-and-gold liveried servants stand at intervals along every wall, as silent as ghosts. I pass one bloke with a bulbous nose and leering squint like a gargoyle.

The Margrave sits at one end of a long table that could seat twenty or more. He wears a simple cream shirt with the cuffs folded up once. The material is finer than anything in the Undercity, and fitted, tracing his chest and tapering to a point below the table.

The skin at his collar is lightly tanned, golden. There's more color in that exposed clavicle than in all of the Undercity. His arms rest on the table, his biceps relaxed but bulging beneath the light fabric.

Despite myself, I'm drawn to his throbbing masculinity, to those marble-carved wrists, to the shape of those muscles. If he was a normal human being instead of a psychopathic angel, I might even toss him a smile.

A place is set beside the psychopathic angel, presumably for me.

He doesn't bother to look up when I cross the room, and my gut curdles. Suddenly eating seems like a bad idea—I might bring it up all over his smug face.

I scrape the chair out as noisily as I can, really screeching those wooden legs across the stone, trying to carve parallel lines in the floor.

That gets his attention. He looks at me, watching like you'd follow a lame dog with your eyes. No doubt he'd laugh if I lay down, rolled over, then begged him for food. Well, he won't get the pleasure.

Be the opposite of a lame dog, I tell myself. I fold my arms across my lap, not even glancing at the food, although the smells are intoxicating. Roasted chicken, roasted pigeon, buttery caramelized vegetables.

Crap, I hope my nose isn't twitching.

I calmly pour water from a jug into a glass, then sip. Cool, delicious, sweet. Even the water here tastes better than back home. I guess it hasn't been filtered through cave moss and then left to stagnate for a few days.

If he thinks I'll be the first to speak, he's wrong. I won't make conversation with a murderer, even if he does provide good food.

"Help yourself to the potato." His deep voice reverberates through the room.

I wish I could make my voice echo like that—it sounds so

authoritative. I decide to give it a go. "I prefer mattroot," I say grandly, but the words don't repeat from the chamber walls. "Not that you care anyway."

Maker-be-damned, now I sound like a petulant child.

"Indeed," he agrees.

I serve myself a heaping of mattroot and chicken, leaving the pigeon for him—I'm not a fan. The food is good, but the chair is hard, and the edge cuts into the backs of my thighs. It's obviously crafted for somebody taller than me... and without regard for what guests it might seat.

My lips press in a thin line. "What the hell am I doing here? You clearly hate me as much as I hate you, yet you're putting me up in a soft bed with warm blankets—"

"Is this a complaint or a thank-you note?"

"—and now you're feeding me a feast. Just let me go. You don't want me here, and I certainly don't want to be here."

Is he worried I'll tell everyone the truth about him? That the grand ruler, the Margrave of Malanox, is an angel? I mean, I'll try, but I'll be laughed out of the Undercity.

There must be another reason.

The Margrave's jaw works up and down slowly as he calmly chews. It's infuriating. I have plenty of time to marvel at his dark three-day growth, so unlike the fashion among Hightowners. His face is rugged but pristine, an off-putting combination.

When he's good and ready, he locks me in his piercing green gaze. "You're not going anywhere. Is that clear?"

I try to mirror his calm tone, but my blood jumps like a lake of lava. "It is far from clear. You seem to be under the mistaken impression that you can order me around. Let me help you with that." My chair scrapes satisfyingly as I take my feet, throwing my napkin onto my plate.

"Sit." His voice is dangerous now, making it even more gratifying to ignore him. I'm halfway across the chamber when he says it.

"If you leave, I will kill your father."

My fire turns ice cold, arctic. My thumping pulse stops dead, and I can't feel my fingers. Slowly, I turn, a tingling returning to my extremities.

He doesn't need to repeat himself, but he does; he's clearly enjoying himself. "If you attempt to escape, I will have your father murdered."

"You'll never find him." It's desperate and weak and, even worse, completely untrue.

"Luca Bradson Farmer of the South Undercity, sleeping hub S2A7. Dogsbody for the council, picks blyberries at dusk. I think I'll manage to locate him."

My mouth goes dry. I sit beside this monster, thinking frantically, but it's like churning butter, and my ideas can't gain traction. So I eat. I shovel calories into my body so I'll have the energy to handle whatever comes up next.

"Don't eat so fast," he growls at me. "It's disgusting."

That's one instruction too many. "How dare you tell me how to chew and swallow? I'm not an object you possess."

I drag a hand across my mouth, deliberately smearing chicken fat onto my cheek.

He looks away, but my anger can't be stopped; it's like an erupting volcano.

"Or maybe I'll stop eating altogether." I'm shouting, but he doesn't even look at me. "Then I'll die of starvation, and you won't be able to threaten me anymore."

The monster dabs his mouth, still playing the little lord. The tendons in his corded wrists tense, and the soft cream shirt shifts across his biceps. When he finally looks at me, his face is plastered with a sneer.

"I'd be delighted if you'd die of natural causes. Or, indeed, self-inflicted ones."

Again, he's taken the wind out of my sails. He's turning my own threats against me, and all I have are useless splutters and huffy breaths. This is the most enraging conversation I've ever had.

"Why not just kill me, then?"

And now I'm suggesting he murder me. I've definitely lost control of this situation. I need to beat a retreat and figure out a different approach.

Silence seems the best answer, for now. Unfortunately, it suits him too.

The food, of course, is impressive. The main meal is followed by blyberry crumble and cream.

"A not-so-subtle reminder about my father? Really, you stoop so low," I say.

He's already admitted he knows my dad collects berries, and this dessert is clearly intended as a parry.

His eyebrows come together, and he studies me over the top of his bowl. "Hm. You're less stupid than I thought. Yes, it's a gentle reminder of what's at stake. Honestly, I didn't think you'd pick up on it."

I put on my prettiest smile. "Oh, Margrave, thank you for your esteemed compliments." My eyelashes flutter. Frankly, I doubt he'll notice my lack of sincerity—he is not exactly attuned to others.

He surprises me.

"Hm. Humor. Maybe the next fifty years won't be so boring

after all."

Cream splutters all over the table, ejected at speed from my mouth. "What? Fifty years? What are you talking about?"

I've posed it as a question, but the answer is perfectly clear—it's staring me in the face like a life sentence in the undercell. He intends to keep me prisoner until I die.

"Don't worry, it's just an expression. A figure of speech."

He's clearly underestimating me again. If he thinks I'll buy that oxencrap, he's dumber than skitter beetle.

My monster is fattening me up, keeping me fed and happy, and keeping me here in my gilded cage for the next fifty years.

Until I die.

Scarla

I am the Margrave's prisoner.

For life.

The rest of dinner passes slowly, each minute dragging by as though on the end of a chain. Even the damn blyberry crumble won't go down my throat no matter how many times I chew it.

I am the Margrave's prisoner for life. And if I try to escape, he'll kill my dad. Kind of ruins a girl's appetite.

The Margrave eats in silence, and I don't just mean his lack of chat. He moves like he's hunting mountain lions, all fluid and stealth. No sound filters the air except the pounding of my own heart and heavy breathing.

The stillness in the room is as unnatural as the angel in it. Every time he spoons dessert into his mouth, ripples flow from the movement like disturbed air inside a tomb. His soft cream shirt flows over and around his movements like it was all pre-ordained.

His white-purple glow shines as brightly as ever. But if I focus on him, I can ignore the shine and see through it to his marble features, which are just as perfect and unnatural as ever.

I rock back in my seat and examine him. Broad forehead, long nose, a chiseled jaw lined with stubble, and full lips that mesmerize me when he speaks, and those menacing green eyes.

With his short dark hair and the whisper of black wings behind him, he looks more like the devil than an angel.

The Margrave's aura—if that's what it is I can suddenly see—dances as I stare at it. I can make it flicker. Shivers strobe my spine.

A pair of red-and-gold servants enters the dining hall to remove our dirty dishes. Another pair brings coffee. Suddenly, I'm aware that I'm giving this Margrave all my attention, and I tear my gaze from his face and see a servant standing against the far wall behind his shoulder.

Something about the servant snags my attention. He's one of many standing at intervals around the room's perimeter. He is boyishly handsome with a flop of sandy hair across his forehead. He smiles at me, and I grin back. This is the first time anybody has shown me a hint of kindness since I entered the castle, and I can't help but respond.

Sandy-hair holds my gaze, leans to the servant standing nearest to him, whispers, and then winks at me.

Before I can wink back, the Margrave seizes my attention again.

His purple shine deepens to black, and I'm fascinated to watch the transformation. Black flames lick through the darkening aura, giving the impression he is simultaneously amethyst and ash. I try to focus through the glow to see his features, and when I do, my breath intakes sharply.

His eyes have changed from green to black, and my heart forgets to beat. The male is terrifying.

The Margrave rises to his feet in one movement and draws his long silver sword from the scabbard at his hip, ringing with power. Before I can let out my next breath, the Margrave is across the room, blocking my view of the sandy-haired servant.

All I can see is the broad sweep of the Margrave's back, the cream shirt stretching across his deltoids as he raises his sword, pointing to heaven. His stance is wide, and a zipper toggle on his black pants swings back and forth across his ass cheek.

The Margrave raises his sword and slashes, then spins and strides back to the table, taking up my entire field of vision. He stares at me, those black eyes alive with menace.

My mouth is dry.

"He won't speak to you again," he tells me coldly, then strides the length of the room, his footsteps making no sound upon the stone floor.

I blink and breathe, then see blood pooling beneath the injured man. He lies face down, and I can't tell whether he's alive or dead from this distance.

The other servants remain at their stations along the edges of the walls as their master takes his leave.

Before I know it, I'm running across the room to the fallen servant. "What the hell are you all doing? Move!"

I fall to my knees on the hard stone floor and slide into the red pool. I lay my hands on the man's head, seeking the drumming of his heart.

A faint beat pulses through my fingers. Alive, barely. I try to channel healing energy into him, but I don't know if it's working. I'm not skilled at this—I'm usually the girl who heats people up or cools them down, not the one who repairs pumping wounds. Besides, I'm too emotional to focus properly.

Still the servants haven't moved. I turn to the nearest one. "Go and fetch Molly," I snap because it's the only thing I can think to do. She's the only person in this whole damn castle whose name I know.

While I'm waiting for her, I take a look at the man's injuries. The sword slashed him diagonally from armpit to hip, but judging by the amount of blood spilled and the lack of intestines, it wasn't too deep.

Not deep enough for a quick death... but probably about right for a painful, lingering one.

Molly arrives, with the freckle over her top lip dancing.

I point at two servants. "You and you, pick him up." Sandy-hair groans as they jostle him. "Carefully," I snap. Turning to Molly, I see she'll be of no use unless I boss her around. "There must be somewhere we can take him." My fingers drum against my thighs, fueled by impatience. "Come on, Molly. Do you have a medical wing?"

She shifts her weight and looks at her shoes. She's obviously hiding something.

"Look, I don't care if the room is filled with angel feathers and sex swings. Just take me somewhere that I can look after him. Somewhere with hot water and bandages and a bed. He can't recover here in the middle of the dining room. It'll put people off their food."

She gives a quick nod. "Follow me."

I expect her to turn and head out to the corridor, but she goes to the wall behind me and sweeps aside a tapestry, revealing a door.

"Through here."

Intrigued, I peer inside the tiny space, breathing the stale air. The door leads to a narrow passageway within the thickness of the castle walls. Molly ushers the men inside, and I follow. Stone brushes each of my shoulders as I hurry behind Molly.

Fascinating. There is a hidden series of corridors inside the very walls of the castle. I wonder how many miles of secret passageways there are—it feels like we're traveling several. My inner little girl is excited at the discovery.

The two servants carry Sandy-head awkwardly between them, and groans of pain punctuate our flight.

"What is this place?" I whisper. Something about the hidden nature of this place keeps my voice low.

"The inner maze," Molly says, replying in a whisper too. "It was built for the servants to get around without disturbing the Margrave."

Fury washes over me at yet more evidence of the Margrave's sense of superiority, but I push it aside. Now is the time for healing energy, not anger. If I want to help the poor man that bastard sliced open, I'll need to get control of my emotions.

We clamber over a pointless set of stairs. Five narrow treads lead up, then across a yard or so, where we are up near the ceiling, then down again. When we come to a second stile, I look to Molly for answers.

"What's with these stair bridges? Just extra hassle for the servants?"

"They're doorways," Molly whispers.

Suddenly it makes sense. We are walking an inner maze inside the castle walls, so we have to climb above a door wherever we come to one. Explains why the doors are so small.

We begin to descend a narrow staircase in a large, curving arc. There are no windows and very little light, other than the occasional high sconce, but given how long and round this descent is, I imagine we are curling around the outside of one of the towers.

We pass a fork in the labyrinth, then spill out of the inner maze into the castle proper via a stone door. Glancing behind, I watch the door close and disappear into the wall, leaving the barest crack of an outline. It would be impossible to detect if I didn't know it was there.

Just how many of these secret doors are there?

I try to make sense of our location. We must be on the first floor near one of the towers. My instincts tell me it's the northeast tower, and I trust them. Earlier today, Molly told me this was the servants' area and "not for the likes of me."

Well, here I am.

"Down here," Molly says, and I follow her into a room with no windows and eight beds around the edges. Only one is occupied—an elderly woman sleeps peacefully on the cot nearest the door.

"Is this the infirmary?"

Molly shrugs as the two porters lay the sandy-haired man onto a mattress. "I wouldn't go that far. We don't have a healer. It's more like...."

The gruff voice from one of the porters breaks in. "It's where we go to die. I reckon that's what Robin here will do now." This bloke isn't exactly brimming with emotion, and neither is Molly. I feel like the only human among a castle full of half-animated statues.

"Robin, is it?" That's the injured man. "And you are?"

"Gerard."

I recognize Gerard as the man Robin whispered to just before the attack. Curiosity digs her fingers into my brain. "Why did the Margrave attack Robin? What did he say to you?"

Gerard shakes his head. "He should never have said nothin'.

127

They say angels can hear a skitter beetle a mile away. He shouldn't of said nothin'.'"

"But what did he say?" My voice is harsh.

Gerard glances at the other porter like he's seeking an escape. "He shouldn't of said nothin'."

I'm furious that the Margrave would attack somebody for whispering in his dining hall—especially when that somebody had just smiled at me and was probably the nicest bloke in the whole castle. The anger tightens my muscles and hardens my voice, and it's all I can do not to curl my hands into fists. "What did he say to you?"

Why does everybody in this godforsaken place have a secret to hide?

"He... he said that your clothes are disgusting... but he'd take a piece of your ass, even if he had to cut it off himself."

Molly gasps, a timid mousy sound that infuriates me. But I don't follow down that rabbit hole... My anger is leading me nowhere today. First, it got me kidnapped; now it's gotten me protecting a sandy-haired man who's turned out to be just another leering prick.

Anger rushes out of me like a deflating balloon, and I slump onto a bed. "Get out," I say, and I'm pleased that the men scurry away. Maybe I'll develop a mean reputation here too.

I glance up and see Molly is still there. Clearly, she's not such a timid mouse after all—she's got more balls than those sacks of testosterone that just walked out. I like her more and more.

Molly clears her throat and shoots me a straight question. "Do you have healing powers?"

It's my turn to shrug. "Sort of. I work in the underwing. That's the hospital wing of the Undercity."

128

She considers that for a few moments, arms crossed over her small chest. She nods toward the bed. "Are you still going to fix Robin? After what he said about you?"

Yes. Of course I will. A crude tongue shouldn't carry a death sentence. I bite my lip. "I can't yet. If I lay hands on him now, I'll probably kill him."

The truth is, I have to wait until my emotions are under control until my anger subsides.

Then I'll lay hands on this idiot and try to revive him. After all, he doesn't deserve to die.

The Margrave, on the other hand, is a different story.

Scarla

The Margrave is mind-boggling.

He elevates callousness to a new level. I can't believe how little he thinks of others. Mere mortals, he considers us, treating us like insects to be used or trodden on at will.

This line of thinking doesn't help my anger subside. I take a deep breath to try to relax, but my shoulders are still hunched, and my fingers twist on my lap. I'm sitting on one of the spare beds, trying to control my emotions.

I look at Molly, standing quietly to one side. "Why do you stay here? How can you stand it? The way he treats you and everybody around him. Why don't you just get the hell out of here?"

Molly is as placid as ever. Her expressive eyes look at me with pity as though I'm a child who doesn't understand the real world. "This is my life. I was born here, like my parents before me. It is my duty to serve the Margrave."

"To hell with duty," I snarl.

Molly's gaze burns me, and I wish she'd look away. "Duty isn't a burden. I know how the people outside the castle live, and it sucks. I'm lucky to be here, serving the messenger of heaven."

There must be a flaw in her logic, but my tangled mind can't find it. Instead, I snort. "Messenger from heaven? More like a king with a horn stuck up his ass."

I don't know why I'm describing him this way. It sounds petty, petulant, like he's a meanie and I need a nap. When really, he's an avenging angel, and what I need are answers.

"What is the Margrave's true name?"

Molly glances at the doorway, preparing to confide a secret. I shift on the mattress, but I'm disappointed.

"We call him Margrave or Sir."

Irritation creeps along my scalp. "I didn't ask what you call him. I want to know his true name. Please, it's important." I don't trust her enough to tell the whole truth, that a man named Zaden was involved with my sister's death, and I suspect that man is the Margrave. "Please."

I'm not above begging. I'll get down on one knee and kiss her shoes if she wants me to.

Molly shakes her head. "I don't know his true name. And you shouldn't ask around about it if you want to stay out of trouble."

The expression on her face is neutral enough, but I can't tell if she's issuing me a warning or a threat. Her face is impassive, as though she witnesses death on the daily. "You don't seem that bothered by this."

"The Margrave is an angel."

"That doesn't mean he gets to kill whoever displeases him."

Molly looks at me like I'm an idiot. "Yes, it does. Robin was a fool, and he deserved what he got."

"Wow. You are ice cold."

Molly is unfazed. "When the Margrave loses control, he loses his guard. We're just lucky he didn't go into a killing trance and murder us all."

131

I snort. "Lucky. Yeah. That's the word I was thinking of too."

This place just gets better and better.

Molly twitches a finger toward the cot where the injured man still bleeds profusely. I'd better do something about him now before he dies, even if my anger isn't entirely controlled.

I rise and approach Robin's cot, then place one hand on his forehead and the other across the gaping wound in his belly. I don't know if I'm doing the right thing, and I've never had training in medicine, so I just follow my instincts.

My eyes close, and I concentrate on the body beneath me, trying to command the blood back into the flesh, attempting to staunch its outward flow. It feels like I'm squeezing butter through a pinprick-sized hole in a canvas, smooshing and smashing and getting nowhere fast. Like I'm using a sledgehammer when I need an eyedropper.

Before long, I'm exhausted, and I have no idea if I've made any impact.

I come away, open my eyes, and take in the room. Molly's still there, watching me in silence.

"Did it work?" Molly takes a step closer and peers at the man.

He's covered in blood, and now I am too. It adds another layer of grime to my already soiled clothing.

"No idea. I'll be back later to help the old lady."

I don't know when I decided to come back and heal her, but I know I'm too tired to do it now. I exit the room into the close stone corridors. The hallway is narrower here than upstairs, clearly designed for servants.

I can't picture the Margrave deigning to scurry through here.

Molly trails me. "Where are you going?"

"My room. Why? Do I have a choice?"

As I suspected, we emerge from the corridor into the fancy foyer, with the big wooden gates and the ornate rugs. I climb the grand, curving stairs and wander to my room.

Molly runs a few paces to catch up with me and walks beside me. She is silent, which I appreciate, and I find her presence comforting, even though I know she's really my jailer escorting me to my cell.

True enough, she locks me in my bedroom and takes the key, leaving me alone in the gigantic chamber.

A fire is set in the grate, blazing and throwing warm light across the stone room. There's a thick carpet underfoot and that enormous bed that I'll never get used to.

The stone bath in the adjoining room is empty, worse luck, but somebody has put a basin of freshwater on the ornate bamboo nightstand. I splash my face and arms, trying to scrub off the sandy-haired servant's blood.

Who knows what tomorrow will hold?

The Margrave

That mortal is a puzzle.

She is immune to my charms, which should be impossible. I suspected it in the carriage ride and confirmed it at dinner last night. The woman exists beyond the natural order. When a human comes near an uncloaked angel, they should fall to their knees. Should beg to be touched, should beg to serve.

That's why I breed my own servants. They are exposed to me from birth and, therefore, capable of meeting my needs without collapsing or pleading. Certainly, I have to release the ones who cannot resist my celestial lure, but the ones who remain are useful.

But this new mortal, Scarla, should have no such resistance. When she first saw me without a glamor, at dinner last night, she should have fallen to her belly and prostrated herself before me.

Or, at the very least, stripped off her clothes and pressed her naked flesh against me.

I will have to consider it some more.

"Servant!" A butler is permanently stationed outside my bedroom door in case I need something.

I pace to the window and survey the land. I chose the

northwest tower for my private quarters because it looks away from the dirty scum of the city with its crawling insects and instead shows a wild vista, with Penngrove Forest and the Dead Desert beyond.

I much prefer to overlook a vast desert where nothing can survive than the teeming streets of a filthy mortal town.

My door swings open silently, but I hear the movement of the air. "Yes, Margrave?"

"Lay out my blades. I intend to practice." My hand flows to the hilt of Ashmodu, but I won't use it today. "The steel and the copper."

"Yes, Margrave."

My fingers tap impatiently against the window ledge as I listen to the footsteps climbing to the floor above, selecting the swords I've requested, and setting up an array of targets.

My gaze falls on the bookshelf beside my bed. It has been years—decades, perhaps—since I pulled a tome from that shelf and indulged in reading. I no longer have patience for stories about mortals. Their failings and shortcomings are innumerable, and I find no joy in subjecting myself to them.

The bookshelf is little more than a table for my forest lilies. They remind me of an earlier life, and they are wilting. If a servant doesn't fetch more from Penngrove Forest this dusk, I will spill blood.

Footsteps patter down the stairs, and I cross the room in a few strides. I fling the door open to the surprised face of a servant.

"Th—the gymnasium is ready, Sir."

I brush past the fool. I have no need of being told the damn obvious.

Upstairs, I assess the layout the foolish servant selected.

He—or she, I can't recall—has placed a number of obstacles out among several targets.

Fine, that will do.

I pull off my dark shirt over my head and fling it aside. I flex my arm muscles, feeling pleasure in their strength. The one joy of being cast to earth is having a solid form that brims with power.

The copper. I snatch the red-brown sword from the cushion and throw it from hand to hand, feeling its weight. A copper blade is perfect for practicing deftness and precision. If I lose control and strike too hard, the finely wrought blade will bend.

I plan my route through the course, then leap over a pommel horse, spin, duck under a bar, and strike through the heart of a mannequin. Perfect.

The metal catches the light streaming through the window, reflecting coppery tones remarkably similar to Scarla's hair. There's no question about it. I shall have to dissect her abilities until I understand them well enough to control her properly. Her resistance to me is irritating.

I duck under another bar, then whirl around and stab at a sack of grogan. I pull back too late, and grains pour from the bag onto the floor. The blade is dented.

Damn that mortal.

"Servant," I call.

The door swings open. "Yes, Mar—"

"Tell our guest she is dining with me tonight. Tell her not to be late."

"Yes, Sir."

I swap the copper blade for the steel—I have no patience for precision work today. I whirl and leap and strike until sweat flows down my chest. I master my breathing and focus on the

136

challenge, honing my skill.

I will treat the mortal's abilities as a series of obstacles, and I shall overcome them. Starting at dinner. I shall unleash my seductive powers until she is a quivering mess. The thought of her haughty face melting into desire has my lips curling upward.

I will master her yet.

Yes, that mortal is a puzzle. And I intend to solve her.

* * *

The mortal slinks into the dining room with her infantile attitude, shoulders thrown back and feet stomping.

I'm already seated at the table's head, and I keep gazing out the window at the darkening sky, careful not to switch my attention to her. But I'm aware of her scowl, and the thought of her irritation is a warm ball of light inside me.

She's certainly not immune to being ignored.

"Do you intend to acknowledge me?" Even her voice is tinged with emotion. Honestly, the lack of control these mortals exhibit is pitiful. But she can control her response to my presence.

Interesting.

I let her wait before turning my face. She wears fitted black pants that hug her hips and an emerald green shirt of the softest silk that cradles her breasts, then sweeps in to her stomach. As I planned, the green shirt plays well off her copper hair.

Providing her with clothing is one more way to control her, of course. She shouldn't complain—it's all far finer and more flattering than her originals. I must remember to have those burned.

Interesting that she chose trousers instead of a dress. She has a wardrobe full of clothes that fit her perfectly, yet she has chosen the ensemble that most closely resembles her own filthy outfit.

The longer I stare mutely, the more her color rises. She stands at the far end of the table, hand on her hip.

Temper, temper, little mortal.

Rather than reply, I send a tendril of magic toward her and brush it against her cheek. Her blush rises further, but it seems to be anger, not arousal.

"Have the decency to reply, Margrave." She injects venom into my title.

Still immune, then. Interesting indeed.

I run my tendril of magic down her neck and can sense the softness of her skin and the intake of her breath. Moving slowly, I stroke my power down the swell of her breast and circle her nipple. I can sense it tightening, coming to life, and I wait for her to come to me.

She does not.

I speak low, husky. "Won't you join me, Scarla?"

She stares as though unsure of her next move. I thicken my magic and, with it, trace her nipple, then make bigger circles, feeling the fullness of her breast.

Finally, she moves toward me, and I take note to remember the amount of power necessary to compel her.

But she doesn't sit in my lap or drape herself across me as a normal human would. She falters, then sits at the place laid out for her. She is on my left side with a view out the window, but she is staring at me.

"How lovely of you to invite me to dinner." She emphasizes

the word invite as though there is poison in it.

"My pleasure," I purr. "You look stunning tonight." I soften my magic from a tendril to a swirl of smoke and wrap it around her, watching her to see the effect.

She stiffens, and her lips part. Her chest rises and falls rapidly, those breasts straining against the soft green fabric. I can see the stiff peaks of her nipples.

Finally, she's responding as she should. It feels like a victory.

She reaches for a glass of water, knocking it over. Liquid splashes across her lap, and she moves quickly to dab it with a napkin. The spell is broken.

For now. But I intend to keep testing her until she is entranced. Completely and forever.

Then she will have no thoughts of escape and will remain a contented prisoner until she dies.

Scarla

I want to slide face-first across the dining table and land with my tongue licking the Margrave's chest.

He'd sweep aside the plates and have me right here on the table. Legs wrapped around him, his corded thighs supporting him as he thrusts into me. He could rip off my trousers and slide the crotch of my panties aside, then push into my wet, wet core.

Fucking hell. Thank the Maker I poured cold water all over my lap; otherwise, I might enact that little daydream.

It doesn't help that the Margrave looks sexy as sin. A chocolate brown shirt is open at the collar, hinting at the sculpted golden chest I know lies beneath. Matched with the rugged three-day growth he always seems to have, he looks brutal and masculine and like melted cream would drip down his torso in delicious rivulets that I would have to clean up with my tongue.

Fuck. I am losing control. I grip the table hard, trying to focus on the woody grain beneath my fingers. His magic engulfs me, swallowing me in a mist. I can't decide if it's better or worse than the finger of power he traced along my breasts.

I pour myself some more water and hastily take a sip. Cold

liquid seems to be the antidote I need.

Thankfully, a train of servants arrives and distracts me, and the Margrave retracts his dark magic. They bear platters of meat and vegetables, far more than the Margrave and I could possibly eat. The thought of all that waste leaves me cold—thank the Maker.

I've already witnessed enough waste today—all those eggs at breakfast and then a ream of paper being thrown away in the afternoon. Honestly, if the Margrave hadn't summoned me to dinner, I would have dived into the trash and retrieved the paper, soiled or not. That stuff grows on trees.

The red-and-gold footmen place their dishes on the long table in silence, steaming meats and colorful vegetables. I want to grab hold of the woman who puts a plate of greens near me and beg her to stay to shield me from the Margrave.

How do these servants resist him?

All too soon, they are gone, leaving nobody between him and me. Footmen are dotted around the room's perimeter—minus the sandy-haired Robin—but the Margrave is closer. Near and urgent.

Immediately, he sends his cloud of sensual power to me, and my body responds with liquid warmth between my thighs.

"Take a bite," the Margrave purrs, and I almost choke. He definitely isn't talking about the food.

His voice reminds me of a mountain lion stalking prey, all deep and powerful. The skin along my legs tingles deliciously, robbing me of strength. If I wasn't sitting down, I would probably fall.

I busy myself with serving, plating food that I have no appetite for. Best keep my hands occupied with something other than pleasuring myself.

The Margrave leans forward, and the pressure between us builds like the air has nowhere to go. He rests his elbows on the table, clasps his hands, and his muscular forearms snag my attention. That chocolate brown shirt hugs his biceps. I look at my plate but don't see it—my focus is entirely on those powerful arms, those thick wrists, those large hands.

His hands look skillful like they could penetrate my defenses in an instant... or in a long, extended session. Stroking my neck, caressing my breasts, squeezing my ass, circling and teasing my clit.

My breath comes faster, and my skin is alight with sensitivity. I squirm in my seat, relishing the delicious pressure at the top of my thighs, feeling the silk of my shirt kiss my nipples gently, all too gently.

I'm staring openly at him now, no longer pretending to look at my plate.

I can't remember why I'm trying to resist him. I'm a grown-ass woman with sexual needs, and he's an attractive man. A fucking attractive man. Why shouldn't we indulge in pleasure while we're living and sleeping in the same place?

"Tell me what you're thinking," he purrs.

I can't do that, can I? I'm thinking we should ravage each other here and now, but that's not exactly polite dinner chat. Besides, there was some reason I shouldn't succumb to this pleasure, but my mind can't recall it.

I'm so wet now—and not from the lapful of water I spilled. Neither of us has touched our food. My fingers run along the wooden table, back and forth, feeling the smoothness with enhanced awareness, as though I've never touched polished wood before.

"Are you going to take a bite, Scarla?"

My gaze travels up to the Margrave's face. His lips are so full, and when my name falls from them, I shiver, straining against my shirt for more pressure on my breasts. His scent surrounds me, lilies of the forest but with a musky undertone, like he's lying in a wooded glade, sexually aroused.

A thrill runs through me that I, my femininity, my body, can get this perfect male aroused.

"Yes," I breathe. "As long as you promise to bite me back."

His full lips turn up in the hint of a smile. "Interesting."

Something in the tone of his voice jolts me from my haze. He's toying with me, seeing how far he can push me, as though I'm some sort of science experiment.

What a dick.

I stop caressing the wood and push a forkful of food into my mouth, chewing mechanically. Anything to take my mind off him. I force myself to remember why I'm here. To find Zaden, the angel who killed my sister.

"Are you Zaden?" I blurt out. I'd planned to be more subtle when I finally broached that subject with him, had intended to find the information I need with wiles and finesse. Instead, I shout it out. Like it will defend me from his seduction.

And, in a way, it works.

The sparkle from the Margrave's eyes vanishes, and his lips compress. The movement is slight, but I catch it. "The walls have ears, Scarla. We do not discuss Zaden here."

Those simple words are a revelation. Taking a sip of water, I try to unpack them. Firstly, he knows Zaden—that's a triumph in itself. A victory for me—I've been looking for that asshole for months.

Secondly, the Margrave isn't Zaden. I think. He didn't really make that clear, but he implied it. Unless he's one

143

of those arrogant guys who talks about himself in the third person—which I wouldn't put past him.

And thirdly, something is going on in this castle beyond the Margrave's control—otherwise, why would he say the walls have ears. It definitely sounds as though somebody—or somebodies—is working against him. And he, presumably, doesn't know who they are. I saw what he did to Robin last night; he definitely wouldn't hesitate to strike down his enemies. So the fact that he hasn't means he can't find them.

Perhaps I can find whoever is working against him and ally myself with them. Your enemy's enemy is your friend, and all that.

My appetite comes roaring back, and I snap a crunchy bean between my teeth. Things are looking up. Last night, I learned that he intends to keep me prisoner for life, which was a blow, I'm not gonna lie. But tonight, I'm finally finding the answers that I came for. When I have them, I'll escape, with or without killing someone first. Plain and simple.

The Margrave might think he controls his universe, but cracks are starting to appear.

And I intend to exploit them.

With my mouth full of chicken, the Margrave sends a powerful thread of magic toward me. Seriously, when will this guy give it a rest?

His power snakes around me, a purple-black coil of sexuality. My body immediately responds. Traitor. I focus on the thickening ribbon of magic so I can remember that he is trying to manipulate me. He isn't arousing me because he finds me attractive; he's doing it to control me.

That damn ribbon strokes my thighs and even finds its way right to my core, pressing and cupping me as though it were a hand. Fuck. I wriggle in my chair and dig my fingernails into my thighs, latching my focus onto the pain and ignoring the arousal.

Or trying to.

When I can't last a moment longer, I scrape out my chair with the backs of my knees and stand at my full height. I plaster a smile onto my face, digging my fingernails into the palms of my hand. "Thank you for a lovely dinner."

The frown that flits across his broad forehead delights me. Suck it, Margrave. If I hadn't been looking for his reaction, I wouldn't have seen it because the furrowed brow vanishes as soon as it appears. But I saw it. It gives me power.

I manage to escape the room, almost bursting with glee. I award myself five gold stars. Best of all, I think I've figured out the trick—keep a watchful eye on his magic, cause myself pain, and remind myself what an arrogant prick he is. The trifecta.

By the time I reach my room, my thrill has retreated into fatigue. It took a lot of energy to resist that male. I close the door behind me, knowing Molly will come and lock it later. I slump onto the sofa and remove my boots.

The bed looks so soft, so wondrously cozy. It beckons me like a siren's song but, despite my exhaustion, I can't sleep.

There's something else I must deal with first.

Scarla

It's a perfect torture.

And I've devised it for myself. Sitting on a hard wooden chair and staring at my bed but not allowing myself to climb into it. As the minutes pass, my head droops, and I shake awake. It happens on repeat.

Even all the demons in the Margrave's hell couldn't devise a better torture.

I jerk awake, and the light in the room seems different. The fire has burned low, and a smoky fog fills the room.

Wearily, I get to my feet and cross to the window, then fling it open and lean out as far as I can, kneeling on the soft sofa. It's past snowfall, and a white, crystalline blanket drapes across the world, reflecting moonlight. I take some deep breaths, inhaling the sweet cool air. This is my favorite time of day. I can imagine I am the only person alive and that the world laid at my feet was crafted just for me.

Below me, the river emerges from beneath the castle then runs in a wide arc all around it, acting as a protective moat, before wandering off past the town and away into the distance. It has already frozen over, which means it's time for me to act.

I cross to the bowl of water. It ain't so fresh anymore but streaked with blood and dirt. Even so, I splash some onto my face to wake myself properly.

I strip off the soft clothes that the Margrave gave me and step into my rough-spun pants and home-dyed blue shirt. Fancy clothes won't help me where I'm going. Then I pull on my ox-hide boots and shrug into my jacket.

Beaming with my own cleverness, I strip the pillowcases from the pillows. I stuff the cases into my jacket pocket—they will come in handy later.

Time to get to work.

Several large tapestries hang on my bedroom walls. The nearest one depicts a host of angels battling a swarm of demons in a complicated dance of archery and magic. I sweep it aside, amazed at its heft, and push myself between it and the cold stone wall, resisting its weight while my fingers seek an artificial break in the natural stone.

It's dark here and smells of the vinegar used to make the tapestry dyes fast. It's all I can do to force myself to slide deeper behind the wide tapestry while I look for the door that I hope is here.

That must be here.

The stone is cold and rough beneath my fingers. And completely unyielding. I emerge from the other end of the tapestry with mussed hair and fraying nerves.

The next hanging depicts a woman on a mountain top battling a single angel and, although the mortal has no hope of winning, I hope she does.

I heave the edge of the tapestry aside and slide behind it, and again the whiff of acetic acid greets me. The stone is just as cold and unyielding as everywhere else. Chisel marks show some poor slave has chipped away at the forbidding rock, like the girl facing a seemingly insurmountable opponent on the mountain.

But the slave beat the rock into submission, which gives me hope.

Maybe I'll beat the Margrave too.

The chisel marks and the rough stone make it impossible to detect any tiny cracks, and my hopes fall through the floor. I allow the weight of the tapestry to press me against the wall and slump.

There must be stranger places to sleep, but I can't think of any. My eyes flutter closed when a sense of falling startles me awake, and I find the wall is falling inward, opening.

I'm wide awake now, my heart pumping hard. I retrieve a pillowcase from my jacket pocket and lay it on the floor—it will prop the door open a crack so I can find my way back.

The torches have been extinguished, which should leave the inner maze in pitch black. But, luckily, the walls glow faintly, which must be from the magic that regulates the castle's temperature.

Thanks to years of living in an underground maze, I'm good at navigating half-blind. My sense of direction is as good as any Undercity-sider, and I get my bearings quickly.

Keeping my fingers trailing along each wall, I walk until I find the secret, curling staircase that hugs the outer wall of the northeast tower. It will take me to the first floor, at least, and I hope to find a hidden external door that will spill me out into the open air.

My footsteps echo in the close, stone passageway, so I end up walking like a crab in high heels to muffle the sound. It must look ridiculous, but at least it makes my giant ox-hide feet quiet.

The staircase descends to the first floor, where the servants sleep, and I look for the fork I spotted earlier. Heart fluttering, I take the second passageway, but it ends in a solid stone wall. Damn. Perhaps they meant to build an exit here but never got around to it?

"Lazy bloody slaves," I muse, making myself smile.

Sighing, I retreat to the servants' floor. The whole castle should be asleep. Judging by the moon's position in the sky, it was well after midnight when I left my room. Even the servants who have to rise early to cook breakfast and set fires won't be up yet, so I should be safe enough.

I risk poking my head out into the main corridor on the servants' floor. I walk a complete circuit of the castle, walking in my awkward silent pose in these ridiculous thick boots for a hundred feet along three of the four sides of the castle's square—keeping clear of the foyer which will be guarded—until I return to my starting point.

There are no external exits. Not even a single window on this floor.

"Maker-be-damned."

I must have missed something. I again head down the fork in the inner maze but find nothing but that annoying stone wall.

Then again, stone isn't always unyielding around here. I lean against the wall and push with all my might, but it doesn't give. I run my fingers along the edges but can't find anything. I even try falling asleep against it, but that doesn't work again.

Grunting, I sit on my bum cross-legged and stare at the wall. Just like the rest of the stone in the castle, it glows faintly, and staring at it is mesmerizing, like watching a rippling ocean. It's the visual equivalent of white noise, and my eyes begin to close. At the edges of my vision, I catch a shape in the rippling

149

waves of light.

The shape disappears when I stare at it, so I heave to standing and run my fingers along its outline.

It's a latch. I tug on it, and a section of stone the size of my forefinger hinges forward. I pull it, and the whole wall opens toward me.

Fumbling in my haste, I pull the second pillow slip from my pocket and lay it on the floor, hoping it will be enough to keep the door open. I stumble outside, tripping over a knee-high blanket of snow and landing flat on my face.

"Elegant as always, Scarla."

Lying flat in the snow, I'm tempted to wiggle my arms and legs to make an angel, then I remember how much I hate those celestial bastards and just clamber to my feet instead.

The door has already closed behind me, but I can just make out its outline against the dark stone. The moon has passed its zenith and smiles down on me, casting its serene glow across the glittering white world.

Trudging through snow is hard work, so I'm soon huffing and swearing.

"Where's a bloody horse and carriage when you need one?"

The river forms a circle around the castle, like a noose. By the time I reach it, I'm sweaty with effort and ready to nap.

I give myself two minutes sitting in the snow at the river's edge to gather strength, but I give up after one. My sweat is icing over, forming a sheen of frost on my face.

"Extra elegance," I mutter.

Iced sweat. That's gotta be new.

Luckily, the frigid temperatures have also iced over the river. I slide down the bank on my bum, which is now soaked through. After a long negotiation with my legs, I slip and slide to my feet and cross the frozen water. Thankfully, the layer of snow makes the ice less slippery—which is just as well because if it was any more slippery, I'd be better off coated in butter.

Finally, I'm across the river and climbing out onto the streets of Malanox.

Here in Hightown, all the rich folks are tucked up safely in bed, sleeping on thermal mattresses, as toasty as hell. In a few hours, their servants will rise, light their fires, and cook their breakfast like mini castle slaves.

Every man's house is his castle. Or, if you look at it from the servants' perspective, every man's house is his prison.

I make my way quickly through the streets of Hightown, sticking to the narrow alleys in case any patrols are out. With access to all the best materials—and sorcery, I now realize—the Margrave sometimes has guards patrolling Malanox, and I can't risk running into any tonight.

It might be my paranoia, but I see movement in the shadows and duck into Taylor's Lane, hoping to throw them off. My heart rate is already maxed out from exertion, and now I'm hearing scary noises. Heart attack, here I come.

Every dark window is like a soulless orifice, a dead eyeball watching me flounder along Taylor's Lane. I scurry, sticking to the walls, but those dark openings keep me in their sights, and I can't shake the feeling of dread.

When I round the corner into Main Street, my alarm intensifies. Deep snow keeps me moving slowly, like a sticky berry trap for catching insects, only I'm the bug. And those damn window eyes in the lurching stone buildings just stare at me.

Finally, I clear Hightown and enter Lowtown. Skitter beetles don't come out at night, and the snow muffles all sound, so I should feel as though I have the world to myself. But the sense of being followed and watched never leaves me, even as I skirt the snowmelt wells and head toward the Undercity.

Out here in the open, there is nowhere to hide. I glance behind me and see nothing but the distant huts of Lowtown and the stone edifices of Hightown beyond. Plus that damn castle, which is always watching.

Is that a movement in the shadows near that hut? It's too cold for mountain lions and too cold for skitter beetles; too cold for anything with a heart.

But not everything has a heart.

Shaking my head at my own foolish imaginings, I break into a run.

"I'm in a hurry," I pant, but that doesn't explain the pounding in my ears or my skyrocketing heart rate.

The snow isn't as thick on the road to the Undercity. The road was built with a steep camber, so the snow falls off to the sides. If I stepped off the edge into the ditch, I'd be buried in snow to my neck, but I know the road better than I know my own name, and I stick true.

A noise behind me has my jog becoming a sprint, with my heart racing too.

Panting, I come upon the Undercity puffing and spluttering and not even stopping to make fun of the mouthguard. The two men on duty wave me through, sharing a glance at my awkwardness, storing up another tale of my eccentricity to share around the fire later.

I don't even care; they can heap shit on me all day if they want, as long as they don't let whatever is following me into the Undercity.

I thrust aside the ox-hide hangings, soaking up the warmth, letting my fingers and toes thaw out, and my fear too.

Now I just have to find Dad and warn him that he's on the Margrave's radar.

Then I have to get back to the castle before my escape is noticed.

Otherwise, my dad will really have to watch his back.

Scarla

The ox-hide hangings are heavier than I remember—or I'm getting weaker.

I shoulder aside the second curtain and walk into the Undercity proper. The main cavern stretches before me, dotted with bonfires. Halfway along, the South Undercity peels away to the right and the North to the left.

My gaze is drawn right, where the old folks gather around the fire telling stories of the past. Or so I imagine. One woman catches my attention. I don't recognize her, but something about her looks wrong. Crows feet walk from the outsides of her eyes, and years of laughter line her face, but it isn't those features that attract me. It's the sheen emanating from her.

I approach her, completely sidetracked from my reason for risking my neck by coming here—and my dad's neck.

The old lady seems to be glowing, and I reach out a hand to see if it's real.

"What you doing, girl? Don't attack me." Her voice cracks with age, like her face.

Hard words lick my tongue, but I bite them back. "Sorry, Fra," I say instead. Surely a little kindness here won't ruin my tough reputation with Sadie's gang.

The sheen on her face reminds me of the Margrave's glow;

only hers is a subtle orange, not his vivid purple.

"Quit peering at me, girl."

I drop my arm to my side. "I work in the underwing. Are you unwell?"

She cackles, and the sound echoes off the walls. "I ain't sick, and you can't have it."

I cock my head. "I can't have what?"

The flames flicker off an old man's face across the fire, catching on his gappy smile. "Don't worry about Fra Fielding. She's not quite right up here." The man taps his temple.

I stare at the orange-tinted woman, and the longer I peer, the more the glow fades until it's nothing more than sun rash.

I shake my head. I was imagining things.

I turn and walk away, needing to find Dad and return to the castle before my absence is noted. As usual, the air is dank, making it smell safe. Homey.

Dad should be on night shift, so hopefully, he's hanging around somewhere near the dining hall. Otherwise, he could be anywhere, and I'll have a hell of a time finding him. Sometimes Dad covers shifts in the mines, sorts goods in the warehouses, or processes hides in the factory center. Oftentimes, he works closely with the Undercity Council, so he could be off on an errand for them.

As I cross the main cavern, the ceiling extends above me, giving the impression that I'm entering a large cone. My fingers pat a tune against my thumbs, channeling my nervous energy, and I glance left and right, looking for my dad.

No sign of him. Noises from the kitchen draw my attention, and I figure I might as well ask around.

The duty chefs are Pa and Fra Stollen from my sleeping hub. They look like siblings but—I really hope—they aren't. Both have short faces with narrow noses and dull gray eyes atop short, thin bodies.

"Hi, Scarla."

Fra Stollen looks at me without friendliness, and a pang of loneliness strikes me. Suddenly I regret my reputation for sullenness. Folks don't make conversation with me because they don't want their heads bitten off, and now I'm reaping the reward.

Either I'm Little Miss Sarcasm or Little Miss Bitch.

"Fra Stollen." I toy with the idea of asking after her kids or her health. "Where's my dad?" It comes out more aggressive than I intended.

"No idea."

I must've heard Fra Stollen gossip a thousand times to her friends in sleeping hub S2A7, and it irks me every time, but now that I need some information out of the woman, she won't spare a syllable.

"It's really important," I say.

Her face softens. "Sorry, love. I haven't seen him since dusk."

I sigh. "Okay. Well, if you see him, let him know I...."

I suddenly don't know what to tell this woman. I barely know her, and she could be a spy for the Margrave for all I know. If I tell her I'm trapped in the castle, word will definitely get back that I escaped. On the other hand, if I don't get a message to my dad, he won't know to stay out of sight and change sleeping hubs.

Indecision makes a fool of me.

Fra Stollen's face hardens again, and her lips press into white lines. Her gray eyes lose some of their dullness. "Yes?"

"Don't worry," I mutter. The world has shifted on its axis

these last 24 hours, and I no longer know who to trust.

Time is running out. I don't have enough hours to run through the warehouses and the factory district, let alone the miles and miles of mine shafts. Besides, the mining tunnels are one maze I haven't cracked yet.

My belly twists with rising anxiety. I have to be back at the castle well before dawn, and who knows how hard it'll be to locate the secret entrance? Not to mention how slow it is trudging through knee-high snow.

I'll check the sleeping hub, then I'll have to make a call—leave a message and risk being exposed, or don't and leave him in danger.

Either way, I'm risking his life. And mine.

I stride across the cavern fast enough to make my copper hair flow out behind me. From the corner of my eye, I glimpse a familiar shock of red hair emerging from the tunnel that only leads to the underwing, the mines, and the stairs up to the council chambers. A moment of uncertainty furrows my brow because he doesn't have business being in any of those places, but it washes away instantly.

"Leo!"

Relief courses through me, and my belly untwists. Finally, somebody I can trust.

I throw myself against his chest, rub my cheek on his rough shirt, and wrap him in my arms, breathing in his familiar grainy scent.

"Heya, Scar. How's it going? You all right?"

I wriggle free of his strong embrace and look up at him, reeling in shock. His complexion is sickly and green, and he's coming from the hospital wing. His freckles have vanished under the green hue. Up close, even his hair color looks wrong.

"Are you sick, babe? You look awful. Were you coming from the underwing? What were you doing in there?" I can't stop the barrage of questions, and my gut twists tighter than ever. If something happened to Leo, I don't know what I'd do.

"Gee, thanks. Awful did you say?"

I put a hand to his cheek and press, expecting the flush of fever, but he feels normal. "What were you doing in the underwing?"

Leo never showed any interest in the hospital ward before his long journey across the desert to Desert's Maw. Since his return, he's spent longer and longer by my side, watching me work with the patients. I always assumed it had something to do with his developing feelings for me, but that doesn't explain what he was doing there without me.

He blinks a couple of times before answering. "I was looking for you." His eyebrow twitches in a gesture I've recognized since we were kids. It's his tell. He's lying.

But why?

"Are you sick?"

I squint at him, but that greenish hue has faded from his cheeks, and he looks as ruddy and healthy as ever.

"Sick without you," he jokes, smirking, his freckles dancing in the firelight.

I swat at him. "Cut it out. Listen, there's something I need to tell you. I've been kidnapped by the Margrave and taken to his castle."

I stare into his deep brown eyes intensely, watching for the moment that the knowledge hits him. He'll be infuriated. Probably, I'll have to convince him not to come and rescue me.

It never happens. He blinks some more, then throws back his head and roars in laughter, loud enough to wake the Gods.

Dumbfounded, I watch his shoulders heave and his throat bubble and listen as he laughs at my misery. "Cut it out."

He finally gets himself under control. "Good one, Scarla. I needed that."

I shake him, gripping so hard that my thumbnail digs in below his scapula. That gets his attention.

"I'm not joking."

"In that case, I think *you'd* better go to the underwing for a checkup. Because I got some news. You're not kidnapped in a castle. You're right here."

Understanding washes over me, and I'd laugh too if I wasn't filled with terrifying adrenaline. "Right. Well, I've escaped, but I have to be back before dawn. I just need you to pass on a message to my dad. He needs to change sleeping hubs because the Margrave knows where he sleeps and is threatening to kill him." The laughter washes from Leo's face completely. "Can you tell him that? And tell him I have to stay in the castle for now, but I'm working on an escape. Tell them not to do anything, just to keep safe. Can you tell him that?"

While I've been talking, Leo's been deflating. He is crest-fallen, a smaller and sadder man than he was a few moments ago, and I'm sorry to have been the cause of it. "Are you serious?"

I nod.

Leo grips my arms. "Of course I'll tell him, Scar. Holy crap. What's going on? Why has the Margrave... taken you?"

I shrug, and Leo drops my arms like hot embers. The relief of having passed on my message to someone I trust has me sagging. I could curl up on the hard floor right here in the main cavern and go to sleep. "I'm still trying to figure that out. But he's treating me well. Good meals and a soft bed."

Leo's mouth twists. "But not as many moonlight walks."

Leo knows those are my favorite, and it's sweet of him to think about them. I take his hand. "Well, I got one this evening."

Leo puts his other hand on top of mine and holds tight.

"Don't go back. The Margrave is dangerous, Scar. You don't know how dangerous. He's not the man you think he is, and you'll never be safe in his castle."

"Babe, he's threatening my dad. He'll kill him if I don't go back. I saw him slice down a guard for opening his mouth, and he'd murder my dad in an eyeblink. I can't risk it."

Leo's big brown eyes shine in the reflected firelight. His grip on my hand tightens. "I can take you across the desert—I know how to get across. We'll take your dad too. We can get to Desert's Maw and start a new life there. You and me and your dad. Say yes, Scarla. Just say yes, and you'll never have to worry about the Margrave again."

A future flashes before me where Leo and I live with my dad in a stone house aboveground in Desert's Maw, which I think of as being identical to Malanox—a lack of imagination, I guess. But I can't see myself with Leo. Not yet. Maybe one day.

Leo is offering me his future, tied with a bow, but I can't accept it. I can't let Leo unroot his entire life—his family, his friends, his job—just to rescue me from the Margrave. I can't destroy Leo's life like that. Not when I can't offer him my heart on return.

And I can't leave with all these open questions buzzing through my brain. My sister's death has occupied my thoughts since she drew her last breath, and I need answers that only the Margrave can provide.

Besides, I don't think running away would work. I'd never really feel safe. The Margrave is powerful and determined, and I can't see a puny desert stopping him.

Leo's hands are clasping mine in a vice, and his gaze hasn't left my face.

"I can't, Leo." I shake my head.

He releases my hand like he's throwing a ball. I've clearly upset him. That green tinge in his face flares up, and I shake my head to disperse it. I need sleep.

"Fine. Run back to the Margrave. But never let down your guard. Angels seduce mortal women and make them fall in love with them. If he seduces you, you will never be able to escape. Do you understand? If you sleep with an angel, you'll be enraptured, and you'll never get free. Never. Keep your defenses up always. Do you promise?"

A shiver runs down my spine. That's a shitload harder than it sounds. "I promise. And will you make sure my father doesn't try to rescue me? I can't lose him too."

Leo's shoulders drop like a man defeated. "I promise. But Scarla?"

"Yes?"

"Meet me at dusk tomorrow. I need to know you're okay."

"I can't keep leaving the castle. It's too dangero—"

"What if your dad doesn't believe me?"

I watch Leo's chest rise and fall several times, thinking it over. He didn't think I was serious, so why would my dad? I need to convince him face to face.

"Okay. Meet me in Hightown at dusk, on Washmaiden Lane." I have no idea if I'll be able to get away, but I'll cross that bridge when I come to it.

My internal clock tells me that dawn is approaching. I

punch Leo lightly on the shoulder, channeling some of that playfulness we used to share so easily. "Thanks, babe. I've gotta go."

His lip twitches in an attempt at a smile. "Stay safe."

I smile. "Promise."

I turn to leave the Undercity, hoping that's a promise I can keep.

Scarla

Melting snow is a real bastard.

By the time I reach the castle, I'm soaking wet, and my coarse pants are dragging me down. The sky is more gray than black.

The going is easier in the slush, and my track has melted into obscurity, masking my escape. When I see the bedraggled pillowcase poking out between two stones, I release a sigh I hadn't known I was holding. I found it!

The pillowcase has left open a tiny crack in the wall, and I grip it with my fingernails, pulling with all my might but having no effect on the mass of stone.

"Think, Scarla. What would Leesa do?"

Leesa wouldn't be in this mess in the first place. She would push her blue-black hair behind her ears and frown.

What about Mom? What would she do? Unfortunately, I have no idea. She died when I was young, so I don't have a clear image of her, other than her auburn hair that used to glow in the firelight. I always thought she was a fire spirit. Her name was Rose, so I used to imagine her as a red rose licked with flames.

Sometimes I think Mom never died at all but only left on a grand adventure and will return one day. I certainly don't have any clear memories of her death.

I sigh. Reminiscing doesn't help.

I take a step back from the wall and squint at it. When I focus, the dim light within the stones glows, and it's brighter in a tiny patch near the crack. I prod at the spot, and a latch pops open.

Grinning, I grab on and yank the door open. With one last glance at the sky, I allow myself to relax. I've made it.

I gather the sodden pillowcase—that will be hard to explain—then wearily climb the stairs. That soft mattress in my bedroom beckons.

Up on the second floor, I head south along the inner maze toward my bedroom, keeping an eye open for my second pillowcase and a chink of light. It feels as though I've been in this corridor for hours, plodding through the dark and clambering over doorways. I turn another corner. Surely my bedroom will be here. In my fatigue, my sense of direction is crap.

Turning another corner, I stop in my tracks. I'm back at the servant staircase. I've made a complete loop of the inner maze.

A figure emerges from the gloom, his broad shoulders blocking the entire corridor. His voice is croaky, like he's just finished a breakfast of gravel. "You looking for this, little rabbit?"

In the dim light flickering from within the stone walls, I see his lips tighten, exposing crooked teeth, and he holds something up.

My pillowcase.

"Somebody's been a very naughty little rabbit."

My heart rate picks up, and my breaths come fast and

shallow. I quickly look around for options. My usual trick of delaying until the sun rises or sets won't work here, so I can either race down the curling stairs or let this creepy hunter catch me.

I choose the stairs.

I fly down, two at a time, and spill out into the servants' corridor on the first floor. It's wider than the inner maze but not as grand as the corridors throughout the rest of the castle.

A moment of indecision kills me. The hunter hooks a meaty arm around my neck, pulling me close to his chest.

He smells of soap. Why is this brute so sparkly and fresh? I kick out at him, aiming for a heel to his knee, but ending up flailing like a frost beetle on a line.

The servant's corridors are lit with a few torches—somebody must be already awake—so I can see my hunter's arm is red with gold trim around the cuff. He's wearing the Margave's livery. A servant.

How can I already have made an enemy? I've only been here a few days, and already people hate me. Not just this guy, but Lord Xerxes as well.

Maybe they're connected?

He tightens his forearm around my neck, and I gurgle, gasping for oxygen.

His breath does not smell of soap—it stinks, and it's steaming up my ear. "You're coming with me, little rabbit. But keep struggling. I like the ones with fight."

I shout for help, but his sausage fingers clamp across my lips, and a deep chuckle reverberates from his chest and down my spine.

Calm the fuck down, Scarla, I tell myself. Flat panic never got anybody out of a tight spot.

165

But, strangely, swearing at myself doesn't make me more relaxed either. My eyes dart around the corridor, and I try to bite down on his fingers but only earn another chuckle.

Where is he taking me? And who is this man?

If this guy would just let me speak, I could probably talk my way out of the situation or at least get some answers.

He drags me backward, yanking me by the neck. Both my hands are on his forearm, trying to support my weight, and blood is pounding in my ears. I stumble a few paces. I know I'm helping, in a way, but I can't lift my legs or I'll strangle.

Wriggling, biting, and kicking, I still make no impact on our progress and only seem to make the hunter happier.

I feel it before I see it—a thrill of power coming nearer and stronger.

The Margrave rounds the corner in a swirl of energy. It's too dark to see them, but I'm sure his eyes are as black as coal.

The hunter's laughter crumbles into dust.

The Margrave fills the entire corridor, his hair brushing the ceiling and his shoulders feathering the walls. His presence is commanding, intoxicating.

"Put her down."

There is no question of disobeying. The hunter releases me, and I land in a crouch. Without even glancing at me, the Margrave strides past, his eyes burning with electricity.

He wears black pants that drape from his hips and nothing else. Bare-chested, as though he dressed in a hurry. Perhaps he heard my muted cries for help?

The firelight glimmers off the Margrave's golden muscles, bunched with potential energy. One hand holds a sword glowing with power, black veins and purple smoke dancing along its blade.

His muscles flex as he raises the weapon.

"Wait," I cry. We need answers from this man, like who he's working with and why the fuck he attacked me. As much as I'd like to see him dead, killing him won't achieve anything until we have answers.

But the Margrave is deaf to my command. The sword strikes, slicing through the hunter, spraying his blood across the walls.

Shock numbs me, and I can't feel my feet, but I take a step forward anyway.

The hunter is dead. His insides are on the outside, and vice versa. Even if I could—and if I wanted to—there is no healing him now.

"You shouldn't have killed him."

The Margrave turns his blackened face to me, pulsing with power, rendering me mute.

He is in a killing trance, and I want to flee, to follow my sensible flight instinct right out of here. But my damn feet are frozen to the floor.

The dark magic inside the Margrave ebbs away, and his face returns to that of a man, not a god. His black eyes lighten and sharpen into that piercing shade of green, seeming to glow with their own inner light. He lowers his sword, and his muscles relax. Raw aggression transforms into contained power.

He runs a hand across his rough jaw, and his voice is harsh. "Sentimentality has no place in Malanox Castle." He drops his hand to his side and turns his focus on me.

The angel has never looked more dangerous. His chest looks even bigger in the flesh with no fabric to cover it. All bulging muscles and hard lines, sculpted to perfection. But, with splashes of his victim's blood, those muscles definitely aren't just for show.

I shudder. I may have been better off going with the hunter.

The Margrave's gaze travels down my legs and back up. "You're wet."

I'm wet from running through the snow, and I have no excuse ready. I'd planned to be back in bed before anybody saw me. And I'm probably splashed in the servant's blood. I can barely think.

"It's not sentimentality," I splutter. "I need to know where he was taking me. And why."

The Margrave stares at me for a heartbeat, as unmoving as stone, insight swirling in the depths of his eyes. I wonder how much he knows and what he isn't telling me. "You don't need to know. Now go get yourself cleaned up before breakfast. I don't want to dine with a vagrant."

He dismisses me with a flick of his wrist, making heat rise in my chest.

"I'm not some servant you can discard."

His face snaps back toward mine. "No?" He considers me again, and I silently curse myself for drawing his attention back to my bedraggled state, which I can't explain away.

I try anyway. "Somebody left some water in my room," I say, as though any sensible person would pour the water all over their dirty clothes while still wearing them.

He crosses his arms over his broad chest, flexing his muscular forearms. I imagine running a finger along their contours, wondering if they'd feel supple or firm.

Firm, I imagine. Hard. His entire body looks like rock.

His voice snaps my attention to his lips, which are twitching in a smirk. "Go down to the bathing pool and clean yourself up."

Heat is in my cheeks, and I'm ashamed at how quickly I was entranced. Just one look at his forearms almost had me down on one knee proposing marriage. Doesn't help that below his hard stomach, I can see the top of a sculpted V diving down inside his pants.

Leo's warning against enchantment flow through my mind, and I know I have to be on my guard around this angel.

I nod. "Okay."

I can't help it. Before I leave, my eyes drop down to that V again, lingering on its outline.

I tear my gaze away and turn. "Maker help me," I whisper.

Scarla

Master has commanded, so the slave must obey.

Whether I like it or not.

The only way down to the lake is via the central staircase. It is extra luxurious compared to the cramped servants' quarters—and that claustrophobic inner maze that I hope never to see again.

Frankly, I'd rather crawl into bed and sleep for a thousand years, but the Margrave ordered me downstairs, thinking I'd had a full night's sleep, and I can't make him suspicious.

Besides, it will be heavenly to get out of these filthy clothes. Being provided with a wardrobe full of fine clothing by your jailer isn't so bad.

The underground lake is pristine, even more beautiful than I remember. Cool, clear water bubbles up from deep underground and sparkles under the glowing blue walls. The ground slopes gently into the lake, firm and smooth underfoot.

It feels like a small piece of heaven, and I understand why the Margrave chose this castle as his home.

I let my pants slide to the floor, then wriggle, so my panties drop onto them. I pull off my shirt and throw it down too. It's hardly blue anymore, more like a grimy brown. The lot of them should be incinerated. Even soiled, they make a cozy little heap on the ground, and I wonder if they'd make a good pillow.

Sighing, I dip a toe into the water. It's cool and inviting. The rock floor slopes downward gently, so I can wade in. When the water reaches my thighs, I shiver.

A sense of freedom washes over me. Apart from cleaning in this oasis, I haven't been completely naked in years. Sharing living quarters with a bunch of families makes everybody expert at changing in stealth—top first, then the bottom, so part of our bodies is always covered.

And living from snowmelt means bathing is done in parts too. A scrub here and a dab there.

I hadn't realized what I was missing out on. I stretch my arms above my head luxuriously, entwining my arms. I never knew how sensational fresh air could feel when pressed against every inch of exposed skin.

I want to be clean, so I dip my hands in the water and wash my face, rubbing away the dirt and grime. Next, my armpits. The crystalline water washes away the stench, leaving me clean and free. I splash water on my breasts, and my nipples stand out, sensitive to the cold water.

The water is sensual, the droplets tracing the curves of my body in rivulets, making me aware of my tingling skin.

Maybe the water is magical? Or perhaps it's the lingering image of the Margrave's muscular forearms. My breasts are yearning for touch, and I place my hands gently on them, increasing the pressure to satisfy the craving but finding no release.

Silken warmth pools between my legs, and I catch my nipples between two fingers, arching my back and picturing the Margrave's hands on my flesh.

Powerful heat swirls around me, and I squirm, trying to place pressure on my core from the movement of my hips, clasping my full, yearning breasts.

A throat clearing from behind me has me turning in an instant, dropping my hands and burning in shame.

The Margrave stands at the foot of the stairs, watching me. His eyes burn black, and I fear I've triggered a killing trance, but he makes no move toward me.

"Enjoying yourself, mortal?"

He's pulled a loose black shirt on over those hip-hugging black pants. The material is plain. But the look on his face is purely exotic, like sin personified.

For unending moments, we stare at each other. I am in thigh-deep water, facing him, legs apart, completely naked.

For the briefest moment, I think I see the outline of massive black wings behind him, rising from behind his shoulders and touching the rock ceiling. I could use those as a blanket, wrap myself inside the feathers and have sweet, sweet dreams.

My knees weaken, dipping me into the lake. The water reaches the apex of my legs, an excruciatingly gentle caress.

I snap to my senses and let myself plunge into the water, although the translucent blue liquid does little to cover my nudity.

The blackness in the Margrave's eyes disperses, and he clears his throat again. "I came to check on you."

Came to seduce me, more likely. "And it didn't occur to you I might be naked?"

I wish he would blush, or stutter, or stumble, but he just stares at me blankly. Then a cheeky smirk lands on his face. "Oh... it occurred to me."

He takes another step forward, and I respond by backing

away. If he keeps this up, I'll go so deep my head will go underwater, and then I won't be able to breathe and I'll drown. Perhaps that's what he has in mind.

Maybe I'm already entranced because I can't tear my eyes away when he removes his shirt. He reaches an arm to the nape of his shirt then pulls it over his head, revealing sculpted golden muscles and shoulders that look even broader without clothes. His beauty is breathtaking, enchanting, and suddenly I want to be enraptured by him, seduced by his magic.

The hard planes of his chest bathe in the reflected glow from the blue water, and I'm struck by an impulse to stroke their contours, outline their muscular shape, run a finger around his nipple. Just to see how firm the muscles are and how soft the skin is—purely for scientific purposes.

I run my gaze down the lines of his chest, over the ridges of his abdomen, to the firm plane of his stomach. He tapers at the waist, then broadens, and a sharply defined V draws the eye down.

My breath quickens.

Languidly, his hand moves to his belt buckle, and my jaw drops open. I catch the amusement in his eyes, so I jerk my face away and show him my back. I can't have him thinking I'll fall into bed with him... I can't have myself thinking that either.

Splashes of water behind me indicate that he's wading into the lake with me.

Amusement imbues his tone. "It's safe. You can turn around now."

Gingerly, I rotate, careful to keep everything from my neck down below the water. I see his pants on the rocky floor beside his shirt, and my pulse double-times in my neck.

"Are you always this squeamish around men?" His voice is deeper and huskier than I recall, and it takes all my courage to look at him.

"Only around evil angels."

"Evil?" He cocks his head.

I count his deeds off on my fingers. "Kidnap. Murder. Concealing your identity. Murder. Oh, and did I mention? Murder."

He splashes water on his face. "That's quite the list."

I take another step away. "Yes. Do I need to add sexual assault?"

His smirk turns to a scowl, and dark waves of energy roll off him. "I don't take what isn't given freely."

I float into shallower water and plant my bum on the rock, pulling my legs in close to hide my breasts. Considering his severe response to that sandy-haired servant who talked shit about me, I think the Margrave is telling the truth.

"That's good to hear."

As though I've passed some kind of test, the Margrave's dark mood passes, and his features relax. I think his good moods are either smirk or relax, and his bad moods are either brood or kill.

Relax is the best of the bunch.

I swirl my arms in the water, marveling how it flows over and eddies under, imagining this is how it feels to fly. "Why am I here?"

Why is he so protective of me? Why did he rescue me from the hunter? Why did he injure the sandy-haired footman? What the hell is going on?

One question at a time.

I don't expect him to answer, but the words tumble from my

mouth. "Why me?"

The Margrave dives under the water and disappears from view. The seconds pass, but he still doesn't emerge. Panicking, I stand, and water gushes off my body, but all I can see is the shadow of the male lying on the bottom of the lake. He has been under too long without breathing. He must be dead.

I should be relieved, but I'm jumpy, anxious, like the whole world is spinning out of control, and I can't do anything about it.

As suddenly as he disappeared, the Margrave emerges from the deep with his hair slicked back and snarls when he sees me standing naked. "Sit down."

Startled, I do as he commands. That's really annoying. I must take better care not to obey him in the future.

He watches me. "You're a vestige."

The rock is hard beneath my bum, so I push off and float in his direction. "What's a vestige?"

He puts a hand to his head as though he's wrestling with how much to tell me. "A vestige is created when an angel dies."

My back stiffens. "No. I've never seen an angel die. I'd never even seen an angel before you."

He looks at me sharply. "The vestigial powers are inherited from father to son. Or in your case...." He gestures towards my breasts. "From father to daughter."

I can feel my brow crease. "So my father saw an angel die?"

The Margrave nods. "Or his father before him. Or his father's father. The vestigial powers wax and wane through the generations."

I shake my head. This dude must have me confused with somebody else. I don't have any celestial powers—I didn't even believe in angels two days ago. And now this giant of a man with wings and a massive cock is telling me I'm part angel.

The Margrave shakes his head. "You're not part angel."

Shit. "Can you read my mind?"

He doesn't bother answering. "A vestige is like a conduit for power. Like a tub that can have power poured into it if the circumstances are right. If you are present at the death of somebody with powers, you inherit those powers."

I'm shaking. If I expected a comforting hug, I don't get one. The Margrave's stare is as stony as the castle itself.

"So, I'm like a big well, and you want to fill me up?"

The Margrave almost chokes when I say this, and he looks away. Finally, he's allowing emotion to show—other than murderous rage. He clears his throat. "I wouldn't quite put that way." He glances away. "And no, I don't want to...fill you up. I'm just interested in the powers you've already obtained."

I shake my head. "I don't have any powers. Sorry to disappoint, babe."

"None?"

Now I know he's got me confused with somebody else, so my shock subsides. I'm not even shaking anymore. In fact, I'm doing a decent impersonation of a brave person. "I think I'd remember if I could fly or cut down my enemies with a single blow."

He doesn't even crack a smile. "I see. Do you like this pool?"

"Way to change the subject, buddy. Yes. Your underground lake is charming. I can see why you had it installed."

He quirks an eyebrow. "The water's not too cold?"

As though responding to his gravelly voice, my nipples tighten at the memory of the chill when I first entered the lake.

"No."

"None of the servants bathe here," he remarks mildly.

I try to mimic his smooth style and push water away to the sides to propel myself forward, but I don't go anywhere. "Perhaps if you gave them some time off, they'd be able to go for a swim."

He watches me closely, making me feel a fool, so I stop splashing about and try to look sophisticated.

He smirks again. "No. It's because it's too cold for them."

My whole body freezes. Shit. I've given myself away. I hug my arms. "Yes, it is quite cold. I think I'll get out."

He nods once, then turns and rises from the lake like Poseidon. Water streams from his muscular back and his tight, round butt. A sensual waterfall. He sweeps down an arm and snatches up his clothes without breaking stride, then disappears up the stairs.

He yells over his shoulder. "I'll have some clothes sent down to you."

And, just like that, I'm alone again.

The Margrave

I leave the pool with my back to Scarla so she doesn't see my massive erection. Without turning around, I call instructions over my shoulders and stride up the stairs while I still have control.

She's just a mortal woman, so why are her curves engraved on my retinas? Why is the sway of her hips and the line of her neck so mesmerizing? It's supposed to be the other way around.

Angels seduce women, and that's that.

What's more, she should be throwing herself at me, pressing her full breasts against my chest and begging me to hold her.

She should be licking my chest with her perfect tongue and calling my name on her lips.

I shake my arms out, and droplets splash the stone walls. Perhaps it's a vestigial power she inherited? Yes, that must be it.

It's more fodder for my study of her, and even if her resistance is frustrating, it is also interesting.

Refusing to hide my arousal like a teenager, I march through the castle in my full glory. My staff is bred and trained to look away, but more than one servant reaches up and touches my chest as I pass, unable to resist the naked angelic allure.

So what's with Scarla? This experiment is becoming frustrating.

I pull my clothes on and snap at a staring servant. "Take a fresh gown down to the pool for our guest."

As soon as I laid eyes on her down in the lake, my control almost slid away. In the moment before she knew I was there, she was swept away in her own pleasure, her arched back making her breasts and bottom more voluptuous. Small moans reached my ears, so quiet she was probably unaware of them herself. Her skin looked like cream over velvet, and I felt my magic snaking around her body, increasing her arousal.

Shaking my head, I march along the corridor, feeling my sorcery awaken at the very idea of her.

I stop in my tracks. Cowardice comes in many forms, and scurrying off to my tower to avoid a mere mortal must be the worst kind. I turn on my heel and retrace my steps, heading toward her chamber.

I burst into her room without knocking, making sure she knows damn well who's castle this is. She's fully clothed, thank the Maker, but I still see the image of her naked and arched in pleasure, with her hands pressed against her own breasts.

Pressing my lips thin, I growl. "Good. You're out. But what are you wearing? I sent you a dress."

Her shoulders press back, and the thin shirt pulls tight across her chest, making me harden. It is mustard yellow with a scooped neckline, exposing a swathe of pristine flesh below her white neck.

"I'm not some doll for you to dress up as you please. I won't be paraded about in skirts—they're as restrictive as any prison cell. I insisted that Molly let me select trousers

179

from the wardrobe, and if you have a problem with that, you can damn well wear a dress yourself and see how you like it."

Her chin is thrust forward, and anger clouds her face, which should be repellent. It's a mortal's face, an insect's visage. But hers is full and round and soft in all the right places, and I can barely drag my eyes from her lips.

The truth is, she looks better in pants. They hug the shape of her legs and draw attention to the place where they meet, making it hard for me to think.

Just making me hard.

Damn her vestige powers.

"Wear whatever you please. It means nothing to me."

Liar.

She stands on one foot, thrusting her hip out, and all I can see is the memory of her hand running down her naked flesh. "Why are you here, Margrave?"

That's an excellent question. But not one I'm about to answer. She will never have the privilege of hearing that she arouses me when thousands of mortal women have failed to do so over centuries.

Never.

Nor can I admit my true purpose—that I intend to seduce her to make her a more willing prisoner. A bewitched mortal causes no trouble.

"It's my castle. I won't justify my movements to you."

Her lips twitch in a damn smile, and I sense that she's mocking me. When did she get control over this conversation? But still, I can't draw my eyes away from that curved mouth.

I step closer, and she backs away, fear registering in her eyes. "Are you here to seduce me?"

"Seduce you? Now, that's a good idea."

I stop my advance because it only makes her press further away. Instead, I look at the tapestry on the wall. It's the one that is supposed to remind us angels that we are not infallible: it depicts a human woman battling Samael, and it always makes me shudder.

A mortal should never have that much power.

Suddenly, Scarla is beside me, and her blyberry aroma envelops me, making my breath hitch.

Transfixed on the tapestry, I pretend not to notice how close she is, but warmth radiates from her like a furnace, and I feel my magic rising in response.

"Will you tell me a secret, Margrave?"

She's breathing on my shoulder, and when I turn to face her, only inches separate us. "No," I say firmly.

She beckons me down, and like a tame puppy, I bend. Best to keep her happy, after all—a happy prisoner is a compliant one.

Her lips are a whisper away from mine, and her scent is all-encompassing. Her tone is lilting, and her lips curving. She is an interesting experiment indeed.

She reaches up and rests a cold hand on the back of my neck. "Please."

Finally, my seduction is working. She strains to reach me, and my magic springs in response. I close the distance between us and press my lips against hers, tasting her sweet, blyberry lips, which are softer than the ripest peach.

She bites my lower lip, and I become fully hard, straining at the fly of my pants.

"What's your name, Margrave?" She's talking through the kiss, and her lips are pressed against mine again.

Burning awareness of her every limb scorches me. I have

one hand on her hip and the other on the small of her back, applying gentle pressure, but not enough to ease the aching in my cock. "Zaden."

Her hand is around the back of my neck and the other on my chest. But when I speak my name, she freezes and then pushes me away.

It takes every ounce of celestial strength I possess to let her pull away, and my magic coils around her, beckoning her, but somehow she resists. Irritating mortal.

Her face is unreadable, and the only thing that I can tell from it is that it doesn't want to be kissed.

She points to the door. "Zaden, you may leave."

Like a fucking tame pet, I do. I cross the room and get out of there. But if she thinks she can order me about in my own castle, she's wrong. And if she thinks she can resist me, she's wrong.

Seduction is the master art of angels, and I intend to make her my puppet.

Scarla

The heat at the apex of my thighs turns icy cold when he says his name. "Zaden."

I point to the door and make him leave, and, thank the Maker, he does.

The door closes behind him with a thud, and I stare at it, trying to make sense of what I heard. Dread surrounds me in a cloud, a halo of bitterness.

I was starting to hope that the Margrave and Zaden were two separate people. The Margrave has been so protective of me, shielding me from his servants with a ferocity I can't understand. Part of me thought that maybe, just maybe, he found me desirable and... liked me.

And that kiss—oh, God, that kiss.

"Idiot!"

I'm still standing like a statue, frozen to the spot. The only thing I knew two days ago was that Zaden was involved in my sister's death. Now I know that Zaden is the Margrave.

This answers one question, but so many more crowd my mind, clamoring for answers. Like why did he even tell me his name? Why did he kiss me? Was it just to seduce me so I'll be a willing prisoner? Why am I here? And, most important of all, did he kill my sister?

Like ice cracking, I finally move and flop onto the soft bed. I'm here because I'm a vestige—that's the only possible explanation. I try to let that sink in, rolling the concept around in my mind as I wriggle an indent into my pillow, getting comfortable.

I possess the vestigial power of an angel. Magic associated with the death of an angel courses through my veins. And some aspect of this vestigial power is important to Zaden.

Or he's full of shit.

Using as little strength as possible, I kick off my boots then crawl under the heavy comforter.

I didn't even know that angels could die. That's good news, at least.

My eye lands on that tapestry of the lone woman battling the evil angel. Does she think she can kill him? How does an angel die? This question is becoming less hypothetical with every passing hour.

My gaze flits to the other tapestry, the battle between the angels and demons. It's colorful and dramatic, but the question is... Is it historically accurate? Tales of celestial battles are as common as gadflies, so there must be a kernel of truth in them.

This means angels can die.

And other angels can kill them.

My eyes flutter closed.

Sleep descends like a hammer blow.

* * *

A spike of adrenaline floods my body when I wake.

My internal body clock has gone haywire, and I have no idea

if I've missed my dusk meeting with Leo. Sitting bolt upright, I blink to clear my head, but it doesn't help. The room feels off-kilter, like something is wrong.

I cross to the window and fling it open, breathing in the sweet fresh air from outside. The deep gray of the sky pierces my foggy thoughts, and I realize that dusk is near. I must have slept for ten hours straight.

The bowl has been replaced with fresh water—"Thanks, Molly"—and I splash some on my face. I use the piss pot—"Sorry, Molly"—then pull on my boots.

I slide behind the tapestry of the girl battling an angel, resisting the weight and accidentally breathing in too much of the vinegary air and coughing.

Pillowcases won't work again—they are too much of a giveaway to my enemies, whoever they are. No, I'll have to memorize the way.

I fumble for the latch and pull open the small stone door, marveling at the soundless movement. I close it behind me.

The air is disgusting in the cramped, dark corridor inside the castle walls, even worse than the dank stuffy oxygen in the Undercity. Here, it smells like stale sweat.

I take a deep breath. I'll have to count the steps to the staircase inside the walls, so I can retrace them on the way back. Glancing at the stone, I have another idea.

I stare at the door and try to unfocus my eyes, looking through the door like I'm peering into another dimension. Sure enough, that hazy blue glow appears, and I can see the outline of the secret door.

I drop the trance and clamber to the top of the nearest staircase bridge, then unfocus my eyes again. From here, I can see the length of the corridor. Two additional ghostly, glowing doorways lie between here and the nearest corner, making mine the third one down.

"Three. Even I can remember that."

I head north, clambering over the stone bridges over doorways, and make my way to the inner maze staircase. Brimming with confidence in my new I-can-see-shining-walls skill, I'm outside the castle in no time.

The ground shimmers with residual heat, but the thick soles of my ox-hide boots keep me comfortable. Without snow, the trip to the river is easy, but I have no way of crossing it.

"Bugger."

I didn't think this through. Without the frozen river, I can't get across to Hightown. The only way to cross the water is via the bridge, guarded by the Margrave's men. Zaden's men.

Zaden already knows I'm impervious to the heat and cold, so it won't take him long to figure out that I can leave the castle anytime I want. This could be my last time out, so I might as well make the most of it.

I travel the river's curve until I reach the central gate at the bridge. At this point, many women would get their flirt on, slapping on a smile and charming the guards. Not me—not today. I don't have a lick of charm in me right now.

I go the direct and confident route instead. "Good evening, gentlemen."

Two men in red-and-gold guards' uniforms with metal breastplates stare out of their insulated hut, mouths agape. The taller one, a rake of a fellow with a bushy beard, puts out a hand to stop me.

"You can't leave, milady. Margrave's orders."

His colleague, shorter, rounder, and dumber, just points. "Ain't you... hot, milady?"

I nod curtly, channeling all the authority I can muster. "Put those two ideas together, and you'll figure it out."

I give them a couple of moments to think it through, knowing there's no way they could come up with the answer I'm proposing, but trying to make them feel stupid so I have the upper hand.

I frown. "I am here on the Margrave's orders. He has spelled me to withstand the heat for a short while. Obviously."

The round dude stares at me, then nods. "Obviously."

I nod again, then march onto the bridge, keeping my footsteps slow although my heart is running.

The sun dips behind the horizon just as I reach Washmaiden Lane, but I have to wait ten long minutes before Leo rounds the corner, puffing.

He looks sickly again, a dull green color that would look better on a pumpermelon, but light shines from his eyes when he sees me.

"Scarla! You made it."

"Yep. Where's Dad?"

Leo pulls me into a grain-scented hug and speaks over my shoulder. "He couldn't make it, but I passed on your message, and he's going to change sleeping hubs and mix up his routine for a while."

I sag against Leo's chest, my cheek resting against his pectoral muscle. For the first time, I notice the strength in his back, the power in his arms wrapping around me.

"Thanks, babe."

He squeezes me tighter, then lets go. "How's it going in the castle? Are you staying safe? Are you staying away from the Margrave?" Leo obviously sees something in my face because his brow creases in concern. "What did you do? Did he seduce you?" Jealousy rages behind his eyes, and I shake my head.

He didn't, not really. If anything, I seduced him. I needed to know his true name. But I can't tell Leo about the kiss. "He says I'm a... a vestige. It's a descendant of somebody who saw an angel die or something. It sounds crackpot, I know, and I'm sure he's wrong. But... it would explain my heat resistance."

I expect Leo to roar in laughter, but he doesn't. My words don't seem to even register as news. He just nods at me. "Yeah, I thought so."

Heat rushes through me. "You thought so? You knew about vestiges, and you never told me? Even though you thought I was one?" My voice rises in a squeak.

His smile drains all the fury from me. "I heard about it over in Desert's Maw, but I never really thought it was real. Do you have any other... powers?" Leo peers at me intensely, scooping up one of my hands so I can't get away.

I avoid his gaze. Since he returned from Desert's Maw, he's hated my powers—well, at least that makes sense now. But I'm worried about how he'll react to this one.

Still, he's my best friend in the world.

My only friend... Unless you count Molly, the servant whose parents will be tortured and killed if she isn't nice to me.

"I can... see things."

Leo chews his mouth. "That's not very impressive."

I slap his hands away and put mine on my hips. "Things that aren't there. Like glowing stones and even glowing people. Like the Margrave—he is so bright it hurts my eyes unless I shut it out. Some people in the Undercity too."

I squint at Leo, and his green hue shines, but I don't mention it.

Leo narrows his eyes, and his lips form a thin line. "It's the

188

Gaze."

The Gaze? I suppose that's as good a name as any for my new way of seeing people's inner shine, or whatever it is I can do.

How in Hades did Leo get so knowledgeable about this stuff? And why has he never talked about it before? I used to have so many questions about the mysterious Zaden—and I still do—but now they're swirling around my oldest friend, too.

My whole world is fracturing, and I don't have enough glue to stick it back together.

Leo looks up at the sky, assessing how much longer he has. "Come with me. You can't go back to the castle; it's not safe. You need to come away with me, and I will protect you."

I want to laugh. When we were kids, Leo once pushed me in front of a skitter beetle so he could get away. He is not the protecting type. But I don't laugh because he's acting strangely and has done ever since he returned from his voyage.

I shake my head. "I can't come with you. He threatened my father, you know that."

"The Margrave is dangerous, Scar."

Leo doesn't know the half of it. "The Margrave is Zaden." My heart thumps while I assess Leo, waiting for a response. "He killed my sister."

Leo's head snaps up. "You don't know that for sure."

"Sure enough. I have to kill him. The Margrave."

"No. He's an angel. You can't kill him. Just let it go."

Anger flares within me, and I shove Leo away, hard in the chest. He barely moves. He's acting weirdly, like an overprotective hound, but I can't help confiding in him. "I have to. I don't care if it kills me. I don't care what happens to me. I just have to kill that asshole angel."

My oldest friend glances at the sky, obviously worrying about how much longer he has. But he holds out placating hands to me. "I'll help Scar. Whatever I can do. You know that. Just don't try anything until you have a plan."

"I always have a pl—"

"A *good* plan."

Sighing, I nod. Sure, no problem, I'll just come up with a *good plan* to kill a celestial being, handcrafted by the Maker out of muscle and anger.

The only thing I have on my side is my ability to make angels shine. Brilliant.

I squint at Leo again to see if I can make that glow return. I feel like this Gaze power can be trained because I can already squint and focus and jiggle my eyesight to make things visible or not. Adjusting my focus so I'm looking beyond Leo, his shine glows brighter than I've ever seen it.

A thought startles me from my focus, and the glow vanishes. "Are you an angel?"

Now that throaty laughter comes, rumbling throughout the little alley and echoing off the tall Hightown houses. I can't help but smile in response, and my shoulders relax with the release of tension. Suddenly, it feels like we're on one of our famous expeditions into Hightown, like we used to embark on as teenagers.

The sky is turning gray, and Leo has to go. He winks, keeping it light. "Meet me again at dusk tomorrow. Same time, same place."

I shake my head. "I can't get away again." Those guards are sure to report my escape, and I can't keep risking my father's life.

Leo's brow clouds. "Okay. Well, keep an eye out for Count

190

VanDyke. He's on our side."

"Who? What do you mean?"

"Gotta go." If he stays any longer, he'll freeze before he makes it home. So, with that mysterious message, Leo is gone.

This meeting has raised more questions than answers, and I'm starting to see a side of Leo that I never glimpsed before. He is more complicated and inscrutable than I realized... and more muscular too.

I cross the bridge and pause briefly to talk to the guards.

"Hey chaps, I just thought I'd let you know that the Margrave didn't send me out here, and he doesn't want me out here. He forbade it, as you probably recall. So if you tell him you let me through, he'll probably kill you. Bye."

I smile with fake cheer, then head back to my room, hoping that will keep those guards silent.

Scarla

Molly is on the edge of my bed, weeping.

When I slip into my room via the secret tunnel, she looks at me, her eyes rimmed with red. Her tall frame is folded over, and that freckle above her lip jiggles sorrowfully.

When a realist cries, you know she's distraught. "Where have you been?"

I hook a thumb over my shoulder. "Out."

Molly twists her fingers. "Outside? You sneaked out of your room and right out of the castle? Bloody hells below, Scarla! If the Margrave finds out, he'll–"

"He'll torture your family, I know."

Molly's voice quavers. "This isn't a joke. Please don't tell the Margrave you escaped."

I sit beside her on the mattress. "I wasn't planning on it."

She leaps up, leaving me alone on the bed, reminding me that she's not my friend—just a servant who fears for her family's life.

She dries her eyes with the palms of her hands. "You have to get ready. The Margrave is taking you out. Your gown is in the closet."

I flop back onto the mattress and wiggle my legs. How do they make this so soft? "Out? Where to? And I don't do dresses.

I already told the Margrave that."

From beneath my lowered lids, I see Molly fidgeting and worrying again. For a strong-ass woman, she sure frets a lot. I suppose the perpetual threat of flogging will do that to a person.

I sit up. "Fine. Just this once. And just for you, I don't want the Margrave getting any ideas about me wearing frocks all the time."

Molly's face collapses in joy. "Thank you. You'll need help getting it on."

I sighed. "Oh. It's one of *those* dresses."

Molly hops from foot to foot. "And... you'd better hurry. Here, I'll get it for you."

The dress is deep purple, an exact match to the color of Zaden's aura. I wonder if he knows. It is deliciously smooth to the touch, reaches the floor, and has a bunch of ridiculous buttons up the back.

Once I'm restrained in it, Molly appraises me. "The neckline shows off your creamy shoulders."

"Really? That's all you have to say? I would have said... that skirt makes you look useless in a fight."

Molly doesn't need to know that I *am* useless in a fight.

Her lips twitch, and I wonder if maybe, just a little bit, she *is* my friend.

I weave through the corridors, ready to make my big entrance. Zaden barely glances up when I descend the curving marble stairs to the castle's fancy foyer. "You're late."

I fan my face with my fingers and giggle coquettishly. "Why, thank you. You look gorgeous too."

I hope to Hades he gets my sarcasm and doesn't think I'm paying him a compliment. With this man, who could tell.

Gone is the bloke who shared truths in the under-castle lake, replaced with the monosyllabic twat I know so well.

He is dressed more formally than I've ever seen him—finely tailored black pants that hug his package—oh Lord!—and a tapered purple silk shirt that hugs the rest of him.

When I reach the ground, he swirls his long black cape around his shoulders. Watching him there, in flesh and blood—or whatever stardust he's made from—I can't imagine slicing a sword through his heart or a hammer into his brains. But I'll have to. At some stage.

I shake my head to clear it. I need to focus on the evening and just get through it, then figure out the details of his execution later.

Zaden turns his back. "This way."

I force a smile. "Wonderful! With such excellent conversation, I'm sure the evening will pass in the blink of an eye."

He leads me to his horse and carriage, then ushers me in. I don't look forward to jostling about like a stone in a child's sack. He climbs in beside me, and a footman closes the door gently, then we're off.

True to form, the carriage door slams into my temple as we cross the bridge. I groan. "How do you stand it? Do you have some sort of angelic power that makes these seats feel soft? If I kill you, will I get that power too?"

Finally, Zaden turns to look at me, and our eyes meet for the first time since I ordered him from my room after that kiss. That God-awful, hellish, spectacular kiss. His lips are so close, so full, so delicious. I could just tip forward and meet them with my own.

"It's not a Celestial power."

I shake my head. "Then how do you do it?"

He shrugs. "Lack of cowardice." He snaps back to face forward, shutting me out again.

I refuse to be made a fool of by the man who may have killed my sister. "Did you..."

I can't ask him flat out. I sigh. No need for him to make me look a fool; I'm plenty ridiculous on my own. Plus, I need to get the truth from him, and I don't imagine an idle request for it will work.

Bumping around in this windowless carriage is making me feel nauseated. I close my eyes, willing myself to sleep, but it doesn't come. As usual, my circadian rhythms are out of whack.

Zaden's voice is as deep as a canyon. "Aren't you wondering where we are going? Or why you're coming?"

I peel one eye open and regard him. "You're not usually in the habit of answering my questions."

He ignores the jibe. "Tonight is a gathering of the Cloaked Court, and I need you to use your Gaze."

Leo was right. The vestigial power I inherited from Fra Perkins is called Gaze. Apparently, everybody knew except me.

Understanding floods me. Zaden wanted Gaze for himself—that was why he kept visiting Fra Perkins on her deathbed. And when I received it instead of him, he kidnapped me to control Gaze for himself.

"Why do you need Gaze?"

He deigns to glance at me. "Gaze lets you identify angels and vestiges. He raises an eyebrow. "Surely you've noticed?"

He thinks I'm an idiot.

"Of course I've noticed," I snap. I focus my eyes through him like I'm staring into a dimension behind him, and his

195

purple aura blazes so brightly that I have to blink it away so I'm not blinded.

Two new pieces of information are clear. One, that I must glow myself, though I can't see it. Two, that old lady by the bonfire in the Undercity and Leo are both vestiges, whether they know it or not.

Still, I'm curious to learn more. "Can't you identify other angels?"

He breathes deeply. "I know most of the angels in Aubia, but only because we have all been around for centuries. When somebody stubbornly remains alive, they are clearly an angel."

"But if a new angel is...."

"Fallen? Then I would only recognize them if they used their powers in front of me. That's why I limit my use of magic, because knowledge is power."

Of course. It's all about the age-old game of power. A bunch of rich assholes is vying for control by exposing each other and trying to keep their own secrets hidden.

I close my eyes, weary of the idiocy of rich jerks. "So you want me to tell you who the angels and vestiges are at your Fancy Council—"

"The Cloaked Court."

"The Fancy Council, so you can have power over them and become king? Have I got that right?" I can't even bear to look at him; it's bad enough I have to share a carriage with him.

"No."

That has my attention. I stare at him, looking for a sign that he is lying, but I find none. Just that chiseled jaw with its dark shadow and that smooth forehead. "So, what do you want?"

His head jostles over a bump. "I am a fallen angel, Scarla. Part of my soul was ripped from me when I fell, like a gaping wound. Every day I lose more of myself, like blood gushing from the hole. Every day I forget a little more about the angel I once was. I've been here for centuries, and I... I want to go home."

His tone is so straightforward, and his expression so pained that my heart clenches. I've never imagined the Margrave having emotions—other than hatred and anger. Seeing him vulnerable and in pain twangs my heart strings. Right now, I can't reconcile the male before me with somebody who might have hurt Leesa.

"And Gaze will help you get back into heaven?"

"Yes."

"How?"

He sighs and looks at me. "Don't you ever run out of questions?"

I bite my lip. "Don't you ever run out of excuses to stop answering them?"

He rubs a hand along his jaw and suddenly looks exhausted. "I don't really know how, Scarla. But with Gaze, you can see the gate to heaven."

His vulnerability reels me in. "Dammit. Fine. I'll help."

The emotion leaves his face, and he nods. "Thank you."

We must have left Malanox hours ago. I can only imagine we're heading south to Solren. North of Malanox is the Dead Desert which, if rumor is to be believed, shouldn't be crossed in a ballgown.

So, south it is. My nausea ebbs and flows, and if I could fall asleep, I would, but it's not only my zingy brain that prevents me from doing so but also the damn carriage wall which keeps banging the side of my head.

Zaden looks to be napping, so I prod him awake. "Why don't

you kill me?"

I feel perfectly safe asking the question because I believe there's a logical answer. Since he kidnapped me, he's been protecting me and has already said he will never murder me. Clearly, he plans to wait until I die of natural causes and inherit Gaze from me. That's why he will never let me go.

Come to think of it, he could have murdered Fra Perkins too, but he didn't.

He sighs as though I bore him. "Vestigial powers can be good or evil. Gaze, for example, is used to identify magic. That's why you can see angels and vestiges."

"And the magic imbued in the castle walls."

He darts a glance at me. "Really?"

I nod, pleased to know something he doesn't. Perhaps that's how I can see the gates to heaven too. "So, I'm guessing that's the good brand of vestige?"

He nods. "Yes. If you are present when a vestige dies of natural causes, you inherit the good brand of their power. If you murder them, you inherit the evil brand."

"Which is?" He looks at me but stays silent. "What's the evil brand of Gaze?" I might as well know what I'm up against, what somebody stands to gain by murdering me.

"The mirror side of Gaze is called Watch. Somebody with Watch bears witness to the worst sins of every person they meet. It sends most people insane after a few years, observing all the obscenities of which humankind is capable."

A massive bump bounces me off the seat, and I land hard. "What? If somebody murders me, they will inherit Watch?"

"Yes. And every time the Watcher meets somebody, they'll see the worst sin that person has ever committed."

"Bloody hells below." I shiver. Knowing the mirror of a

198

skill that resides inside me could send a person insane within years is horrific, like somebody told me my mom was a mass murderer. It feels like evil resides in my cells.

At least it keeps me safe, I guess.

Another bump jostles me into the Margrave, and electricity shoots along my arm. Why does that happen every time we make contact?

I shuffle away from him, keeping strictly to my half of the carriage. "So if you kill me, you won't get my Gaze and be able to find your way back to heaven?"

He nods.

So I'm safe. He can't kill me, and he needs something from me. Steel enters my voice. "If you harm a hair on my father's head, I will make sure you never inherit Gaze. One day, maybe twenty or thirty years from now, I will kill myself while you are out of the room. And you will never get back to heaven."

Darkness burns in the Margrave's eyes, turning them as black as sin.

But I'm not finished yet. "If any harm comes to my father, I swear you will never get Gaze from me. If, on the other hand, he leads a long and happy life, then you may have my Gaze willingly."

There's no way in Hades that I'll keep up my end of the bargain, but Zaden doesn't need to know that. As long as it keeps my father safe, I'll do anything.

Even make a bargain with an avenging angel.

Scarla

The palace—if that's what this building is—is disgustingly ornate.

The carriage rattles to a stop, and a footman releases us from it. We step onto a well-lit courtyard of hand-carved pavers outside a palatial building with decorative features even more unnecessary than those in Malanox Castle.

Other guests are arriving too, the men in suits with funny little bows around their necks, and the women in evening gowns as restrictive as my own. Opulence is the word of the evening.

At least my gown doesn't have the puffy sleeves that so many others do. I check the men's feet—back in Malanox, the richest idiots wear trousers so long they trail in the dirt, but that fashion doesn't seem to have taken off here. Or, more likely, it's already passed.

It's full night, and I've never seen so many folks out after dark.

I put a hand on the Margrave's arm, feeling the muscles coiling beneath, and he flinches. "Are all angels impervious to the cold?"

His brow clouds while he considers my question, then it clears. He gestures all around. "We're in the sealed section of

Solren."

"The sealed section? What's that?"

He sighs. "I forget how naïve you are. It's the section right at the heart of Solren with a thermal seal so mortals can walk around."

I bristle at his insult, but I'm too intrigued to give him the silent treatment. "You mean people can go outside any time of the night or day? That's amazing!"

He grunts in acknowledgment.

I peer at the sky, noticing a slight shimmer all around. "Is it a magical seal?" I imagine an invisible dome plunked over the Hightown of Solren, and that glimmer in the distance tells me I might be right.

I've never heard of anything like that. The sun dictates our lives in Malanox, with everything centered around dusk and dawn. Watching these people is like seeing aliens or people from the distant past. Except they look just like Undercity skanks, only better dressed.

Also, these folks saunter as though they've nowhere to be. In Malanox, if you're outside, you're running because time is limited, and if you hang around too long, you die.

But not these people. Some glow with vestigial power and one woman across the courtyard is almost as bright as Zaden.

"See any vestiges?"

I nod. "And an angel."

Zaden smiles, and I feel like a performing monkey who has pleased his master. Bristling, I follow him up the broad steps and through large double doors into a palatial hall.

The interior is more sumptuous than the exterior. The ceiling reaches the heavens, and the large rectangular room would barely fit into the main cavern of the Undercity, although the pillars here are made of marble and gold rather than rough-hewn stone. A mezzanine balcony lines all four walls, and a curving staircase leads up to it. Itching to climb it to see the view from above—and to get out of the throng—I stare at the winding steps and don't notice the second angel arrive until Zaden introduces us.

"Scarla, this is Count VanDyke. Count, May I introduce my companion, Scarla."

I jump at the name VanDyke. This is the man Leo mentioned. He said the Count was on our side, whatever that means. I assumed it meant the Count was against the angels, but that can't be true—Count VanDyke's orange glow is almost as bright as Zaden's purple one. Clearly, he is an angel too.

Does Zaden know? The potential of Gaze dawns on me. Knowledge is power, after all.

Even without Gaze, I might have recognized the Count as celestial. He is well over six feet tall, though still shy of Zaden's height, and broad. Bright blond hair frames his symmetrical features like a halo.

A long, ivory cloak brushes the tops of his pale shoes. He is a vision of gold and cream. In fact, he looks like those paintings you see of cupids with the curly blond hair and the bow and arrow—but all grown up and pulsing with testosterone. I can practically count the muscles beneath that cloak.

The Count's smile is genuine, but I don't miss the tendril of orange magic he coils around me. Despite myself, I tingle in response. A thread of desire weaves through me, connecting my honeyed warmth with his body. I focus so I don't step toward him.

"I'm so pleased to meet you, Scarla. Any friend of the Margrave is... An acquaintance of mine."

The angels laugh, but the tension between them is palpable.

I nod at the angel, refusing to speak. The count's snaking magic is coiled around me, and my skin is alight. My nipples tighten under my soft dress, and I shift so that the silk brushes across them.

There's no doubt his orange tendrils are filled with sensuality. I worry that I'll ask for a kiss if I open my mouth, so I keep it pressed shut.

As soon as I'm able, I duck aside, getting as far away from Zaden and VanDyke as I can. The last thing I want is to spend all evening being introduced to a bunch of politicians and rulers who only care about power.

Okay, that's the second last thing I want. The last thing I want is to throw myself at a passing angel and stick my tongue down his throat.

I weave through the beautiful people to the staircase, keeping my hands and tongue to myself, then ascend, taking those marble steps one by one. Up on the mezzanine, I find a good spot to lean against the railing and observe the party from above.

It's a blur of dull mortals with the occasional shining light, but at the room's center is a glow so bright I can barely look at it.

Squinting, I make out figures walking beneath a shimmering dome. Angels. Their combined glow could blind an earthworm.

And what's with the shimmering dome? It is exactly like the one I imagine covering the sealed section of the city, all twinkly and gleamy and barely visible. Is that the VIP section of this party? Can just anyone walk in? Maybe I'll give it a go and see what those angel snobs do.

Can anyone else even see the shimmering dome, or is that part of my Gaze?

Blinking to clear my vision, I turn my attention to the rest of the room. Gray-and-yellow liveried servants carry trays of drinks and food, bobbing and being polite and keeping out of the important people's way. I hate that. I hate everything about it—the injustice, the carefully manufactured divisions in society, the sly underbelly of every slimy conversation.

Leesa used to say that hell is other people. I amend that.

Hell is a room full of angels.

The irony isn't lost on me.

I feel it before I see it, that snaking orange magic of the Count. I'm not surprised when he slides behind me, resting his elbows on the balcony, his arm parallel to mine and mere inches from it. It dwarfs mine, bulging with muscles—as I suspected. His shoulder is higher than mine.

"Hello, Scarla. I watched you come up here. I hope you don't mind me joining you."

His blond hair halos his face, a foil to the dark intensity of his eyes. His clothes are light and bright, tailored cream pants and a light gold shirt of the softest weave. He must have ditched his ivory coat with a servant.

His magic is strong, and he makes no effort to tame it—he's trying to tame me. Every inch of my skin is on fire, and I can't resist leaning toward him so our arms touch from elbow to shoulder. I even rub against him like a dog. The silver scabbard strapped around his waist pokes into my hip.

Horrified, I jerk away and keep an eye on his snaking orange magic, hoping that seeing it will provide some defense against it.

He laughs. "Don't be embarrassed, Scarla. I just want to

find out about your relationship with the Margrave."

I squirm. "I don't have a relationship with that man. He kidnapped me and took me into his castle. That's all there is to tell."

I trust few people in this world, and Leo is one. Maybe the only one, other than Dad. If Leo tells me the Count is on our side, I believe him. Otherwise, I wouldn't speak this openly.

"Can you please retract your magic?"

The count cocks his head, regarding me with curiosity, and I figure most people can't see his snaking tendrils. But, thankfully, he does as I ask, and I'm able to relax.

VanDyke's expression is earnest. "The Margrave and I are not on good terms either. Perhaps I can be of assistance to you if you ever need it."

"Oh. What do you mean?"

He blinks. "The Margrave deals out death without thought. He considers mortals beneath him and has no hesitation in stamping them out. I disagree with his methods, and… we have an agenda that goes a long way back. If you ever need help, I will endeavor to provide it. In any form necessary."

I slam my dropped jaw shut and try to look like I have political life-and-death conversations every day. "Thank you." I look him over from head to toe, and my gaze snags on his sword. Those tapestries in my room depict angels with swords too. An epiphany strikes.

"Can your sword kill another angel?"

VanDyke regards me with a smile playing on his lips. "My sword is Jonshu. And yes, a celestial blade can strike down an immortal being."

"Sweet. Do you, er… could I maybe borrow it one day?"

My ears ring with music and laughter, the nonstop chatter

and chirping of the wealthy and oblivious, and my ribs contract in anticipation. There's no doubt I'm playing in dangerous territory.

The Count's brow furrows, and he leans closer, brushing me with his magic. His voice is almost inaudible above the background hum. "You would be wise not to speak of such matters. We celestials have supernatural hearing."

Oh crap. He's right. Zaden sliced open that sandy-haired servant Robin for muttering under his breath; to his ears, my quiet words are like a shouted broadcast. Zaden can't kill me to retaliate, but he could make my life a whole lot worse—I dare say Malanox Castle is built on dungeons, even if I haven't found them yet.

VanDyke leans against the railing. "I believe we have a mutual friend. I will deliver him the parcel when the time is right."

He's talking about Leo. And I guess the package is his sword.

"How will you know when the tim—"

"Speak no more of this."

The Count nods then glides away as though he's flying, but I call out to him. "Wait. Can you tell me what that is in the middle of the room?" I point to the shimmering dome. Surely we can safely discuss that.

He tilts his head, watching me closely. "That's where the Cloaked Court meets."

Really? "In the middle of the ball? Don't they want privacy? I thought it was all cloak and dagger and top-secret negotiations."

He laughs, exposing straight white teeth that match his hair. "They are meeting under an invisible shield that prevents eavesdropping. And they get to be the center of attention. The rest of us get to look at them, so it's win-win."

"Invisible?" I can see it shimmering, plain as day.

He narrows his eyes. "Yes. But trust me, it's there."

I decide not to show my hand and admit that I can see it. I bite my lip. "Shouldn't you be in there too? Aren't you one of the movers and shakers of Aubia?"

He grins wolfishly. "Indeed. The only person more powerful than me is your Margrave. The Maker only knows why he chooses to live in obscurity out there in Malanox. But, if it were up to me, he'd stay there." He glides away, saying over his shoulder, "And yes, I'm heading back to the meeting now. I just wanted to have a private chat with you."

With that, he is gone, leaving me even more to think about.

Like how long until I get my hands on his blade.

Scarla

Count VanDyke transforms into the perfect courtier.

I watch him descend the stairs and rejoin the revelers below. His beautiful face instantly transforms into a mask of politeness, with twinkling eyes and broad grins. I can imagine the compliments he's paying the ladies, judging by the twitter of excitement that ripples through them as he passes. One or two press against him, and he graciously fends them off.

He makes his way through the not-so-invisible barrier in the room's center, which billows slightly as he does. Strange to know that nobody else can see it except me.

I wonder how rare Gaze is? I guess angels don't die often, and Zaden has been seeking it for centuries... so I'm feeling pretty special. Pride brims within me, and I let it. No harm in seeking some joy from this shitfight my life has become.

Several nobles below shine with varying degrees of brightness, though none so stark as the angles in the central bubble. I watch them go about their business, discussing politics and power with the other celestials of the Cloaked Court.

Strange to know that life in all of Aubia is dictated by a bunch of fallen angels. Strange to know that all the rulers of the land are really celestial beings. Strange that I didn't even believe in angels a few days ago, and now I can barely restrain myself from unbuckling their belts and letting loose on their cocks.

Occasionally a party guest stops to watch the angels, craning their neck to listen, but they don't last long. Liquor and canapés are more appealing than failing to eavesdrop.

But I can see more than just talk. Tendrils of power snake from Count VanDyke as he speaks, handing him the rapt attention of the other angels. Most angels use their magic to influence their peers, with their own personal color of shine.

Faces turn to Zaden—it's his turn to speak. I wait to see him influence them with his magic, but he doesn't. His glow stays close to his body, and I can't help but admire that. He doesn't use his angelic prowess to intimidate or convince; he relies on his words alone.

On the other hand, he thinks mortals are insects and doesn't give a fuck about our politics. I guess he's saving his energy for more important things, like beheading his servants.

My belly rumbles, and I get bored of watching the game of politics. I descend the staircase holding onto the banister—I'm not used to wearing heels, and I don't want to tumble ass over tit with all these rich bastards watching... That would be one more reason for them to despise me.

Safely on the marble floor, I wend through the crowds, trying to avoid bumping into silken women and shaven men. But mostly failing.

I don't know how everybody else bloody does it. Before I've gone ten paces, I've spilled somebody's bubbly wine and planted a shoulder in someone's plate of food.

I wasn't cut out for fancy balls.

Giving up on making it to the food tables, I abort my mission and head out the nearest doors. They're big, glass, and paneled with intricate designs. They lead out to a patio overlooking a garden sprinkled with fairy lights, as though hundreds of fireflies are watching the party from the trees.

I take some deep breaths, enjoying the crisp air and the lack of perfume. A slight breeze ruffles my hair, and I turn toward it. Obviously, the seal over this part of the city doesn't stop the wind—unless that's an artificial gust... I can't take anything for granted anymore.

Not even the fact that I'm a normal human.

The door behind me opens, letting the party's roar escape until it shuts.

"Here. I brought you some food." Zaden hands me a plate piled with roasted chicken, mattroot, and at least five other foods I don't recognize. "I know you don't like pigeon, so I got you chicken."

"How do you know I...? What is ...? Thank you."

Jesus. Nobody will ever accuse me of being eloquent.

I search his hard face, but it is expressionless, as usual.

"I noticed you didn't choose pigeon at dinner on your first night, so I figured you prefer chicken."

He noticed that? He hadn't spared me a glance all evening and seemed oblivious to my presence until he'd slashed that sandy-haired footman almost in half.

I take the plate. "I love chicken."

As much as I hate to admit it, this irritating angel is not as cold and emotionless as I'd like to believe. His stony expression is just a mask, and a flowing stream of feeling runs beneath it.

Maybe I'm wrong about his role in Leesa's death. All I know for sure is that the Margrave's name is Zaden, and he is an angel. The rest is just conjecture.

I rest my plate on the railing and survey the garden. This

food is delicious. The chicken is plumper and juicier than I've ever tasted back home, and these colorful orange vegetables are salty with a hint of sweetness. Why does that remind me of Zaden?

"There are a bunch of angels in the room," I tell him as a kind of payment for his thoughtfulness. "Inside the central dome. It's so damn bright in there I can barely see."

He leans on the railing beside me, just like the Count did upstairs. But the energy rolling off the two men couldn't be more different. The Count's magic snaked around me, drawing me into a seductive dance. But Zaden's aura stays close around him, tightly coiled. I sense his veneer of control masks a raging rapid of raw power.

He nods. "We've been circling each other for centuries; I know all about them. Occasionally one masquerades as a mortal for a few decades, wearing a disguise—"

"Like a wig and a big nose?"

"A glamor. A magical facade."

I nod. "Got it. An angel wig. Have you ever done that?"

Zaden chews his lip, which is very distracting. I zone out and think about his mouth for a while, those straight white teeth, those full lips, and whether he'd taste like those forest lilies he smells of.

He's still talking. I tune back in and realize he's telling me that he once spent fifty years as an old woman.

That knocks me out of my sexual reverie. "An old woman? Really? Why?"

He shrugs. "Why not?"

"But wait." I gesture to his body, allowing myself to look at his fitted black trousers that sit so snugly around him. I happen to know they cup his butt perfectly. The formal pants are such a change from his usual practical clothing with all those pockets and thick buckles.

This clothing is more fitted, finely spun, and hangs low from his hips. It looks like I could only just slide a hand into the space between his belt and his stomach. I could squeeze it in there beneath his purple silk shirt and...

It's only when I notice the bulge of his packet growing that I realize I'm staring. I could touch that. Seriously, just one stiff breeze would tip me into him, and my fingers could hold onto that.

Where's a strong wind when you need one?

I shake my head and check for his snaking magic. Nope. This reaction is all me.

He's smirking, of course, by the time I finally get my eyes up to his face. "Yes?"

"Yes what," I snap.

"You were saying something about me being an old woman."

"Was I?"

"You were."

"No, I was thinking about... Okay, sure, you're an old woman."

Zaden flexes his muscles slightly, and his pectorals show through his light silk shirt. "Not at the moment, I'm not."

"Wait." I hold out a stop-sign hand and close my eyes until I'm under control. I can't have those damn chest muscles in my face while trying to have a conversation.

When I open my eyes, I focus on his irritating smirk. That keeps me calm. "Is this your real form?" I circle my hands around in the air but keep my gaze squarely on his annoying, gorgeous face.

"No."

"What? Really?"

"But it's as close as I can get outside of heaven. Up there, I'm always naked and even sexier."

His voice is hot as hell right now, and I try really hard not to picture him naked. That fucking chest.

"And, let me guess, you're also even more arrogant?"

He laughs, but it is tinged with a frown. "I can't figure you out, mortal."

I shrug. "I was born in the Undercity. I grew up in the Undercity. Same as the next skank."

"Not quite the same." He turns to look out over the gardens, at the shape of the trees that are just visible in the dark, at their glittering lights. He shifts the conversation as easily as his body. "What about the people outside of the dome? Are any of the nobles vestiges?"

I accept the change in conversation greedily, like I've been rescued from a mistake. I grope for the plate of food he brought me and swallow a mouthful of creamy deliciousness before I answer.

"Yep. The strongest was an old guy with white hair and a big white mustache, balding on top. He was quite a strong red color."

Zaden looks at me. "They have different colors?"

I take another mouthful. Now that I've started eating, my hunger is sparked. But I'm trying to be elegant, so I swallow before answering. "Different colors and different brightnesses. I guess the brightness is their magical strength, and maybe the colors represent the type of magic."

Zaden steals a grape from my plate. His fingers avoid brushing mine, for which I'm thankful. But I'd like to test how soft they are. "You're not as stupid as most mortals."

I don't bother swallowing this time, and food flecks onto his arm when I shout. "Just when I was beginning to like you. You take that back."

A corner of his mouth lifts. "Okay, I take it back. You're precisely as stupid as most mortals. Dumber than some."

I wipe a chunk of white vegetable off his sleeve, and a bolt of electricity passes through my touch. "That's not what I meant."

He smiles. "The truth is, Scarla, you're not like most mortals. You're a vestige. That's why I can have a decent conversation with you."

His green eyes deepen, and his magical glow expands, tickling the edge of my arm and the length of my leg.

I can't help it. I turn toward him and arch my back ever so slightly, finding it impossible to resist his pull. Man, he is hot. He's the most handsome male I've ever seen, and he's right next to me, his attention searing my face.

My nipples are the closest part of my body to him, and I watch as his tendrils of magic snake around them, bringing them fully erect.

"No," I say, but I've lost the thread of the conversation. I'm just sure he was being disagreeable—that's a pretty good bet with Zaden.

"A vestige," he repeats, and I watch his lips form the words, wondering if he's thinking about kissing me.

I step away from him so I'm out of his aura cloud, and my mind clears. He said mortals can't hold conversations. "Mere mortals can form sentences, you know." I remember my stumbling and bumbling at the start of this conversation, so I amend that. "I mean... usually."

214

I know I have to keep my distance from him—Leo told me that if I succumb to an angel's seduction, I will fall in love with him and be unable to leave. Sensing Zaden's power, I have no doubt that's true.

Even so, I'm disappointed when he steps away from me. "Time to go."

I watch his back as he walks, paying attention to the movement of the purple silk over his muscular frame, and I wonder if I'm already lost.

Scarla

On the carriage ride home to Malanox, I invent a new yoga pose. I call it sitting-bolt-upright-while-sleeping.

It sucks. But my fatigue is overwhelming, so I nap despite being trapped inside a giant jackhammer.

Even so, when we return to Malanox Castle, I fall into bed for a few more hours.

I'm awoken by a maid tiptoeing around the room, emptying the pisspot and re-filling the water bowl.

"Morning, Molly." I'm too tired to even open my eyes, but she is near the top of my list of almost-friends, so I play nice.

My only answer is silence. I peel open one eye to find it isn't Molly at all. A shorter woman with generous curves scurries around my bed, furiously avoiding eye contact.

I sit up, holding the sheet to my chest. "Hello. Where's Molly?" The maid doesn't even glance at me, but she flinches, so I know she can hear me. "Hello. What's your name?"

She hugs the walls and ignores me.

Irritation makes me snap. "Answer me, dammit. What's your name?"

The poor maid bobs a curtsy, and her long ponytail swings. "Abby, milady."

Shame sweeps aside my irritation. The last person I want to

become is an entitled lady who makes servants pee their pants. I coax gentleness into my voice. "Sorry, Abby. And please, call me Scarla."

Abby throws a frightened glance my way, then scurries out the door without another word.

Sighing, I get dressed then follow my stomach to the dining room. The place is abandoned, so I head downstairs to the kitchen, keeping an eye out for Lord Xerxes the Fuckwit.

All clear. The grainy aroma of baking bread reminds me of Leo, and I smile. I hope he's doing okay.

"Hello," I call to the bustling room but only earn the turning of a few heads. I grab a bread roll and stuff it into my mouth, hating that I'm too scared of Xerxes the Fuckwit to savor it slowly. On a whim, I head to the main foyer.

A deep voice rumbles behind me. "Will you join me for a walk?" The Margrave. The scent of forest lilies surrounds me. He's back in his practical black pants, matched with a marle gray T-shirt that highlights his biceps.

"Sure." I try to hide how excited I am to leave the castle, but when the Margrave heads up the curving stairs, I blanch. "We can't walk inside. Let's go out."

He stares at me appraisingly, clearly assessing my abilities. He already knows I don't feel the cold, so I'm not giving anything away.

He nods. "Outside, then."

The castle doors open, and midday heat sears my skin.

Zaden looks at me, and I think that's concern in his sparkling green eyes. "Are you sure you're okay?"

I step into the full sun. "Yep."

Strolling outside in the midday sun is about the worst place to be, even for me. But I can't stand being in that castle for a moment longer. I can't handle being imprisoned. And I especially can't admit that weakness to the Margrave.

Automatically, I take a step toward the bridge. "To town?"

The Margrave says, "No," and marches off in the exact opposite direction.

Dammit. I'm torn. I don't particularly want to visit the town, but I definitely don't want to trail after the Margrave like a duckling.

I groan. Curiosity wins out, and I follow Zaden around the back of the castle.

He waits around the corner by an expanse of red dirt with patchy shrubs. He grins. "Beautiful, isn't it!"

Politeness isn't my strong suit, and simpering agreement is right down the bottom of the pack. "No. It's ugly. I prefer the world blanketed in snow, so you can imagine all kinds of wondrous plants growing underneath."

A twinkle in his green eyes shows that he isn't annoyed. "I agree. But I hate going into town during the day—those skitter beetles give me the heebie-jeebies."

When the humans take cover for the day, the armored bugs reign supreme. They are dark brown insects as big as my foot with insulated carapaces. They're drawn to the snowmelt barrels in Lowtown—they clamber over the lip and plummet inside. At this time of day, the thunk of their shells hitting the lid sounds like constant heavy rain. I reckon the worst job in all of Malanox is the poor schmuck who has to climb down and clear out the carcasses every dusk, so the nightly snow doesn't wash the skitter beetles into the drinking water.

Even so, I laugh. "Really? A powerful avenging angel is scared of a couple of bugs?"

He falls into step beside me, and we walk out among the

dotted shrubs. "Well, in my defense... they're disgusting."

I refuse to fall for this easygoing façade, so I straighten my spine. I need to find the nerve to ask about Leesa. I just need to know if I can ask Zaden or if I need to go around him. The problem is, I haven't made a good impression with his right-hand man, Lord Xerxes the Fuckwit, and I doubt any of the servants would know if Zaden killed Leesa.

Or why.

Judging by the maid I had this morning, Abby, most of the servants here would faint if I tried to ask them a question.

Besides, I'm growing to believe he didn't kill her, and there's another explanation for his name on her lips.

I start with an easy one. "What happened to Molly?"

Zaden veers around a measly bush, taking his shadow with him and casting me into full sun. "Who's Molly?"

Is this guy serious? He doesn't know the name of a woman who's worked for him her whole life? I take some deep breaths. "She's one of your maids."

He shrugs. "Try the infirmary. And if she's not there, tell me."

Well, that ain't going to happen. I won't land Molly in trouble with her asshole boss.

Zaden's long shadow falls over my face again, bringing blissful relief. "Why do you hate mortals so much?"

His shadow falters for a moment, then resumes sliding across the barren ground. "I have no opinion whatsoever about mortals. They mean nothing to me."

I snort. "Liar."

His head snaps toward me, and black fire flashes in his eyes. He controls himself before answering. "Mortals know nothing of the world and bring nothing to it. They live for the blink of an eye, each new generation forgetting what the previous generations learned. I have no time for their nonsense. Tell me, Scarla, do you invest feelings in the life of a gadfly?"

I don't love being compared to a gadfly, but I see his point. He has been on earth for centuries and in existence for even longer. It must be hard to care about the mistakes of humans, which repeat ad infinitum.

"But to treat mortals with such viciousness. You slash them down without mercy. I saw you kill a man in the streets of Malanox when I was a girl. Hatred burned in your eyes."

His tone sharpens. "Do you kill a mosquito that buzzes you at night? Do you hate that mosquito, or do you just want to be rid of an annoyance?"

I don't know if it's my sense of self-importance, but I still don't buy his explanation. "There's more to it than that. It's as though a mortal once did something terrible to you."

I'm inviting a confession from him. I tell myself it's because I want to know all of his weaknesses so I can exploit them... But maybe that's just another lie I tell myself. Because the truth is, I yearn for intimacy too.

Walking beside him, without the intensity of a face-to-face conversation, I find the courage to ask the question that will change my whole life. It's the whole reason I followed Zaden that day in the Undercity and the whole reason I'm still here. It's the question that has shaped my every action for the last year since she died.

And now, for the first time, I think he has enough depth of character to answer me honestly.

"I need to clear up something with you so we can get back to the part where you keep me prisoner until I die."

Zaden looks up sharply at the change in topic. Of course, he doesn't say anything since he's a shit conversationalist. But he's *my* shit conversationalist, so I try not to take offense.

He just raises an eyebrow. That's his way of saying, *Sure, go on, happy to chat.*

"Did you kill my sister?" My voice is stronger than I feel.

Zaden's footsteps beside me falter, and I want to shake the answer from him.

But I dread what it might be.

Scarla

My feet keep their rhythm, but my heartbeat is syncopated, stumbling uneasily. The heat on my face is burning, and I wonder if my temperature insensitivity has gone. I focus on the red dirt and just try to suck oxygen in and out.

I finally found the ovaries to ask Zaden whether he killed Leesa.

And the suspense is killing me.

He opens his mouth to answer, and I hold my breath. "No," he says, loud and clear.

That's it. One word, one syllable. I should be elated, but I feel empty. I'm still hot and uncomfortable, and now I'm walking next to a dude I have no reason to hate and no reason to stay near.

Apart from being his prisoner, of course.

The Margrave, Zaden, the angel, didn't kill Leesa.

Our footsteps kick up puffs of red dust as we walk, and the castle is hazy in the distance behind us.

We're almost at Penngrove Forest, a vast expanse of trees with a wealth of wildlife sheltering beneath their canopy. The sight disgusts me. If I could muster the moisture to spit, I would. All the hatred I've been nurturing to release on my sister's killer emerges now, and I'm directing it to a bunch of trees.

I spin on my heel and turn my back to the forest, retracing our steps toward the castle.

The Margrave comes with me. He's clearly reading my mood, which is surprising. "Why do you detest rich people so much?"

I jerk my thumb over my shoulder. "Because of that."

"Because of the forest?"

"Because there's a forest with abundant wildlife minutes from town, and nobody is allowed in except the mighty Margrave of Malanox." I shoot daggers at him. "That's you, in case you're not paying attention."

"I see."

"I hate them because there's a sealed section in the center of Solren where only the rich folks are allowed to go, while the poor scurry about in the dark underground like rats. Because there were five types of vegetables on my plate last night that I didn't recognize. Because my sister died in a cave."

The Margrave watches my outburst dispassionately, clearly uncaring. He hasn't even worked up a patch of sweat on that gray T-shirt. He doesn't give a fuck about anyone except himself, rich or poor, so why should he care if a cave dweller like me has never seen a grape?

Why should he care about anything?

If I don't constantly pump life into the conversation, it dies. My mood has soured, so we trudge back to the castle in silence.

By the time I step into the cool air of the castle, I am drenched in sweat and desperate to clean up. But there's something I need to do first.

The Margrave takes a left, probably heading to his tower, so I take a right. Petulant? Probably. Satisfying? Definitely.

The guard lets me into the servant corridor—my reputation

as a healer helps. I duck along the passageway and around to the small northern room of the castle infirmary. Sure enough, Molly lies in one of the cots, looking weak and pale.

"Oh, babe. You're sick."

She smiles when she sees me, but it's a watery thing like her happiness is diluted. The freckle above her lip barely moves.

I lay my hands on her to see if I can help, but her illness feels slimy and strange to my touch, not like the usual fevers or chills that are my wheelhouse.

Her voice is croaky. "How am I doing, Fra?"

I remove my hand from her forehead and take her fingers in mine. "You'll live." But I don't know if that's true.

Her eyes flutter closed, and I examine her chest. It rises and falls with little energy, as though tired after too many days of life.

It reminds me of the outbreak in the Undercity a couple of years ago. It swept through the hubs for weeks, killing the young and healthy as often as the old and frail. We called it the Sighing Sickness because it squashed its victim's lungs until their exhales came with a whistle.

Molly isn't sighing yet, but her symptoms look the same. I close my eyes and focus on the feeling of the slippery sickness in her body, trying to find something to grasp onto and yank out. But it's no use. It's like trying to pull raindrops out of clouds. I can't heal her.

During the Undercity outbreak, Fra Wang spoke of herbs that could be brewed into a tea to help the Sighing Sickness, but of course, we didn't have access to Penngrove forest.

But I do.

The mattress squeaks when I stand, and Molly's lips mutter a goodbye. The old lady from yesterday is still here, so I tend to her next. I can ease her chills quickly, and I pull an extra blanket from an empty cot and lay it gently over her. She's too ill to thank me, but her watery eyes say it all.

The sandy-haired prick winks at me when I tend to his wounds, but he doesn't say anything—too scared of being overheard by the Margrave, I bet. I don't speak either—I save my words for people worth talking to.

At least his injuries are straightforward, and I just need to encourage the flesh to knit together. There's no sign of infection—he got lucky. So I sit for a few minutes with my hands on his chest, eyes closed, sensing the strands of skin weaving together and helping them along. It's like singing alone under the moon before snowfall, quiet and meditative. I can tell it's helping too, which is satisfying.

But I'd much rather help Molly.

I'll go to the forest to find those healing herbs, with or without permission from Zaden. Preferably without—I'm itching for a fight. Learning that he didn't kill my sister has left me without an outlet for the months of rage I've been hoarding. Who knows where I'll spend it?

First, I need a drink and a splash of water before facing the heat again. I use the curving central staircase to climb to the second floor.

Lord Xerxes blocks the corridor at the top of the stairs like a stone warrior growing from the floor. He has the faint glow of a weak vestige, his aura a muddy yellow hue that makes him look like he ought to be in the infirmary too. He is hunched, and his narrow face is contorted in a scowl.

I could probably dart around him, but I shouldn't have to behave like a criminal in my own home... my own castle... well, my own prison cell.

I sigh. "Did you want a chat, Xerxes?"

A vicious smile twists his pinched lips, exposing his yellow teeth. "Call me Lord, girl. I've already warned you once. I won't do it again." His foul breath washes over me.

I grin. "Great, glad to hear it."

Fury devours his smirk. He moves faster than I thought possible and slams against me, knocking me a pace backward. But he's still with me, chest to chest like we're slow dancing. His rank onion breath makes me gag.

I open my mouth to tell him so—or maybe to vomit on him—but before I can, pain rockets through my mind. My hip is on fire. Xerxes steps away, triumphant. He brandishes a flick knife which is dripping in blood. My blood.

"Watch out, little rabbit." He slinks away like he's sliding on oil grease, and I hobble to my room, clutching my hip.

My hand comes away red, and I slide my pants down gingerly to inspect the damage. The asshole has carved a large letter X into my flesh. There's so much blood that I can't tell how deep the wound is and how much I need to be worrying. It's painful as hell, so I'm definitely worrying a bit.

I know Abby freshened my water this morning, but when I cross to my nightstand, I find the bowl covered in gore beside a rabbit's corpse. The creature's chest has been carved open with a big letter X.

"Fuck."

Zaden sure chose a great right-hand man. Lord Xerxes is a real little gem... good people skills, tolerant of others, and a cold-blooded psychopath.

My eyes dart to the only other container in the room—the pisspot. Did Fra Wang once say that urine was a good antiseptic? I feel faint, and my thinking is clouded, so I might have misremembered that. Probably not the best time to pour fecal waste on my gaping wound.

I lie down before I fall down and close my eyes, trying to heal myself. But the only energy available to pour into me comes from myself, so it's not possible. It's like trying to fill a glass of water using the liquid already inside the glass.

I close my eyes for a few moments. Molly's herbs will just have to wait.

* * *

Even in my sleep, I wince in agony.

My eyes flutter open as the sky outside my window is turning dark. I grimace when I shift my weight, but the intensity of pain in my hip has subsided. Gingerly, I remove the pillowcase and press against it to staunch the blood flow. It comes away red, but the wound looks okay.

Abby sweeps into the room with a fresh jug of water, her long ponytail swishing with every step. Her footsteps falter when she finds me lying in a pool of my own blood, and she gasps—it's the loudest noise she's ever made.

"It's not as bad as it looks. Thank you for the fresh water." I stand up then pour the whole jug of water over my wound. The last thing I want is an infection from whatever nasty bugs were on the Fuckwit's knife.

Abby's eyes are large and round, and when she sees the dead rabbit, she whimpers.

I try a nonchalant shrug. "I like bunnies."

She doesn't appear to know what the hell I'm talking about. I can hardly fault her for that. "I'll get some towels, milady." She scurries from the room before I can make another terrifying attempt at friendship.

I tear a bedsheet in strips and wrap a couple around my hips. If I don't do anything stupid, the wound should heal fine. If.

There's a change of clothes in the wardrobe, so I put on clean pants and a shirt. Dusk is almost upon us, and I'd like to undertake the long walk to Penngrove Forest and back before snowfall, and preferably not in the blistering heat of the day. Now would be perfect.

Abby returns with an arm full of towels and begins mopping up my mess. I bend to help her, but the poor serving girl shrinks in alarm, hunching in on herself. I hold her arm so she doesn't prostrate herself and roll into the corner.

Eventually, I figure the kindest thing is to leave her to clear up alone. She doesn't have the spine of Molly, that's for sure.

She finishes mopping then appears to address the floor. "Milady, the M—"

"Scarla."

"Yes, milady. The Margrave has requested your presence at dinner."

Sighing, I cross to the door. "Tell the Margrave I won't dine with him tonight, or tomorrow night, or any night for the next fifty years. Not even if he gives me a million copper pieces and paints the inside of the Undercity with gold ."

Abby gasps, more horrified by this than by the dead rabbit on my dresser. I guess she won't join my friends list after all. She risks a glance at me, possibly to see if I've exploded into witchy flames, then glues her eyes back to the flagstones.

The insanity of refusing to dine with the Margrave only after I've discovered he didn't kill Leesa is not lost on me, but my whole reason for being here has evaporated. Now I'm just his filthy prisoner, with no cards of my own.

I sigh. "You can rephrase it if you like." Abby bobs a curtsy, but I know she must be panicking. "And tell him if he harms you or your family, I'll kill myself while he's out kissing rich people's babies or whatever he does to drum up support."

She's frozen with fear, and I figure the best thing I can do is for her is leave.

Happy to oblige.

Scarla

I'm pissed off with the Margrave for being an elitist twat who doesn't care about anyone. Plus a psychopathic murderer without morals—even if he didn't kill Leesa. And for his choice of right-hand man. Abby's responses inflame my rage—why is she so damn accepting and passive?

My outraged march through the castle is more of a pathetic hobble because my hip wound jolts in pain with every step, but at least I manage to get downstairs and to the castle gates without running into Lord Xerxes the Fuckwit. When the guards come into view, I bite back my pain and march straight up to them.

They don't barge. When I came with the Margrave, I barely noticed them—they slid aside and opened the doors quietly. But now, their lances bar my way, and their faces are stony.

I adopt an imperious tone with my shoulders back and chin high. "Let me through."

Either I'm a terrible actress, or they're smarter than they look. They don't twitch a muscle or even meet my gaze.

I cross my arms. "Fine. Check with the Margrave if I have permission to leave."

Groveling to be allowed out makes me want to scream, and I have no clue if Zaden will let me go. But since I discovered he needs my Gaze given willingly on my deathbed, the power dynamic in our relationship has changed.

One guard barks at a third man standing in the shadows, who trots off, leaving me standing awkwardly with the two big, silent men. I miss Leo's easy chatter more than ever. All of Zaden's men seem to have had their tongues removed at birth.

"I like your helmet." I gesture toward my own outfit, inviting a compliment that I know won't come. Still, I'm amusing myself. "My pants are quite fetching too, don't you think?" Another granite expression greets me. "It's getting on, and dusk is almost here. I really need to get going, you know...." I lean my weight onto my good leg, feeling the pinch in my right hip. The nearest bloke blinks, mute. "Good idea. Let's just wait for the other guy to come back."

Eventually, the guard returns, trudging at the same pace he left. I wonder if they practice that in private so they look professional.

The messenger addresses the guard who sent him away, ignoring me altogether. Bloody typical around here. "The Margrave gives the lady permission to leave. He also gives her freedom to enter Penngrove Forest."

Dammit. I don't want that male's permission. I hate having to grovel and beg and prostrate myself just for the privilege of going outside.

Gracelessly, I leave the castle without a further word. It's so good to be out here. Sounds of activity from Hightown float over the river, and for once, I like the noises of horses' hooves and rolling carriage wheels. It reminds me that there's a world outside the castle, a world where angels and vestiges are still fairytales, a world where I am an ordinary woman.

Despite the pain in my hip, I make quick time across the patchy ground because the temperature is sublime. I judge it to be around mid-dusk when I reach the tree line and plunge into the forest.

It's cooler here and smells leafy and mulchy, a bit like the dank Undercity but less stale. I venture into the dark space between the trees, and my feet crunch on leaves underfoot. It's like entering another world.

My eyes adjust to the dark, and the sky is entirely invisible from beneath the thick canopy. The only indicator of the time of day is the temperature, which is still comfortable.

I jump at a scuttling, rustling noise, which sounds like a mountain lion walking on grogum crackers. Then I catch sight of a small creature, about the size of a rabbit, but with a long tail. Noises in here are magnified.

I get to my task. I'm looking for Wilton's Dale, which grows in small clumps at the base of yen trees. I hope I'll recognize it if I stumble across it—I've only seen it once in the underwing storage cupboards, and Fra Wang almost bit my head off when I touched it.

I walk in a straight line away from the forest edge, so I'll be able to retrace my steps easily. As lovely as it is in the forest, I don't want to spend the rest of my life here.

A woody, olive stem pokes up from the base of a yen tree, and I fall to my knees beside it, pulling away the fallen leaves. My heart leaps when I see dozens of clumps of Wilton's Dale. I run my fingers along the woody stems to remove the heavy needles and fill my pockets with the herb, carefully stripping only one branch from each plant.

I ignore the crunching in the leaves behind me, figuring it's another small mammal. But the crunches and cracks are getting louder... surely there can't be that many long-tailed bunnies?

Dread courses through me as I rise to my feet, and at a loud crunch, my heart races. I spin around and spot a man in the Margrave's livery. He is a servant, but his face is hidden behind a black mask.

Fear rockets through me, and I rear away from him.

"Over here!" The man's yell is loud enough to wake the dead.

Adrenaline spiking, I dash around a tree trunk and slam into a torso that is just as solid and wooden. More servants' livery with another black mask. The man grabs for me, and I knee him in the balls, putting all of my energy into it, then sprint away, blood pounding in my ears.

I zigzag around trees, adrenaline pushing me through the pain in my hip.

My only hope of beating them is if I wait them out—it'll be getting cold soon, and they'll have to seek warmth.

But I can't keep running. Every stride on my right leg shoots pain through my body, and I've reopened the wound. Blood drips down my leg.

Still, I keep sprinting. Thumps and crashes follow me; they're still on my tail. I need to outlast them, but my hip won't hold for much longer.

"Think, idiot."

I duck under a low tree branch, take a couple of paces, then pull a sharp U-turn. I climb onto the low branch and reach for the next one up. I'll have to jump, then hope my upper body strength holds.

I jump and hang like an icicle for several seconds before I manage to hook a foot over the branch I'm hanging from. I hoist myself up and then climb up to the next bough again. I'm nestled inside the foliage, but I can see drops of my blood on the leaves at the tree's base.

I shake away an image of a goat carcass hanging in the Undercity kitchen, dripping blood.

Pressing on my wound, I try to control my heavy breathing, but it's like trying to see through rock. The huffs and puffs keep steaming from my body, frosting the air at my face.

Before long, the men run past, five or six of them spread out in a line like they are hunting. Which I suppose they are. They all wear black masks to hide their faces, which creeps me out.

"The little bitch is gone."

A liveried man stands directly beneath me, and he yells out a response. "She can't of just disappeared, Bradley."

Bradley. I'll store that name away. These idiots wear masks to disguise themselves and then call each other by name.

Another man who I can't even see replies. That makes at least seven of the bastards. "It's going to be cold soon. The Lord didn't say we had to kill ourselves looking for the bitch. I'm getting out of here."

My breath is so loud in my ears that I keep waiting for the man at the base of my tree to hear it. Or to see the drops of red blood on the ground. When he holds up a finger, I stop breathing altogether. Hell, I think my heart stops beating.

But he drops the finger and turns back the way he came.

I give the men half an hour before I dare to climb down from the tree. The temperature has plummeted, but it's not yet snowfall. I'd like to be out of this forest before then, so I jog in the direction where I think the castle is. I'm a little lost with all my ducking and weaving, but I'm happy to rely on instinct and follow my natural sense of direction.

By the time I reach the forest's edge, my fear has morphed into anger. All that adrenaline is swashing around inside me with no outlet. I limp across the expanse of dirt dotted with spindly bushes, mulling things over. Lord Xerxes the Fuckwit seems to want me dead. Zaden definitely wants me dead so he can steal Gaze. Now that I no longer need revenge on Zaden because he didn't kill Leesa, the only thing stopping me from escaping is Zaden's threats to kill my father.

And I have no doubt he'd follow through.

Fine. I'll take my dad and get the hell out of Malanox. I'll disappear into the desert and never come back.

Scarla

The castle doors swing open as I approach, and I storm through them, filled with rage.

I turn on the poor guard who let me in. "Did you send those men after me? Who's been out of this door since I left? Tell me."

The bewildered man takes a few moments to respond. "I... A lot of folks use these doors."

"Did you send word I was in the woods?"

"N-no. I-I didn't do nothin'. I've just been stood here the whole time."

The head guard peers at me with barely concealed disgust. "Is there a problem here?"

I take note of the head guard's features—a long, curling, black mustache and blue eyes that would be handsome on another man but are just a foil to this man's ugliness. I would bet the clothes on my back that he's in league with Lord Xerxes the Fuckwit. I whirl around, showing him my back, and march straight through the door to the servants' quarters, not even slowing my stride.

Fumbling through my pockets, I retrieve a clump of Wilton's Dale as I enter the sickroom. I shove a bunch of it into my mouth, chewing furiously. It tastes foul, and the sharp needles poke into my cheeks. I guess I have to chew until it's soft—not really sure; I'm making this up as I go along.

Another cot is occupied, this one by a young man. That makes four sick in this room—Molly, the sandy-haired idiot, Robin, who got himself sliced open for insulting me, the old lady, plus the new guy.

"Are you sick?" I demand, poking the herb into my cheek with my tongue. I need to know how many patients will catch this bloody disease.

The man's voice is croaky. His blond hair is so short that I reckon I could use it as a bath sponge. That probably means he's a guard. "Yeah."

Good chat.

Molly looks worse. Bubbles of spit frame her lips, and her thin nightdress is soaked through with sweat. I lay my hands on her forehead and am aghast to find her wild with heat. At least that's something I can deal with. I draw the heat from her, feeling the pulses of warmth along my arms as I absorb her excess energy.

She stops her feverish mumbling and relief courses through me. But she isn't safe yet. The Sighing Sickness doesn't relinquish its victims so easily.

The Wilton's Dale is soft enough, I reckon. I pull the masticated herb from my mouth and prise aside Molly's lips, inserting it inside her gum.

The man with the spongy hair cracks open his voicebox. "That's disgusting, that is. What do you think you're doing?"

I rub Wilton's Dale all around Molly's tongue using my forefinger. "I'm saving her life."

I hope.

"Well, don't you go saving mine anytime soon. Not like

that."

I whirl on him. "Let's hope I don't have to." I finish treating Molly as best I can, then turn back to the newcomer. "Now, what's wrong with you?"

As I approach his bedside, the man cowers into his sheets. "Nothin. Keep your witchy hands away from me."

I sigh. "With pleasure."

When I've treated Molly and checked on the other two patients, I take my leave.

Out in the servants' corridors, Abby passes me and bobs a curtsy. She really is quite short.

"Abby." She jumps at her name. "Fetch me a pen and paper. Quickly."

Urgency is the one thing I have—I certainly don't have any authority—and it isn't difficult to impart it. The girl runs off without question. I lean against the paneled wall and wait for her to return, wondering if she will or if she was just fleeing me.

Soon enough, she returns with the requested items, handing them over without meeting my eye.

I scrawl some lines on the thick parchment. There's no time to compose pretty words, even if I could think of them, so I scratch out a quick sentence or two, then fold the paper.

Before handing it over, I look Abby up and down. She's timid, but maybe that's exactly what this mission calls for. "Can you read, Abby?"

Her face pinkens, and her large eyes dart to the floor. "No, milady."

Thank the Maker for that. I can't have anybody reading that message except Leo. We Undercity-siders may not sleep in silk, but at least we teach our children their letters. "Fine." I hand her the note. "Here. Take this to the Undercity. Lay it in the hands of Leo Billson Farmer in sleeping hub S5A9. Repeat that back to me."

"Sleeping hub S5A9."

"Good. Lay it in Leo's hand and nobody else's. At first dawn. Do you understand?"

Abby looks like she's about to piss her pants, but I have to get this note to Leo. I must stop the plan to kill Zaden. He's irritating as fuck, but he didn't kill Leesa, so fair's fair. I won't kill him.

If I'm hoping Abby will dash along the corridor, note in hand, I'm disappointed. The girl's large eyes widen with alarm, and eventually, she shakes her head. "Leave the castle, milady?" Her voice is quieter than a blyberry falling onto dirt.

"That's right. Your friend Molly's life depends on it."

Okay, so I'm a lying son of a bitch—that note has nothing to do with Molly. And it's a stretch to assume that Molly and Abby are friends, but not a long one.

Abby has shrunk during our chat. She's practically cowering on the floor, prostrating herself before me. But the damn girl still refuses to take my note out of the castle against her precious Margrave's orders. If only she realized I was trying to save his worthless life.

Well, good on her. I suppose. I'm glad she's found her backbone.

"Fine." I snatch the note back and stuff it into my pocket. I'll figure out another way to get it to Leo.

Tomorrow. Right now, I'm beat. Fatigue and hunger war within me, and tiredness wins out. I lumber to the northwest stairs and ascend to the second floor, plodding toward my chamber.

My bedroom door swings open easily. Roasted chicken lingers in the air, and my belly clenches. On the nightstand lies a large plate heaped with meat and vegetables—mattroot plus some of those others I must find out the name of. And seated beside it is Zaden, with a blank, appraising expression.

That pit of heat in my chest surges at the sight of his entitled face sitting in my private chamber, and I stoke it by ignoring Zaden and snatching up the plate of food to take to my bed.

As I sit on the mattress, the note in my pocket pokes into my hip, and I'm suddenly aware of how dangerous this situation is. I cannot allow Zaden to find that letter. Still, I can't exactly throw it into the fireplace without arousing suspicion.

Best thing to do is eat—as is so often the case.

Nothing ever tasted so good. Sweet vegetables, plump chicken, and a rainbow of other delicious foods. I savor the flavors and take my time eating until the emptiness in my belly is gone.

Zaden is still sitting there, watching me. A white T-shirt makes his tanned skin seem even more golden, but I refuse to play his games. I won't be the one to break the silence. He can sit on that Maker-be-damned chair while I sleep the night through if he wants.

When my plate is empty and every bone picked clean, I reach over and put it on my nightstand.

"I see you still like chicken," Zaden remarks.

With my belly full, my energy returns. I arc up at his mockery. "Yes. I suppose that makes me an animal, does it? I don't eat like a lady, and I don't dress like a lady and don't want to be a lady. Nothing about this castle is good except some of the servants—well, just the ones that aren't trying to kill me—and the food. Everything else here sucks. Present company included."

The smirk on his face hardens into a steel slate of anger. "What happened in Penngrove Forest? What do you mean some of my servants are trying to kill you?"

I shake my head. I can't trust Zaden. But glancing at him, I second guess myself. The hard planes of his body are turned toward me, and his concern seems genuine. His green eyes shine like beacons, and something about his presence brings me comfort.

No, that can't be right. I'm just grateful that he brings me chicken. "Why did you bring me chicken?"

He grinds his teeth as though I've asked him the most challenging question in the universe, like what is the meaning of life?

He doesn't answer, but he's brought it because I like it. Bloody hells below. He's being thoughtful and considerate, as well as sporting that caring expression on his stupidly beautiful face.

This male is such an enigma; I don't know whether to punch him or fuck him.

"What happened out there?" He sits beside me on the bed, and I lean toward him, pulled into the dent his massive body leaves in the mattress. His forest lily scent includes me in its cloud. The note in my pocket pokes into my hip.

I shift away. "An answer for an answer. I'll tell you if you answer a question of mine."

His jaw is so cut that I could sharpen a blade on it. He nods, and his green eyes twinkle. "It's a deal."

Scarla

I remember when I first saw Zaden, down in the underwing by Fra Perkins' bedside. My gaze had slid right off him, my eyes unable to focus. But now, I can see his golden skin as clearly as a plane of velvet.

"Why can I see your face now? Is it because I have Gaze?" He tilts his head at me, and I fumble on. "That isn't my question, by the way."

He lifts his head. "Then I won't answer it."

He's infuriating, as always, but with none of his usual spiky barbs. Maybe I've ground away some of his sharp edges... Like a relentless mortar grinding against a pestle. I sure feel like I've been banging my head against his these last few days.

I curl my fingers on my lap. "Okay, here's the question. Why did you leave heaven?"

I glance at him, and his jaw grinds. I can hear his molars scraping, and I wonder if I've gone too far. His eyes are turning darker, which is usually a sign of fury. I lean away from him, but it's like fighting gravity because his dent in the mattress is so much bigger than my own.

His whole body is rigid, and I'm sure he won't answer me.

But I'm wrong. "You make it sound as though I left heaven on vacation." He's trying to keep the tone light, but there are depths to his voice that I haven't heard before. "I was cast from heaven, Scarla. I felt my soul ripped from my body. It hurt, like every drop of blood was forced out through the pores in my skin. The pain was unthinkable. There are no words...."

Zaden stares at my desk, and I look at his face in horror. It is joy's graveyard, bearing witness to the hell he has endured.

It seems to cost him a brutal effort, but he raises his face to mine and looks me in the eyes. His pupils are pools of black, but his irises glow vibrant green. "I don't remember heaven. That's part of the punishment. But I do remember why I was cast out. I entrusted the Ring of Roth to a mortal, and she never returned it."

My breath hitches. "She?" I have no clue why I am focusing on this stupid detail, but I am swamped with pity and horror, and I don't know what else to say.

Zaden's eyes narrow, and he seems to be returning to the present. With a few minute movements, his vulnerability vanishes, and the man before me is as stoic and implacable as the one I first met. "Mortals cannot be trusted. That is the lesson I learned, and I will never forget it."

My hands curl into fists. "And I suppose you think angels can be trusted?"

Zaden stands, and I am jostled by the mattress springing up. He strides to the window and surveys his domain, probably reminding himself how superior he is to everybody else. He doesn't bother answering my question, which is no surprise. Still staring out the window, he says, "You owe me an answer. Which of my servants is trying to kill you?"

I cross to the nightstand and pour myself a glass of water, buying time while I compose an answer. I owe him honesty, but I don't know how far I can trust him. For all I know, Lord

Xerxes is acting under Zaden's orders.

But, deep inside, that doesn't feel right, and I don't think it's true.

"Lord Xerxes doesn't like me. And a number of your servants attempted to kill me in Penngrove Forest. One of them was called Bradley. I believe they were working for Xerxes."

There, that should do it. Honest but straightforward, just the facts and none of the whingeing.

Zaden turns to me, and I can see the dark fire in his eyes from across the room. Black swirls of magic mist around him, but his voice is calm. If it weren't for Gaze and his giveaway eyes, I could mistake him for someone who didn't care.

"Do you have any evidence that it is Lord Xerxes behind this?"

Evidence is a strong word, and I have nothing more than a hunch and a wound on my hip. I shake my head. "No."

"Let me know if you get any."

"Why do you have him living here? Even if he's not trying to kill me—which he definitely is—he's a sniveling power-monger with no morals or personal hygiene. He seems like just the sort of mortal you should slaughter."

Zaden sighs. "It's complicated."

"Try me."

"Xerxes was…" Zaden's smooth brow furrows, and he clearly comes to a decision. "You're out of questions. Let me know if you get any evidence against him. In the meantime, clean yourself up and get to bed."

There's clearly a big pot of juicy tea about Xerxes, but Zaden ain't spilling.

Since he isn't sharing and is ordering me to bathe, I fold my arms, waiting for him to leave so I can do precisely that.

Somebody has filled the stone tub in my adjoining room with hot water. Steam eddies and whirls above the bath, and I want nothing more than to clamber into it, soak myself, then crawl into bed.

I gesture toward the door. "Feel free to leave."

Zaden folds his arms across his chest and leans back against the windowsill, mirroring my posture. His muscular forearms are on full display, and I let myself look at them. "I'm not going anywhere. Not while your life is in danger. You can bathe here since the water is hot, then you will come and sleep in my chambers."

"Really?" My chest feels lighter, and a smile lights on my lips. He wants to protect me.

He nods, then turns to study the landscape while I undress. My sweaty clothes pool at my feet, and Leo's letter lands on top. I poke the incriminating note under the pink silk panties Zaden provided with my foot.

Stepping into the luxurious water, I begin to relax. Gentle waves lap across my skin. The liquid coats my thighs, belly, and breasts, and I sigh in pleasure as I lower myself in.

I run a dark gray bar of soap across my body, lathering bubbles along and between my legs. The day's stress washes away with every pass of the smooth bar across my skin, and my muscles relax.

Zaden is still staring out the window, unnaturally still. His back is broad, muscular, and tapers at the waist. I squint, and for a moment, I see his massive black wings outstretched as though he intends to leap out the window and fly. I see them so clearly—the anchor point where they fuse to his shoulder blades, the tips brushing the ceiling above, the way they soak up all the light in the room.

Those feathers have an instant effect on me. Liquid heat pools inside me, and my hands creep up my body, tracing the curve of my belly, then circle the swell of my breasts, islands in the ocean. My nipples harden into points, and I splash water across them, aching with sensitivity.

When Zaden turns, I jump, and the heat inside my core rushes to my cheeks. I submerge myself completely, but I'm sure he saw me arching in pleasure.

His green eyes darken into black, and tendrils of magic swirl around him. He stares at me, those liquid pools of blackness penetrating me. Without averting his gaze, he stalks toward me, smoldering, and I forget to be embarrassed. My back arches, and my breasts rise from the water, dripping wet.

Zaden's forest lily scent mixes with the steam, musky and earthy, and suddenly he is beside me, bending his face to mine, those black eyes filled with purpose.

Scarla

Zaden scoops me from the bath and into a fluffy, white towel, carrying me like a bride on her honeymoon.

The towel falls in folds across my breasts and legs, a thin layer between Zaden's powerful chest and my naked body.

His eyes are black as pitch, and I know I should be scared, but all I can focus on is the granite of his warm chest and the strength of his arms beneath my back and knees. I shift slightly so the towel falls lower, exposing more white skin, aching for the heat of his gaze on my breasts.

Those twin pools of black stare into my face, then flicker down, and when he catches a glimpse of my white flesh, his jaw hardens, and tendrils of his smoky magic engulf us.

His long strides carry us across the room to my bed. He places me onto the mattress gently, and if I was stupid, I'd say lovingly... I'm trying very hard not to be stupid. But my mind isn't in control, and I sink into the mattress's embrace like into a lover's arms.

Angels have the power of seduction, but right now, I crave it. Consequences be damned.

Zaden's hands are on either side of my head, twin pools of gravity, but it's his hard chest that my eyes are drawn to beneath the folds of his clothes.

"Take off your shirt." The words pour from me like wine, and I can't tear my gaze from his torso.

He stands, and for a horrible moment, I think he's leaving. But at his full height, towering above me, he slides his white T-shirt over his head, slowly revealing the V that points beneath his pants and the sculpted muscles of his chest.

Nobody but the Maker could have made this perfect being.

My breathing comes faster, and I run my gaze across his form, anticipating the feel of his skin beneath my fingers, imagining the velvety texture over the firmness beneath.

Liquid heat pools inside me, and I beckon him closer.

He obeys, and a thrill pulses through me. Zaden sits beside me gently, but black magic swirls around him, and he looks as though he's fighting to control himself. He unstraps his scabbard and places his silver sword onto the pile of clothing on the floor.

I push myself onto my elbows, bringing my whole body closer to him, feeling the towel's fabric strain across my breasts. He is the last male I should have sex with, but I've never wanted anything more than to press my body against his and clamp myself around him. There's no outcome from this moment that doesn't involve our bodies entwined and writhing—and if there is, I don't want any part of it.

"Do angels know how to kiss?" I purr, and he leans closer, scented of musk.

"Let's find out."

I close my eyes to block the sight of his black eyes because I've only seen that look on him when he's murderously enraged, and I honestly don't know if he's going to kiss me or kill me. Even worse, I can't make myself care. I just need to be nearer.

His lips are warm, soft, and insistent, pressing against mine and claiming me for his own. He tastes of apples and honey, luscious and sweet, and I push back hard, kissing him passionately, claiming his mouth as my own.

He pulls away, teasing, just out of reach, and raises an eyebrow. "So? What's the verdict?"

I smile. "Angels can definitely kiss." I raise a shoulder innocently. "I wonder what else they can do?" My shoulders shimmy, and my towel drops lower, revealing a nipple

Zaden's jaw goes slack, and his breathing comes fast. My chest heaves, and my breast yearns for his touch, reaching toward heaven.

With a look of wonder, Zaden traces the swell of my breast, starting from the outside and spiraling in. Is he torturing me on purpose? Finally, his hand brushes my nipple, and a moan bursts from my lips.

I buck into his hand, yearning for a harder grip, and he surprises me by pinching my nipple between his fingers. His face is slack, his eyes lidded and staring at my breasts. A moment later, he takes me into his mouth, sucking hard, running his tongue in circles, and nibbling.

I cry out in pleasure and startle him. He pulls back, leaving me wet and needy.

"Am I hurting you?"

I fall back onto the mattress, and his glance catches my jiggling breasts. "Don't you dare fucking stop, Zaden."

He grins, and I get the sense that he's won the war between us, but as long as I triumph in this particular battle, I don't give a shit.

My fingers find their way to his chest and gently trace the outlines of his muscles. He is solid, like a male forged from steel, but his skin is silk.

"I thought you'd be sparkly or something," I murmur.

He emits a low chuckle, as breathy as a moan. "I'm not a unicorn, Scarla."

I raise myself to sitting beside him, my feet brushing the floor, but he still towers above me. I lean forward and lick his chest from belly to scapula, absorbing him through my sensitive tongue, which finds valleys and mountains in his chest, all covered in velvet.

"You taste like a unicorn."

His chest vibrates against my mouth. "Are you in the habit of licking flying horses?"

I bite his nipple. "Unicorns can't fly. You're thinking of alicorns."

His voice is tight, and his hand finds the back of my head, squeezing. "Trust me. I'm not."

Pleasure ripples through me, and I'm overcome with urgency. I clamber to my feet, holding the towel about me, aware of Zaden's gaze tracking my every movement. I let the towel drop to my feet and stand before him, completely naked.

I feel exposed and vulnerable, but the hunger in Zaden's eyes makes me feel beautiful too. His magic snakes around me, encircling my waist, climbing higher along my back, then down my thighs, exploring my body with a tingle. Zaden's fists curl into the mattress, and his voice hitches.

"Spectacular," he breathes.

But when his magic explores the wound on my hip, he scowls. He falls to his knees at my side, peering at the injury like a demented surgeon.

"Who did this to you?"

Talking about Lord Xerxes the Jerkses isn't my idea of dirty talk, so I delay answering.

"Tell me," he demands, inspecting the wound. "I will take the motherfucker to the clouds and it will rain with his blood."

I shiver at his intensity, trying to shake it off. "That was your best buddy. He signed his initials. Cute, hey?"

Zaden growls. "I'll deal with Xerxes later." He places a gentle kiss on my hip as though tending to a child. But his expression grows hungry again when his gaze roves across my belly. He climbs to his feet slowly, his face just inches from my body. He steals a lick on my breasts as he rises, then my neck, and at my face, he kisses my lips hard.

"Scarla," he whispers, and I can't decipher his tone.

He straightens to his full height, and I lean into his chest, resting my cheek against his pecs, inhaling his musk. A firm hand in the small of my back pulls the rest of my body against him, and his hard length presses into my belly.

I fill my lungs, relishing the slight movement of my breasts against his powerful chest and the shift of my belly against his hard length, earning a moan from him that sends a thrill through me.

My fingers dig into his back, then I step away, leaving a thin gap of shimmering hot air between our bodies. Any sense of embarrassment or vulnerability has evaporated, and I feel sexy and empowered, knowing he is entranced by me.

His gaze follows me to the bed, and he comes shortly after.

I put a hand on his chest to stop him, and he frowns for a moment until I speak. "You're overdressed, Angel."

He smiles but doesn't rush to remove his pants. Instead, he pins my wrists to the bed with his hands and kisses me, achingly soft.

"Do I have your consent to continue?"

I arch my back toward him, frustrated by the distance between us. "You have my fucking consent. Keep going."

He smiles wickedly, then dips his head.

Zaden

Scarla is laid before me on the bed, a fucking goddess.

Her pale skin blends to pure white in the places where the sun hasn't been... her large, bouncing breasts, the tops of her thighs, her mound of Venus. Those flashes of white are intoxicating, pure delight.

I want to cover her breasts with my mouth and press my hands against her thighs. If I wasn't already bursting out of my trousers, that pristine flesh would harden my cock into steel.

As it is, I have to dig my fingers into the mattress to hold myself back. Mortals dent easily.

I run my lips down her neck, and those blue veins running just beneath the skin look so fragile that I raise my head to stop, but she pulls against the back of my neck, encouraging me. When I lick along her scapula, she moans, and my cock jumps in response.

I look up at her face and see pleasure etched across it, her lips parted, and her cheeks flushed. Her arousal is contagious—she's like the fucking flu. I want to study her, understand her, fuck her.

"Why are your irises black?" she murmurs.

My damn eyes signal my desires just as clearly as my

straining erection. Just as well she can't see the black smoke of my magic caressing her.

I put my mouth above her ear, and her copper hair tickles my nose. "Lust," I purr. I'm not usually one for sharing my personal truths, but right now, I'd tell her all the Maker's divine secrets if I could remember them.

Scarla moans again, this time arching into me, pressing her magnificent breasts against my chest, so soft and full that I almost cum right then and there. It's been decades since I last found a person alluring enough to bang. And this one is fucking intoxicating.

This mortal has resisted me for the last time. I intend to dominate her.

Scarla's usual scent is blyberry, which has soaked into her skin since she was a baby, but now her sweet aroma is mixing with her musky core, and it is lighting up every inch of my skin. I inhale her. I work my way down her body, running my tongue around her curves, memorizing their shape.

When I reach her injured hip, with Xerxes' carved 'X,' rage overtakes me for a moment, but I store it for later. I will carve that asshole into pieces when the time is right.

"Does it hurt?"

"No." She pushes my head lower, and the gentle pressure of her hand on my hair, her urgency, sends waves of pleasure outward from its touch.

I reach her soft tangle of hair and detour around it, brushing my lips along the whitest skin of her inner thigh, inhaling deeply. She bucks against me, seeking pressure, and I leave the gentlest of kisses at the very top of her thigh, earning a frustrated moan that sends shock waves through me.

This fucking mortal. I want to ram myself inside her and feel her from the inside, but I also want to understand the extent of her vestigial skills and claim her Gaze. She's messing with my mind.

So I'm happy to mess with hers a little. I tease her with my fingertips, drawing lazy circles on her perfect, white thighs.

"Please," she begs.

And I can't hold back any longer. I press my mouth against her, tasting her nectar, and my cock gets so fucking hard I might burst. I push my hips into the mattress to ease the ache and bury myself into Scarla's core.

I lick her folds, letting my tongue explore. She tastes sweet and salty like sea-washed blyberries, and I want to live inside her perfection. With every moan that escapes her, I thrust against the mattress, needing the friction.

Glancing up, I see Scarla's face contorted and her full, white breasts bouncing and jiggling. My breath catches in my throat. She squeaks, and I realize I'm digging my fingernails into her thighs.

"Sorry." I twitch away.

"I'm not made of glass, Zaden."

Her voice is so fucking sexy right now, throaty and guttural, and my name on her lips is like reentering heaven. She pronounces it unlike anybody else, with a slightly longer 'a' sound and a sensual hum on the 'Z.'

I've removed my fingernails from her legs, but I can't stop running my hands along her smooth skin. "Yes, you are. I was forged in the primordial fires of the stars, and you are just delicate veins and scarred flesh."

A smile quirks her lips. "You're so romantic, Angel."

I know she means it as an insult—as a method of increasing the emotional distance between us—but hearing her call me angel is just as arousing as when she uses my first name.

"And you're sexy, mortal." I try to inject venom into the nickname, but it comes out wrong.

This fucking woman.

My nipples are hard enough to carve ice, so I rub my chest across her calf, earning a soft sigh from her and a wave of aching relief for my chest.

Her whimper is too much for me to resist, so I grab her thighs and lick her slit, circling the nub with my tongue. She trembles, and I sense that she is on the precipice of release.

But I don't allow that—not yet.

I run a hand down her thigh, over the bump of her knee, around the soft curve of her calf, and all the way to her foot. Then, I stand and survey this intriguing woman, laid before me like a sensual feast.

In one movement, she pivots into a seated position and scowls at me. "What the hell are you doing?"

The whisper of a smile plays around my lips. "Just following orders." My hands find my belt buckle. "You said I was overdressed if I remember correctly."

Her gaze follows my hands, and her lips are parted. "Yes," she breathes.

My pants fall to the floor, and my cock springs up, a wave of cool air brushing it. It aches for this mortal's touch, for the softness of her skin, for the pressure of her flesh. But if she goes anywhere near it, this'll be all over. It's been decades, after all.

First, I need to make sure she's back up on that precipice, ready to fall. I need to keep her happy, after all. I need to reap Gaze on her deathbed and return to my rightful place in heaven.

In the meantime, I'll make do with this slice of nirvana on earth.

The sheets feel soft against my length, and Scarla's nub is hard and wet. Spread before me, I feel invited into her, welcomed, desired, and, when I can't resist a moment longer, I pull myself up her body, traveling her soft curves to her face.

I rest the tip of my cock at her entrance while I place my lips on hers.

She places a hot hand on my chest. "No penetration."

"What?"

"I don't want to be bewitched by you."

One inch further and I'd be partially inside her. Her wetness tantalizes my tip, and it takes all my strength to pull away.

But I'm dancing in triumph. She assumes that she will only be bewitched if I thrust myself inside her, but she's wrong. We've probably already done enough.

Just to be sure, I nibble on her breast and earn a gasp, then I extend my wings, and her eyes widen in response.

Smiling, I pluck a feather from my wing, wincing at the painful tug. I hold it aloft, and the mortal arches toward it. If she could fly, she'd hover above the bed to get near it.

Putting her out of her misery, I lower the feather and run it down her neck, then circle it around her breasts. She moans, unfettered and raw, and my cock pulses with every utterance.

I run the feather lower, tracing the curve of her hip. She bucks against it, wild and unrestrained. Her legs are spread, and she is wet and inviting. I brush my feather over her mound and under. When I skim her clitoris, she begins to release.

Her eyes are closed like she's visiting a personal paradise where I can't follow her, and the soft curve of her jaw tightens. I sense her muscles rippling powerfully as she bucks and explodes, panting in ecstasy.

I leave my own pleasure for now—I can sort that out later. The most important thing is this mortal's orgasm, so she will be forever under my control. Even so, my cock strains for release as I watch her climax play out, rippling in a series of waves.

Staring at her, I will her to look at me, searching for a sign that she is enamored. This is her final test.

She raises an eyebrow. "Turns out angels can do lots of things."

Her eyes close, and her mortal flesh turns to sleep.

Yes, angels can do lots of things. Like, ensnare mortal women with sex, so they don't notice they're in prison.

Scarla

My dreams are filled with silk sheets and wet spots and the sound of Zaden's voice whispering by my ear, "Lust."

Somehow, I manage to wake feeling refreshed. The angel lies beside me, a long mass of muscles twisted around the sheets.

"Morning, mortal."

I expected a wham-bam-thankyou-ma'am, but it seems he's stuck around for the aftermath. "Morning, Angel."

His jaw clenches in restrained emotion, but I can't tell what he's feeling. Judging by the sparkling green of his eyes, it isn't rage or lust.

The battle tapestries watch over us, and I recall the plan I set in motion to murder Zaden. I definitely have to cancel that, note or no note. He didn't kill Leesa. And after hearing his story of being expelled from heaven, then our... encounter last night... I feel fondly toward him. Which is hard to reconcile with a desire for his ice-cold angelic blood.

Of their own accord, my fingers reach out and trace the planes of his chest, which tighten under my touch. "You stayed." I shift toward him, and his gaze flicks down to my form beneath the twisted sheets.

His eyes darken, and a snaking tendril of magic caresses

the small of my back, urging me closer. "I have to confirm something."

"You do?"

"Then I'll be on my way."

My hand falls from his chest. "Oh. Okay. What do you need to know?"

He tilts his head, questioning. "Are you in love with me?"

I bark out a laugh and pull the sheets close. "Arrogant bloody angel. No, I'm not in love with you."

He frowns and examines me for a long moment, then climbs out of bed and bends to retrieve his pants, shoving his perfect bare ass in my direction. Last night was... amazing... but I still have a carnal need for his cock inside me. Right now would be just fine—that's a good ass.

Sadly I'll have to make do without. I can't get myself bewitched by him.

Buckling his belt, he turns, still with that wrinkle between his brows. "Why not?"

Is this guy serious?

"Look, Zaden, I'm sorry, but it takes more than a night of... ." Heat creeps into my cheeks, and I rush on. "I'm not in love with you, buddy. Lust, maybe, but...." A memory of him murmuring that word into my ear has me shivering.

He looks into the middle distance. "How odd."

Maker-be-damned, Zaden really is an arrogant sod. "Not really. You can be pretty awful." I'm aiming for post-coital playfulness, but the words come out harsher than I intend.

Zaden crosses to the nightstand and pours himself a glass of water—not offering me one, I notice. "When an angel is sexually intimate with a mortal, the mortal becomes infatuated and does the angel's bidding."

I sit upright, holding the sheets close, wishing I weren't naked, processing this new information. "It's not just penetration? I see."

"You have a rather limited definition of sex if you think it's just about penetration."

"Oh, I..."

"So it makes no sense that you can resist me."

I exhale. "Trust me, it's getting easier and easier."

He sips the water. "It must be another vestige power you inherited. How many people have you seen die?"

I picture all the folks who've passed through the underwing and never made it out. Old folks, mostly, but some young. Infants, too. A conga line of faces marches through my memory. "Enough."

Zaden nods curtly. "Interesting."

"Oh, yeah. Looking at dead people. Fascinating."

He doesn't get the sarcasm or doesn't appreciate it. "I wonder what other vestigial powers you've absorbed."

He's staring out the window, so I take the opportunity to pull a shirt over my head and step into my pants. This needs my full attention, and lying nude in sex-stained sheets near a perfectly formed angelic being is proving distracting.

"You think I might have something other than Gaze?"

"We already know about your temperature resistance."

"Oh yeah."

"And now we add resistance to enrapturing."

My face breaks into a smile. "You can't stand it, can you? Your evil plan to seduce me and make me your slave has failed. Sucked in, babe."

Being used for my body has never felt so good.

He surveys me with his lordly stare, ignoring my jibe. "If

you were a male or an angel, you could become King of the Cloaked Court. You already have Gaze; you would just need Inflict to complete the dyad."

"What? What the hell are you talking about? There's a King of the Cloaked Court?"

The Margrave's sneer is all arrogance. "I forgot how ignorant you are."

"I forgot what a prick you are, but let's not dwell on the details. Who is the king, and why haven't I heard of him?"

Zaden slides a glass of water across the table in my general direction. I guess that's his version of a post-sex cuddle. "The courtly king is both knowing and punishing. That is why he needs the twin skills of Gaze—for knowledge—and Inflict—for punishment. He has power over the whole of Aubia—"

"The whole country?"

"Yes, because most of the city rulers are vestiges. The ones that aren't angels, of course. And they're all installed by us."

Crap. I should have guessed that. Information has hit me like bullets these last few days, and I haven't had the headspace to put it all together. "Except you. You've chosen our tiny town, Malanox. Surely you could have the biggest city you want, like Solren or Desert's Maw?"

He regards me with a cold stare. "I have no interest in the dealings of mortals, any more than I want to be king of the skitter beetles."

"Right, of course. Sorry, I forgot what a twat you are."

"My only interest is in returning to heaven."

I gulp down the water, letting some splash on my cheeks and chin. I refuse to play the lady. "Which you can't even remember. How do you know it's not a big pile of manure up there, with all the angels sitting on dung heaps playing the harp?"

He stares out the window. "It calls to me. I can sense it. And I won't feel whole until I return."

Maker-be-damned, now I feel bad for teasing him. "Tell me more about the king. So he's King of the Secret Club you attended at the fancy party?"

His lips quirk. "The Cloaked Court. Yes. You're not as stupid as you look."

"And you're stupider than you look, but we digress. Go on."

"The king convenes the Cloaked Court twice a year, and all city rulers must attend. It is, as the name suggests, conducted in secret, with its members not fully understanding the others' powers."

"Unless you have Gaze and can see each others' magic."

He looks at me sharply. "You can see my magic?"

"Well, duh."

"Even my... dark magic?"

I shrug, enjoying his unease. "Your sex magic? Yep." He drops his gaze, and it feels like a victory. "And what if you don't turn up to one of the king's little council meetings?"

"I've tried that. The king has Inflict."

"Ahh. I'm guessing that skill doesn't inflict pleasure on others?"

"Quite the opposite."

I follow his gaze out the window, across the river and the stone roofs of Hightown. "I see." Whatever torture Zaden endured at the hands of the vestige king has etched a haunted expression on the angel's face.

"What happens at court?"

"The king metes out punishments and new laws at the

Cloaked Court. He can be very... persuasive."

Our small city of Malanox lies before us, stretching to the mountain of the Undercity but soon giving way to the desert. Before I went to the party at Solren, I thought Malanox was the whole world. Heading to North Undercity or Hightown was the biggest adventure I could imagine. The idea of traveling north across the Dead Desert like Leo did was as wild a notion as I could hold.

But now I know the world is a lot bigger. Malanox is tiny compared to Solren, nothing more than an outer suburb. And even that huge metropolis is just one city in a world controlled by angels and mortals with the vestiges of celestial magic.

I clear my throat, not sure if my lungs are big enough to say what comes next. "And if I get Inflict, I could become king?"

I've never wanted to be on the Undercity Council and never yearned to lead... but the prospect of wielding power over arrogant bastards like Lord Xerxes the Fuckwit has a certain appeal.

"No. Never. You're mortal, although occasionally a powerful vestige has held the role. And you're female. The king must be male."

I whirl on him. "Why? Because men have bigger muscles and smaller brains? That's the worst logic I've ever heard. And I promise you, Margrave, I will put a woman on that throne one day." Obviously, I have no clue how I could make that happen.

He raises his eyebrow as though I'm a misbehaving little girl with grandiose ideas. "Yourself?"

I narrow my eyes and point to the door. "You've got your answer. I'm not in love with you, and I never will be. Now get out and don't come back."

Zaden snatches his shirt from the floor and slips it over his coiling muscles, then sweeps up his precious sword and strides out the door, leaving me staring at it.

Maybe my future holds more than I ever anticipated. Perhaps I'll become Queen of the Cloaked Court and have control over these idiot men who surround me.

For the first time in my life, the prospect of wielding power sounds fucking fantastic.

Scarla

As usual, my body clock is out of sync with my surroundings.

It's no longer because I sleep in a night hub and work odd shifts, caught between the night life of my father and the day life of Leo. Now I'm exhausted from too much sex and too much of being hunted in the woods.

It's not a mealtime, but I'm starving.

I wander along the castle corridor, running a hand along the rough-hewn walls and marveling at the quality of the wall sconces. They seem to grow directly from the stone and cast warm pools of light along the passage.

Tonight, I suppose I'll sleep in Zaden's room—he wants to protect me from Xerxes. Or control me. Or both. I'm curious to enter his tower and see how he lives, what items he chooses to surround himself with—will it be magnificent paintings from Old Masters, or perhaps ancient pottery? Or perhaps he lives like a monk in an austere, dark room. I wouldn't put it past him.

I poke my head in the dining hall, my gaze drawn to the vaulted ceilings soaring above me. Strong daylight pours in unfiltered through the large windows, which lifts my spirits, but there's neither sign nor smell of anything edible.

Downstairs in the kitchen, the strong, greasy aroma greets

me, and my belly clenches in reply. I've figured out there's no community fund here—and Lord Fuckface doesn't take kindly to people nabbing rolls between meals. But they've got enough to go around, so I don't feel bad when I grab an apple and a hunk of ox cheese and stuff them into my pockets.

The dim lighting and stuffy atmosphere give me a pang of homesickness, but I push it down. This is no time for sentimentality. There is a room full of sick people who need my help. At least that gives me purpose.

Outside the kitchen, I dart along the dank hallway, following its twists with ease—I already know this place well. Molly described this area as out-of-bounds, saying it was *not for the living.* That phrase still gives me the heebie-jeebies, so I shuffle along quickly, avoiding the shadows that live in the crevices.

I poke my head inside the sick room to check on Molly. She's not alone. The old lady has gone—cured, I think—but half a dozen other young servants are lying in bed. Plus, my old buddy, Robin.

The man opposite Molly, the one with the blond sponge head, sighs in his sleep, and I shudder. He'll have to accept my masticated herbs now. They all have the Sighing Sickness.

Hating myself for my reluctance, I slowly cross to Molly's bedside, dreading what I'll find. She is pale, floppy, unresponsive. A hand on her forehead confirms that her fever has returned, so I focus on removing the excess heat from her body.

Temperature regulation. Part of my vestigial power. It's one I'm grateful for, that's for sure. I may have witnessed a lot of death, but I've also prevented some of it. Does that mean I owe a debt to the Maker?

I shiver. I've never conceived of having a personal relation-ship with the Maker, but the existence of angels means I have to rethink all that.

I chew on some Wilton's Dale and poke the sodden green mess into Molly's mouth.

"Get better, Molly. You're on my friend list, and it's short." Wow, that sounded selfish. "And, you know, you probably want to get better too."

And that sounded dumb. I'm glad Zaden isn't here to listen to my ramblings. I cross from bed to bed, taking out fevers and poking pre-chewed weeds into strangers' mouths, wondering if it will help or if I'm a lunatic.

I approach the man with spongey blond hair. "Do you want me to treat you?"

He doesn't look disgusted by my nursing methods anymore; he just looks weary. He nods assent, and I do what I can for him.

Footsteps from behind me have me whirling around. Abby stands in the doorway, fretting her hands, writhing them like giant worms. "Will they live?" She is clearly worried enough to forget her simpering politeness and open her mouth for once.

"I hope so."

I move to the next patient and supply some Wilton's Dale, hoping I'm helping. Who knows if I am? Time will tell. Maybe I should utter a prayer, given that angels exist and all that, but I really wouldn't know where to start. Plus, I'd feel ridiculous.

Abby watches me, and I can tell she's searching for the courage to speak.

I spin around. "Spit it out."

"I... I'm sorry I couldn't deliver that note for you. Will she die because of me?"

"Shh." I glance around, but nobody who cares can hear us. "No, of course not," I snap, irritated that I've placed a burden of guilt on this poor woman who doesn't deserve it. I burned that note in my fireplace as soon as Zaden left my chambers this morning, and felt light relief as I watched it turn to ash.

But I never should have told Abby that Molly's life depended on that note. Cruelty lives within me and sneaks out from time to time. Some of the things I'm learning about myself are shit, and I wish I could stuff the knowledge back under the mattress of my soft brain.

She bobs her head. "All right, milady."

I hate being called that. Every fiber of my being rails against it, but this isn't the time to insist that Abby change. Besides, I'm the one with a problem with authority, not her.

"You'd better go, Abby. You shouldn't be in here; the Sighing Sickness is catching."

She backs away a pace. "Won't you get it, milady?"

"No. My family is...."

From the doorway, she pauses, waiting for me to finish. "Are you all right, milady?"

Nothing I used to take for granted makes sense anymore. Maybe my immunity to disease is another vestigial power, not something I inherited from my mom like I always thought. "I'm fine. Just go."

Abby hustles away, and I wonder at her haste. Is she responding to the threat of illness or to my order? The sense of wielding power over others slithers across me like a grease slick, and I don't like the feel of it. I'll have to rethink that whole Queen of the Cloaked Court thing.

With more relief than is seemly, I exit the sickroom and

already dread having to go back. But I will. This afternoon, probably.

I climb the northwest tower staircase. The secret staircase of the inner maze is inside these very walls, a shell around the stairs I'm ascending. As soon as I'm free of the cloying atmosphere of the servants' floor, I pull the cheese from my pocket and bite off a large chunk. Red and gold flash above me. A liveried servant stands at the top of the stairs, blocking my path. He doesn't budge as I approach, and a cold shiver wraps around my spine.

I force myself to meet his eyes, and I don't find any respect there. Just narrowed slits above an unsmiling mouth.

Even one-on-one, I don't think I can take him. Not here, in the cushy, magicked air of the castle, when I can't rely on waiting him out until he freezes or burns. Plus, he has the upper ground.

I try for a commanding tone. "Let me through." Nope, sounds petulant and childish.

The servant is of a medium build, brown hair, narrowed eyes, and now with a nasty sneer. "You ain't the boss, bitch. And the Lord told you not to steal from the kitchens. Do you know what the punishment for stealing is? I'm gonna carve *Do not steal* into your pretty thighs, so you never forget, then I'm gonna take you to the Lord for the rest of your due."

What is with these grown men running around carving letters into women's bodies? Are they short on paper or something?

Candlelight reflects off the man's blade, shimmering. It would be beautiful if it weren't designed to torture me.

I sigh dramatically. "Fine. You win. I'll use the other stairs." My heart races and I don't dare turn my back on this man, so I take a step backward, feeling for the next step with my foot and never taking my eyes from his glinting blade.

I weigh up my options. Stay and fight or see if I can beat this jerk down the stairs and lose him in the castle. The thought flits through me that I should use Gaze on him, but I can tell at a glance he isn't a vestige and can't see what good it would do anyway. Death through staring.

"You ain't going nowhere, bitch."

My back stiffens into steel. "What's with all the gendered name-calling? Your Lord Xerxes is just a sexist prick who's recruited a bunch of slobbering servants to do his dirty work. He's the Maker's ass crack, and you're the fetid shit coming out of it. I've blown smarter stuff out my nose."

Or option three: annoy the fucker, so he really wants to kill me. Clever.

Fire rages behind his squinty eyes, and he lunges at me, but I leap down some stairs, hoping to nail the landing.

I don't. My ankle twists on impact with the staircase, and I fall, smacking my injured hip against a step. Pain pulses through me, and the red-and-gold uniform descends toward me. I glance around, looking for something I can use to my advantage, anything that might tip the scales my way. Nothing.

Panic snaps through me, and I heave myself backward down another step, my heart speeding. He's going to slice through my flesh then take me to Lord Xerxes to kill me.

I can't tear my gaze from that glinting steel blade.

Scarla

I scuttle backward and fall down another step. Pain shoots through my hip. With a smirk dripping with enjoyment, the servant leans down and grabs my ankle.

"You're mine, bitch."

Fear skitters through me, and I try to pull away, but his fingers are like solid rock. I aim a kick at his balls, but he's too far away. I'll save that for when he's carving his words into my flesh. Then I'll punch him in the ear and disappear into the inner maze.

Behind his eager face, black smoke swirls, filling the stairwell, and the servant releases me. A colossal figure looms from the darkness, wielding a black-veined sword, his eyes as black as coal.

Zaden.

The servant bows his head, practically scraping his chest across the steps. "Milord, I caught her stea—"

With one swoop, Zaden swings his sword in a wide arc and slices through the servant's neck, severing his head completely. The headless body pitches forward and traps its head beneath it. At least it didn't roll down the stairs.

I spring to my feet, and pain jolts through my twisted ankle. I lean against the paneled bamboo wall and open my mouth to speak, but Zaden's eyes are still as black as hell, and he stalks toward me with his sword raised.

Those eyes. Pretty sure it's not lust this time.

I hold out a hand to stop him as though my thin bones might be of any use against his coiled muscle and his black-veined sword. "Stop."

His jaw clenches and his shoulders rise as though he's fighting something inside himself—an angel's inner demons must be hectic.

Finally, he gets himself under control, and his eyes shift to green. When his breathing slows, he looks me up and down like he's assessing a thermo-ox that he's considering purchasing at the market. "When the death haze takes me, Ashmodu never stops."

"Ashmodu?" He indicates his sword, which he's clearly named. Honestly, most men just name their dicks.

"I never stop."

The cold wall presses against my shoulder. "Well, you just did."

"Because it wasn't directed at you. Nothing can stop the haze. Nothing."

"Oh."

"What did he want?"

"The dead guy?" Zaden nods. "He had a dagger, and he wanted to carve into my flesh. You know, the usual."

Zaden glowers, and black smoke swirls around him. "What did he say?"

My hip stings, and a hand over it comes away covered in blood. The wound has reopened. "He was going to carve a lesson into my thighs, then take me to Xerxes to kill me."

"Did he say that?"

I'm in pain and pissed off, and I just want to go have a good lie down and a cup of mistleroot tea. "No, he didn't say it. He just thought it, and I read his mind."

Zaden narrows his eyes and studies me closely.

Maker-be-damned, this dude needs to learn sarcasm. "I'm joking. He said it. Out loud. Using words. You should try it someday."

Zaden growls; I remember I'm dealing with a death-loving angel with a robust avenging streak.

I exhale. "He said he's going to take me to the Lord to get my due. He didn't explicitly mention Xerxes by name, but he's the only lord around here. And he didn't detail how my murder would go down, but, again, the implication was pretty damn clear. Is that specific enough for you?"

The black smoke has dissipated, so I guess Zaden is feeling calmer.

Time to poke the bear. "If you hadn't killed the damned servant, we could have gotten more information from him."

Zaden reaches out a hand to me, and I cling to it. "Why do you hate death?" he asks.

"Everybody hates death."

"No. Only mortals."

"Oh, sure. And a smart guy like you can't figure out why we don't like it?"

Zaden helps me sit on a step, and it is bliss to take the weight off my legs. He towers above me. "I mean, why do you hate other people's death? You don't like me killing, and you are trying to save the lives of the sick servants. Why?"

"You know about that?"

He nods. "Nothing happens in this castle without my knowledge."

I think of my explorations through the inner maze and my escape to Hightown. Zaden shouldn't be so sure of himself. "Being mortal gives us empathy. We help others because we don't want to see them die. And they do the same for us. It's part of the deal."

Zaden sits beside me, and heat radiates from him. "No. Other mortals are vicious and wicked. That is why angels exist—to execute the Maker's judgments."

"Which usually involves killing people?"

"Yes. I slew the servant Bradley. I separated his head from his body and cast them both into Malanox River. He deserved it."

It's a horrific description, but I can't say it bothers me. Hopefully, that'll make the other servants think twice about going after me.

I sigh. "Humans are... complicated. We're not all good, and we're not all bad. But we can be wonderful. I'll prove it."

A flicker of interest crosses his face. "How?"

"I'll take you to the dawn market. It's full of small kindnesses. People helping folks carry their purchases or giving free things to the poor. You'll see."

I want him to like humans, for some reason. Defense of the human race, I guess.

"They're not all good." He indicates the body beside us. "But I'll protect you from the bad ones."

"Really?" For a moment, I let myself believe he cares for me and really wants to protect me. My chest feels lighter, and a smile lights on my lips.

He nods. "Of course. I can't have you killed. You must die of natural causes."

That lightness turns to stone. Zaden can't have me being

killed while he isn't present... That would rob him of his precious vestigial Gaze.

He doesn't seem to have noticed the shift in my mood. I guess psychopathic angels aren't well attuned to human emotions.

Zaden leans his elbows against his thighs. "What was the name of the woman you called your sister?"

The change in topic sets my hair on edge. I look up sharply.

Why the fuck is he asking me her name? I thought he knew everything about my family and me.

He knows what sleeping hub my father sleeps in, what he does for the community, and what he eats for breakfast. So why doesn't the Maker-be-damned angel know my sister's name? He's already told me he didn't fucking kill her.

And what an odd way to phrase the question. *The name of the woman you called your sister.* It's like the angel isn't fluent in English. Or like he thinks she wasn't really my sister.

Heat evacuates my body until I'm as cold as the stone I'm sitting on. Words pour from me.

"Leesa Rosedarter—our mother's name was Rose. Leesa didn't have a profession yet, so she just went by Leesa Rosedarter. I always thought she'd end up Leesa Rosedarter Miner, but she hadn't committed. I'm rambling."

"Ahh." Zaden's eyes are shuttered as though he's withdrawing from this conversation. Shadows flit around him, and his green eyes stop sparkling.

Suddenly I don't want to continue this conversation. I wish we'd never bloody started it.

Coming into this castle, I had one goal in mind: avenge my sister's death. And if that meant killing an angel, then that's what I'd do. But since then, he's been... nice. He's protected me and brought me chicken and a brain-blasting orgasm.

But those kindnesses were all to make me stay in the castle until I died. The angel is wholly unburdened by human emotions, so why on earth did I imagine him anything but an asshole?

He told me he didn't kill her. But what's a lie compared to murder and famine? And what did he mean by "the woman you called your sister"?

I pull myself to standing and push away from the wall to stand straight. Pain radiates from my ankle and hip, but I keep the wince from my face. I will not show this male any weakness.

I need to ask the question again. And this time, I'll be specific. "Did you kill Leesa Rosedarter?"

He rises to his full height, and I have to crane my neck to hold his gaze. He has the decency to look me in the eyes. "Yes."

Coldness fills the tower stairwell, and I wonder if it's magic. It is stuffy too, and I can't breathe. I'm sucking lungfuls of useless air into my body but not getting any oxygen. I need to lie down, and these stairs look as good a place as any, but there's one more thing I need to know first.

"How? How did you kill my sister? I mean, Leesa Rosedarter?" I can't stop saying her name. She only lives on through my words and my lips, and I will say her name every day until I die.

"I covered her mouth with my hand and smothered her."

He's doing it now, smothering me, sucking out the oxygen from the castle with his celestial powers. A servant flits past the corridor above us, clearly unaffected, and I realize it's just me.

The Margrave killed my sister. My hands curl into fists,

clenching the fabric of my pants. Zaden killed my sister, and now I have to kill him.

Scarla

I stumble down the stairs. My legs are moving, but I don't feel any pain. Zaden calls my name, expecting me to turn like an obedient slave. Still, I keep walking, navigating the servants' quarters mindlessly until I emerge into the overdressed foyer and the castle doors loom above me.

Through a fog, I'm aware of the guard looking over my shoulder. He must get some signal from the Margrave because his detestable red-and-gold uniform moves out of my way, and the gates swing open.

It's as hot as Hades outside—it must be daytime. Thank the Maker for my habit of donning my thick ox-hide boots every morning; otherwise, the skin of my feet would melt and leave a sticky trail of molten goop.

At least I can breathe now. I suck in lungfuls of searing air and try to think straight. I shouldn't be surprised... I'm not, really. I always suspected the Margrave of killing my sister, and now I know he did. Now it's a fact. I must tell Leesa's friend, Raylee—she'll be sleeping in her Lowton hovel, but she won't mind me waking her.

No, that doesn't sound right. Raylee was never the one obsessed with uncovering the truth of Leesa's death—that was only ever me.

Loneliness punches me in the gut, and I want to be home. Dad and Leo are the only people I have left, and that psychopathic angel almost made me forget it. I lumber along the patchy ground to the bridge. I don't care who is in that guardhouse—they will let me through, or they will die.

There's a bloke inside wearing the Margrave's livery, which makes him an ally of Xerxes or a slave of Zaden's; either way, he's an enemy. He takes one look at my face and waves me through. Whatever expression I'm wearing, I wish I could capture it in a stone jug and carry it with me always because it's my passport out of this castle.

The cobblestones of Hightown torture my ankle, which twists over the uneven ground. Pain returns to me through my fog, bringing rage in its wake.

Unfortunately, I won't make it all the way to the Undercity with my twisted ankle and the searing heat. I limp along to Washmaiden Lane and take shelter beyond the dogleg, leaning up against a building for the sliver of shade it provides.

As my patch of shade grows with the lowering sun, I fumble for a plan. Everything's changed, and the Margrave must die.

I know a celestial sword can destroy an angel, and I think I've arranged to borrow Count VanDyke's. It's the rest of the plan that's a bit hazy.

I recall my conversation with Angel VanDyke. He radiated hatred for Zaden, whom he accused of dealing death to mortals without care. That had proven correct. VanDyke also told me he'd help me in any way necessary and implied he'd deliver the sword to me when I needed it.

Hopefully, he can tell I need it now.

I'd studied the tapestries in my bedroom for hours and concluded that angels could be killed by other angels because of some magic welded into their blades. Only a celestial sword can destroy a being forged in the primordial fires of the stars.

Let's hope I'm right.

I just have to wait for the Maker-be-damned sun to set so I can get to Leo. Together, we'll figure out how to contact VanDyke. And I would take down a mountain lion right now for a glass of water. I stare at my ankle and unfocus my eyes, trying to channel Gaze. I can control it better now—Zaden's light no longer blinds me, and I can see more nuance in the colors it reveals.

My ankle throbs, and I expect to see pulses of bruised yellow light coming from it, but I'm disappointed—it has a dull brown glow that is barely visible against my black boot. I place my hands on it, trying to draw out the sickness as I have with so many others over the years, but it's a flop. A failure. I can't heal myself.

Who am I kidding? I can't heal others either, not really. I can only draw out fevers like I'm some kind of oversized snow bag. And I can see a freaking light show when angels walk past—not super useful. Nothing I do is of much use.

I'm definitely a shit judge of character. I almost fell for that psycho who killed my sister. Leesa. Leesa. Leesa. I expected to feel relieved when I discovered how she died, but I just feel sorrow for the days and years we missed out on. My Leesa.

My slice of shade has thickened enough to cover my whole body, and some heat has gone out of the day. I reckon it would take a full minute to boil somebody's eyeballs. Dusk will arrive soon.

A shadow flicks along the top of the lane, but I don't catch the movement. Probably a skitter beetle seeking water. There it goes again, fast and dark. It's too big to be a beetle, though.

I sit a little straighter and scan for exits. There's only up the lane or down. Or into one of these stern stone buildings where the rich people sip on iced water and play the harpsichord or whatever they do there.

It's a patrol, wearing that awful red and gold. The Margrave's men. Or Xerxes'. There's a man and a woman, both wearing sorcered suits. Is this a standard patrol, or are they looking for me?

I can't lie here and wait. A person lying in the street during broad daylight will catch their attention. I climb to my feet—it feels a long way up—and start hobbling south, away from the patrol. But the other end of the lane is blocked by a second pair wearing the Margrave's livery.

This is starting to feel a lot like an organized attack. But is it coordinated by Zaden or his right-hand man?

My money's on Xerxes.

I duck back into my slab of shade while the two patrols approach me from either side—no point burning while I wait for combat. I'm filled to the skull with anger and don't doubt I'll kill these assholes. I've never been so confident in a fight.

"Did Xerxes send you?" I call.

"He doesn't want to kill you. We don't want to kill you." The woman's voice is muffled through her helmet.

Okay, now I have confirmation of who sent them.

"That's a shame. Because *I* want to kill *you*." Hot rage boils in my gut.

The patrols keep closing in, slow and steady. I should keep them talking to prolong the inevitable, but I'm all out of patience.

I don't care if it's four against one; I'm itching for battle. I channel Gaze and stare at the woman, looking for weakness.

If I can see my sore ankle as a brown splodge, I can probably see any injuries in these guys too.

"Take one step closer, and I will gut you," I yell.

Whatever mania they hear in my voice makes them pause. I try to focus through the woman, peering into the dimension beyond her, scanning her for weakness. She doesn't glow like a vestige, and at first, I can't see a thing. But finally, a dim light ribbons down her spine, a dark blue almost indistinguishable from her clothing.

The dim light pulses weakly, and there is a point at the base of her skull where it narrows. If I could just pinch my fingers around that spot, I think I could snuff out her life force.

The temperature is plummeting. Already, the faint stirring of people outdoors is audible in the distance. The hardiest folks are already outside, going about their dusk. Before long, these streets will be swarming.

Desperately, I swing my attention to the man in the patrol. With concentration, I can see the faint pulse of his life force, a dark, murky gray. Again, it narrows at the base of the brain, an apparent weakness.

But I have no idea how to exploit it.

My empty threat has worn off, and the patrols step closer, boxing me in. They'll want to get this over with before people swarm the streets. This might be a quiet laneway, but it won't be empty come full dusk.

The woman is close enough that I can hear her labored breathing, but her helmet still muffles her voice. "She won't come easy. Conk her over the head."

Heart racing, I back against the building, and the rough stone scrapes my shoulders.

The nearest man raises a long, metal club above his head.

Scarla

My shoulderblades scrape against the rough stone wall behind me, and I realize I've boxed myself in.

Blood pounds in my ears, and my heart races. I take a step forward to give myself some room, not feeling the pain in my ankle or hip at all. Everything has been wiped away by the adrenaline coursing through my veins.

Before the guard can bring his metal club down on my head, I shoulder charge into his exposed belly. I've taken him by surprise, and he stumbles a few paces but doesn't go down.

I wheel around, ready for another attack. But I stop dead at what I see.

Two of the other guards are already lying on the cobblestones. For a split second, I wonder if I subconsciously accessed that weak point at the base of their skulls in self-defense.

Then I see Sadie and her goon squad. Her wild, wavy octopus hair is flapping about in a wind of its own, and her three idiot buddies are grinning and leering. Ralph flops his oily bangs out of his eyes.

Did Sadie just rescue me? What's going on? My whole world has been turned upside down, and I don't know what to believe anymore. Maybe Sadie, my old Undercity nemesis, was one of the good guys all along.

There is no time to ponder it because two guards are still on their feet. I spin around, but they're already beating a retreat. Their feet pound over the cobblestones as they dart up the lane, and they're soon out of sight.

My mind is going a million miles an hour. This isn't a scene I ever expected to see. Two guards wearing sorcered suits lying on the cobblestones of Hightown, and Sadie and her thugs rescuing me.

"Hi, Sadie. Long time no see." I decide to play it cool.

Sadie cocks a hip and smirks. She puts on a falsetto. "One more step, and I'll gut you."

I shrug. "Well, I wasn't about to lie down and give up."

"Really? Because it didn't look like you had many other options from where I stood."

Sparks burst up my ankle, and I lean against the stone building for support. "I had it under control."

Sadie scowls. "A simple thank you would be polite."

She's right, I suppose, although I'm sure there's more to it than pure kindness.

Ralph and long-legged Frank bend down and start tugging the sorcered suit off one of the guards. Manipulating a limp body out of a magical outfit doesn't look easy.

Suddenly it dawns on me. "You just wanted the suits."

Sadie raises a shoulder. "You got me. These suits are nearly impossible to come by. The Margrave's patrols are vicious and put up a good fight. Usually. I can't believe those two cowards ran away."

"They weren't here on the Margrave's orders," I admit.

That sparks Sadie's interest. She raises her eyebrows. "Really? Who sent them?"

If there's one thing an Undercity-sider knows, it's haggling. I have something Sadie wants—information—but I won't give it away for free. "I'll tell you, but I need a favor first."

Sadie's scowl turns into a smile. She recognizes a bargaining table when she sees one. "Whatsa matter, Scarla? You in trouble?"

I don't want to admit weakness to Sadie, but I can't think of any other way to get what I need. I sag against the wall. "I need you to help me to the Undercity." She raises an eyebrow, and I know I'm losing her. "Or... or, fetch Leo for me. I take a deep breath. "My ankle hurts, so I can't get there by myself."

I figure that if Sadie wanted to hurt me, she could've let me patrols finish their job before she stepped in.

But that doesn't stop the glee from overtaking her features. "Well, well, well. The biggest skank of the Undercity is injured. How about that."

I bristle. "Look, Sadie, if you don't want to help, that's fine. I'll take my information about what's happening in the castle elsewhere. See you later."

If I had the energy, I'd fight Sadie for those sorcered suits. At least we should go halves, one for her and one for me to give to Leo. Instead, I watch lamely as the goons strip the suits and stuff them into sacks.

The patrol guards aren't dead, and if they wake up while it's still dusk, they'll make it back to the castle before they freeze to death.

Already, the hustle and bustle of dusk is getting louder and nearer as people go about their business. I'm running out of time. "I need Leo, Sadie. Please."

My fingernails bite into my palms. Begging Sadie for help hurts more than my other injuries combined.

Sadie turns and barks an order to Frank. The tall goon lopes along Washmaiden Lane, covering a lot of ground with each of his long strides.

I breathe a sigh of relief. "Thanks, Sadie."

She leans against the building beside me, flaunting her physical superiority and strength, making sure I don't weasel out of my end of the bargain. "A deal's a deal. Now spill."

I slide to the ground and tell Sadie the tale of Lord Xerxes the Fuckwit who wants me dead.

* * *

Leo canters down Washmaiden Lane on a horse. A horse! His lovely red hair rushes closer, and the sight of his familiar coarse brown shirt brings me joy. When he slides down onto the cobblestones, he wraps his strong arms around me. His grainy scent is as comforting as his strength.

"Scarla. Are you all right? Frank said you were injured."

I wrap my arms around him for longer than I should, reluctant to let go. There are so few people I can trust. I murmur into his shoulder. "It's nothing, just a sore ankle. I'll be fine in a couple of days."

He pulls me to arm's length and examines me, his brows furrowed. "Are you sure?"

"Of course I'm sure." I squint at him. "Are you okay?" Just like the last time I saw him, Leo looks sickly, and I wonder if he's keeping something from me. "Are you unwell?"

Or is that muddy glow from him being a vestige?

He smiles broadly. "Never been better." He winks. "Come on, let's get you back to the Undercity on your majestic steed."

Leo's grown into a strong man while I wasn't paying attention. He slings me over the horse's back, and I land inelegantly with my bum in the air and my legs kicking like an overturned skitter beetle.

Sadie watches the whole thing. "Stylish," she remarks dryly.

I kick my legs and wiggle, and finally, I manage to maneuver myself into a seated position astride the colossal beast. I've never been on a horse before, and it's broader than I imagined.

Leo walks ahead, holding onto the rope, and the horse and I walk behind. The horse's movements are so exaggerated that every one of its steps jostles me, putting me off balance. There's nothing to hold onto, so I grip with my thighs and wrap a fist through its mane. "Sorry, buddy."

Hopefully, having me yanking its hair won't spook the creature—I'm already alarmed enough for both of us.

After a few minutes, my hips find a rhythm that matches the horse's, and we come to an uncomfortable arrangement where I stop pulling its mane, and it stops trying to throw me off with every step. It still takes all my energy and concentration to stay seated.

"I can't believe you got a horse."

"Anything for my damsel in distress."

"But how? Where did you get it from?"

The cobblestones of Hightown make way for the dirt paths of Lowtown, and the proud stone buildings morph into bamboo shacks.

Leo calls over his shoulder. "I borrowed it from the Council."

The Undercity Council keeps a couple of horses for emergencies, but you can't just wander up and borrow them. I have a sneaking suspicion that Leo stole this beast, and I figure there's more trouble waiting for us when we get to the Undercity.

"What do you mean you borrowed it? Do they know that you borrowed it?"

Leo chuckles. "Relax, Scar. Pa Loonta owes me a favor, so I called in. It's all above board. I just wanted to get you home, safe and sound."

I've gone rigid, and the horse's next step almost topples me to the ground, but I recover. "Pa Loonta owes you a favor? What the hell are you talking about?"

Ever since Leo went on his mysterious adventure across the desert, he's been coming up with the occasional sentence that surprises the crap out of me. This is one of them.

Why on earth would the head of the Undercity Council owe a favor to an Undercity farm boy like Leo?

He doesn't answer, and my agitation grows. "What do you mean, Leo? How could he owe you a favor?"

Leo just shrugs in his usual boyish way, but it ain't charming now—it's infuriating.

Even so, warm cider flows through my veins when I catch sight of the entrance to the Undercity. The gaping hole in the mountain means home, and I've been away too long. It's only been a couple of days, but it's been a lifetime of emotion and trouble, and I never want to set foot out of the Undercity again.

I take a deep breath, exhale, and then relax into the horse's back. Finally, the animal's gait is less troublesome, and now that I'm no longer fighting it, I find its motion quite soothing.

The mouthguard nods at us and lets us through without comment, Leo pulling the horse and me astride it.

We walk into the main cavern like that, and dozens of eyes swing toward us. It's not every day you see a prized beast in the Undercity proper, especially not with a couple of nobodies on it.

Scarla

I wait for the gotcha, but it never comes.

The stable master greets us and exchanges mumbled greetings with Leo. I can't believe my old friend wasn't lying about stealing the horse—but it all seems legit.

I swing a leg over the beast's rump and slither to the rock floor. Leo is beside me instantly, offering support, and I lean heavily against him.

"I'll send for Fra Wang."

I shake my head. "Can you just help me to the underwing? We might as well go there. That's where all her herbs and ointments are."

"No."

I snap my head up. It's unlike Leo to go against my wishes. "What do you mean no?"

He smiles. "I have a surprise for you."

I've had a gut full of surprises, and I'd really rather just hobble into my sleeping hub, onto my deliciously uncomfortable grogan stalk mattress, and close my eyes for twelve hours straight.

"Come on, Scar. I promise it's a good surprise."

He offers a hand, and I take it, leaning heavily against him with each step. He steers me toward the narrow stairs that lead up to the Council chambers. I've never been up here before. Dad comes here all the time because he's involved in Council business, but he never lets me accompany him. Most folks never set foot in here their whole lives.

I don't care for politics or secrets. Of course, I tried to sneak up to the Council chambers once or twice as a kid—me and Leo both—but just for the adventure. There's always a guard on duty, and my limited wiles were never enough to get past them.

"We're going upstairs?" My voice rises to a squeak.

Leo nods, clearly pleased with himself. "Yep."

I lag behind. "Can't I just go home and sleep?"

Leo tugs me forward. "Come on. You can sleep upstairs. It's much more comfortable there."

I give in. We hobble up the stairs together. Leo waves the guards aside, and my mouth drops. "Since when do you have authority to come in here and just swan your way past the sentries?" I demand.

He smiles. "Relax, Scarla. I told you, Pa Loonta owes me a favor. I've been working with him a bit, that's all. It's nothing serious." But he definitely looks proud of himself.

The stairs widen out to a mezzanine that overlooks the main cavern below. Several tunnels lead off it in different directions, and a bunch of councilors sit at a table, deep in discussion, and barely register our presence except with a slight nod.

I scan the faces.

"Where's Dad?"

Leo leads me down the middle tunnel. "I'll send him up to you after his shift. He's out picking blyberries."

Yes, of course he is. It's dusk.

After a few twists and turns, we pass another guard who

nods us through. Clearly, we're going deeper into the inner sanctum of the Council.

Finally, we reach a room with a rug and several chairs. A mattress in the corner beckons me, but I'm no longer so tired. Zaden's voice keeps filtering through my brain, jerking me awake.

I covered her mouth with my hand and smothered her.

The same hands that caressed my body, traced the curve of my hips, and cupped between my legs. I feel like a traitor to my sister, having allowed those same hands that brought her death to bring me pleasure.

Leo helps me to a chair. "You look pale."

Leo's eyes narrow, and he looks at me with concern, almost possessively. But he still looks sickly, a murky yellowy-green, like he's bruised all over.

Somebody stamps their feet near the room's entrance, asking permission to enter.

"Come in," Leo calls.

Fra Wang appears, as small and cranky as ever. Her twin gray braids tug on her face severely, and I wonder how many wrinkles they hold back. She carries a parcel of herbs.

My face breaks into a grin. She is a mean old bat, but she might just be a third person on the list of people I can trust. "Fra Wang! It's so good to see you. It must be quiet downstairs in the underwing if they could spare you to come up here and look after my little old ankle."

Fra Wang glances at Leo, then grunts noncommittally. "A sore ankle, is it? And a sore hip, if I'm not mistaken?"

How did she know that? I squint at her, looking for some sign of vestigial power, but see none. She's just an experienced old healer.

Fra Wang attends to my injuries, applying some herbs and bandages, and brewing me a probleroot tea for the pain. "That should keep you going."

"Thank you. I'll be back down to work in the underwing as soon as I am able."

Again, Fra Wang glances at Leo and doesn't respond.

Leo lays a hand on my shoulder. "There's no need for you to go back to work. These are your chambers now. You'll be safe here, and you'll never need to leave again."

I look around at my new bedroom. It's almost as big as the one I had up in the castle, although, of course, there are no windows to let in natural light. It smells dank and moist, but no more so than anywhere else in the Undercity. A large bed occupies one corner, and I have a table and chairs all to myself, plus a narrow opening that must lead to a bathing hub.

I break into a smile. "Really? I can stay here? It's beautiful. I'll be better in no time at all, Fra, and able to get back to work."

Fra Wang glances at Leo, and he nods toward the door, seeming to dismiss her. What in Hades is going on here?

"I'll send Melandra up to check on you later, girl."

Fra Wang exits, leaving Leo and me alone.

He looks at me kindly, smiling. "Drink your tea."

Oppositional defiance is my default position, so I want to refuse to drink my tea. On the other hand, I want to drink my tea.

I take a sip, and it might be a placebo effect, but I can feel the hot liquid easing into my skin and muscle and relieving some of my pain. The liquid is searing, but I take another sip.

"Did you send for Count VanDyke?"

Leo nods. "Yes."

"Good. Because I need to kill Zaden." It feels surreal to

speak so casually of murder. But it's a relief that my plan is in motion.

Leo arches an eyebrow. "Zaden? Are you on a first-name basis with that angel?" His tone is cold, and his jaw rigid.

Well, I definitely won't be mentioning the skull-fracturing orgasm the angel gave me. "He murdered Leesa. He admitted it to my face. So now I have to kill him."

Leo nods, and that sickly aura around him wavers. "I contacted the Count, and he agreed to my conditions."

"Your conditions?" This tea is working, and I'm feeling more alert. I study Leo, sensing something is wrong but unable to pinpoint it.

"That's right. And now you need to agree to my condition."

"I bloody do not." Since when does Leo think he can order me around? "Just get me the Maker-be-damned celestial blade so I can kill the angel and get on with my life."

Leo sighs. He crosses to the table and pours himself a cup of water from a bamboo jug. "You and I are on the same side, Scarla. I just want to end the power imbalance. Take the bastards down. Those assholes up in the castle live like kings in the olden days, sipping wine and eating meat every day. While the people down here scuttle in the dirt like skitter beetles. I just want to put an end to that, to make life fair for everybody. Isn't that what you want, too?"

My heart swells and, if I could walk, I'd cross to Leo and hug him. "Of course that's what I want." It feels so good to be in the presence of somebody like-minded, not that psychotic angel who rains death on humans and keeps all the resources for himself.

Leo smiles. "I know. We're in this together, Scarla. And while you're alive, you can be my queen." That hungry possessive look passes across his features again, and I pause.

"What do you mean your queen? I thought the whole point was to get rid of inequalities."

He smiles, and I guess he must've been joking. Until he continues. "The only way to get rid of inequalities is from a position of power. Ironic, really. I can see that. But can't you see that I can't change the world if I don't have any power?"

I shrink into my seat and put down my cup of tea. "And what do you mean *while I'm alive*?"

Leo crosses to me. "You and I go back a long way. You're my closest friend in the world. I would never want to kill you."

Nausea blossoms in my belly. I channel Gaze and stare at Leo, and that sickly green hue glows brightly. It's muddy and sullied, not the crystal clear color of some vestiges I've seen. Not the unmistakable, radiant glow of an angel.

It's the murky, diseased glow of somebody who has received his vestigial powers through force.

"You're a vestige," I mutter.

Leo spread his arms wide, looking proud. "Of course."

"And you got your powers by killing another vestige." The smudginess of his shine should have alerted me earlier, but I was blinded by my long-standing friendship with him. "You murdered somebody."

My lips feel numb, but my words still seem clear enough. Leo places his mug of water onto the stone shelf with a loud clink.

He takes a step toward me. I've never felt threatened by him before, but that has all changed.

I shrink into my seat.

Scarla

I recoil from Leo as he approaches, his footsteps echoing off the stone floor.

I try to reconcile my two images of him: the sickly green hue of a vestige who murdered to get his powers and the wide brown eyes and red hair of my childhood friend. It's impossible to imagine both Leos residing within one body.

"I just want to help, Scar." That's his voice, and those are the right words, but everything else about him is wrong. "Life isn't black and white. I did what I did to improve Malanox. Can't you understand that? Malanox is in danger from angels like your precious Margrave, and I am the only one who can set things straight. Not just Malanox, but all of Aubia. I need vestigial attributes to gain enough power to make a difference in this world. You were always the one who wanted to make a difference, so why can't you respect that same attribute in me?"

I'm pressed hard against my chair, and I need Leo to back off so I can think straight. "When you said I didn't need to work in the Undercity...."

His smile doesn't crinkle around his eyes. "You will be safe up here. There's plenty of space. There are three or four more chambers that you haven't even seen yet, and they are all yours."

"Why is there a guard on the door?" The guard was an unsmiling man and one I'd never met before. Probably from North Undercity and immune to my charms, such as they are.

"There's more than one guard, and they are there to keep you safe."

Alarm bells ring in my head. "Are you keeping me prisoner?"

Leo scrapes out a chair and sits opposite me. He rests his elbows on his coarse gray pants. "When I first realized you had Gaze, I cried. Can you believe it? I never cry. You know that."

I do. When we were six years old, Leo tried to climb up a stalactite and fell ten feet onto the hard rock floor, conking his head. He sobbed that time, but I can't recall any other occasion he had. He might never be the first to step into danger, but he doesn't weep when things go wrong.

"I cried because I needed it for myself, and I didn't want to force you into anything." His brow clears, and his face softens. "Then I realized that could be a good thing. You and I get along so well. And now we can be together forever."

"Don't be a creep, Leo. You're better than that."

Irritation enters his voice. "Don't fight it, Scar. I just want to help people."

"By keeping me a prisoner until I die."

Leo leans forward and stares at his hands clasped before him, like a man contemplating a higher power. "Not until you die. Just until you... understand that I'm right."

I realize that his changed feelings toward me since he returned from Desert's Maw—where he must've murdered his first vestige—were because he wanted Gaze for himself. That's why he hung out with me so much in the underwing, waiting for the old folks to die.

"Did somebody tip you off on your journey that Fra Perkins had Gaze?"

He looks up sharply. "Perkins, was it? I wasn't sure. And yes, there was a rumor that a Gaze dweller lived within the Undercity, and I figured the underwing was the place to hang out. Having you there was just a bonus." He winks.

I bite the inside of my cheek to keep from screaming. "Who are you?"

He leans back in his chair and looks sad. "I'm the same person I always was. I've just grown up, that's all. You were always the idealist, Scar. You know how important it is to fix things around here." He gestures around the cavern, but I know he means Malanox in general, maybe all of Aubia. "I'm just trying to set things right."

Suddenly I can see the little boy who used to be my best friend, who giggled and pranked and cuddled me, who has his own history and his own heartbreaks at his own family tragedies, and his own hopes for the future.

"Just don't lose yourself in the process, Leo. You're a good man, and I don't want you to forget that."

He smiles, and his sickly green hue turns clear for a moment. "I won't. Thank you for understanding." He calls over his shoulder. "You can come in now, Count."

If Leo thinks I agree with his methods, then he's got another thing coming, but a snarky comment can't get past my tongue because I'm distracted by the bright orange shine of Count VanDyke.

He's dressed all in white, long pants and a loose white shirt tucked into a taut waistband. Combined with his bright blond hair, the effect is truly cherubic but all grown up.

A cherub I'd do every day of the week and twice on Sundays—if he wasn't a prick.

The Count glides across the room, and a tendril of his magic snakes out and brushes my cheek. I can't help it; I cherish the sensation, and tingles run down my body.

"Good evening, my dear Scarla. You look absolutely ravishing, as usual." He takes my hand and presses his lips against it. Sparks radiate along my arm from his touch.

I'm desperate to keep some authority in this shithouse situation. I smile at the angel beneficently. "Thank you for coming." As if I had any say in the matter.

His sword hangs from his hip, sheathed in an ornate silver scabbard. As soon as I get my hands on it, I'll pierce the Margrave's heart, then I'll disappear.

I will never be held prisoner again.

The Count releases my hand. "Have we come to an arrangement?"

He is still looking in my eyes, but he's addressing Leo, who nods.

"Wonderful." The Count's gaze seems to see into my soul, and I wonder if he can tell when somebody is lying. "You may borrow Jonshu to accomplish your task, provided you return her—and Zaden's head—to me."

I shiver. I accept the proffered blade and bear my teeth. "Certainly. It would be my pleasure."

The sword's hilt is icy cold, and it doesn't warm under my touch. I try channeling warmth into it as if it were a person with a chill, but it remains as cold as a grave at midnight.

A sordid agreement clearly links Leo and the count, but I want no part of these underhanded dealings between angels and their helpers. As soon as I have revenge for my sister's murder, I'll be rid of them. I'll head off on my own adventure across the Dead Desert, and I will never come back.

I hope my father will join me, and if he doesn't, at least I know he'll understand.

He'll have to understand.

An image of my mother packing a bag and embracing my father, with tears running down her face, passes through my mind. Did she leave on a similar journey? Was she hounded by angels and vestiges and caught up in a celestial power struggle she wanted no part of?

I shake my head. No, that can't be right. She died.

So why is that image so clear in my mind, as though I witnessed it? The certainty that she died wavers until I'm clear about nothing at all.

"What deal have you two struck?" I'm proud that my voice doesn't quaver.

The count shrugs, feigning insouciance, but I can see that his words cost him. "Leo and I both have our reasons for wanting access to Gaze. He wants power among mortals—"

"So I can end poverty and injustice."

"Quite so, so he can end poverty and injustice." The count has a twinkle in his eye as though he doesn't believe a word of it.

"And you? Why do you want access to Gaze?"

"I will be King of the Cloaked Court," he says simply, as though it is preordained, as though the Maker wills it so, as though nothing can stand in his way.

"But you're an angel. Why do you care about mortal politics?" I hate myself for parroting Zaden's words, but they make sense. As far as I can tell, the Cloaked Court runs mortal affairs. I mean, why bother?

The Count's orange glow turns dark, and his scowl has me shivering. "I am a fallen angel, woman, and I will spend the rest of eternity on earth. I intend to do so from a position of power. I shall rule the mortal realm, and heaven be damned. The Maker will rue the day he flung me from his embrace. I just need the dyad."

Gaze and Inflict.

Anger boils my blood as surely as the midday sun. "I see. And, unfortunately for you both, you can't kill me because Gaze cannot be gained that way."

The Count turns toward Leo, and the darkness in his aura recedes. His pause has my biting my nails. "I see what you mean. She is quite clever."

Leo reaches a hand toward me but leaves it hovering in midair. "I would never hurt you. I... I lov−"

Fury snaps my spine. "Don't you dare say it!" The sword's hilt grows warmer in my hands, responding to my anger. I leap to my feet and take a step, feeling no pain in my hip at all. Either adrenaline is keeping me company again, or that tea was stronger than I thought.

"You'll have your precious Gaze," I lie. "I'll be your eyes for as long as I need to, and one of you can inherit it on my deathbed. But only after I have avenged my sister's murder."

Count VanDyke tilts his head, smirking. "Lovely. I don't expect you'll have to wait much longer. The Margrave should be here any minute."

Scarla

"What in Hades do you mean?" Leo whirls on the Count, spearing him with a look that would send a mortal straight to the underwing.

The Count isn't fazed. "You didn't think you could take the Margrave's precious prize without him trying to get it back, did you? Especially when you paraded her through the streets on the back of that mongrel horse."

Leo's jaw tightens. At his full height, he's still several inches shorter than the angel, but his anger makes up for it. "You arranged for me to take that horse," he spits.

"Of course I did. I had to make sure the Margrave knew exactly where she was. It was the best way to lure him here. You do want to kill him, don't you? Well, that isn't possible in his castle. It needs to be here, where he doesn't have the upper hand."

"I don't care if he lives or dies." Leo shifts his weight dangerously like he's lining up his victim, but I don't see what he could do against an angel. "I just want Scarla back."

In this moment, it feels like my old friend is fighting to protect me, and I have to remind myself that he's just after Gaze too. Gaze equals power.

"A deal is a deal, Pa Farmer." The angel spits the last word like it tastes of coal dust. "I get you the girl, and you give me Zaden's head."

"And who gets Gaze after I die?" I blurt out. This celestial sword hilt burns warmer and warmer with my growing anger like it has a mind of its own and itches for blood. These two men are discussing me like I'm cattle, only good for what I might deliver on my death bed.

And they're conversing about murder as casually as the latest crop of grogan.

The Count is the only one in the room who looks relaxed. "I do, of course. Leo will barely outlive you, compared to my life span." He swings around to face Leo. "I don't know what all the fuss is about. Your girl kills Zaden, who murdered her sister. You get control of the Undercity, and I become King of the Cloaked Court. We all win."

Heat throbs through my palm. "Why don't you kill Zaden yourself?"

The Count glances at me like I'm a rotting pumpermelon. "If you fail, my dear girl, then I will. But why put myself in peril unnecessarily? Angels can be dangerous." He chuckles at his little joke. "Unfortunately, I imagine you will fail, girl. Most mortals do. The Margrave's Lordling was better than most but ultimately useless."

The Margrave's Lordling. What the fuck? "Do you mean Lord Xerxes?"

"Yes. That mortal seemed promising but was ultimately disappointing."

The cave floor seems to hum beneath my feet. "You had Xerxes try to kill me?"

"No, of course not." The Count chuckles, and I want to punch that irritating smirk off his face. "He was trying to kidnap you to bring you to me. I can't have you dying at his hand."

Xerxes was trying to kidnap me? That patrol woman said she didn't want to kill me, but I didn't believe her. Come to think of it, Xerxes had every chance to stab me through the heart when he carved that X on my hip, and he didn't.

I shouldn't be so surprised by all these obvious things that keep happening.

I have to do better.

The Count claps twice. "Now, take your places, everybody." He seems to think he's directing a play. But given that his senses are more alert than our mortal ones, I suspect he can hear Zaden approaching, so I tense and adjust my grip on Jonshu.

A moment later, a bright purple-white light shines along the corridor, and the hilt grows ever hotter under my touch. My pulse is racing, and my blood thumping. Zaden is almost here. The man who murdered my sister.

And, even if it kills me, I will get my revenge.

Zaden enters the chamber, his expression grim. He wears dark pants laden with straps and buckles like he's going to war. A deep green shirt of the softest bamboo clings to his chest and shoulders, and its short sleeves reveal his corded arms. The green of his eyes multiplies above that emerald shirt.

When I see him, a sense of calm threatens to wash away my anger, as though my stupid body thinks he's a savior, not a devil. My first impulse is to run into his arms and have him cradle me against his steel chest. But it's a flawed impulse from a historical Scarla who doesn't exist anymore—one who thought this psychotic angel could be something other than my sister's killer.

304

Anger burns my blood, and the hilt of the sword ignites the palm of my hand. The blade glows bright white. I launch myself across the room. A scream rents the air, and I know it's coming from me.

I raise the celestial blade above my head, ready to strike. Forest lilies surround me, and Zaden watches me passively, making no move to stop me, just moving his lips, talking.

With my hand poised in the air, I scream, "Attack me!" and wait for his magic to darken, for murder to mist his eyes.

Still, his lips open and close, speaking slowly, and he doesn't budge. If anything, he looks calm, serene.

I fight the pounding of blood in my ears and strain to hear his words. I want them to be awful, filled with hatred and disdain for mortal insects, an anchor for my rage. I want to slice that mild expression off his face.

His words filter through my rage like distant drumbeats. "She asked me to do it."

Jonshu is raised above my head, growing heavy now. I falter, and the hilt grows cool. "What?"

"She asked me to kill her. She asked me to. Your sister, Leesa, asked me to end her suffering."

My sister's name pierces the fog of my thoughts, and I drop the blade with a loud clang. It echoes through the chamber and through my brain, and it takes me a few moments to remember how to breathe.

Can it be true? Leesa was in a lot of pain, and no amount of probleroot tea helped her. I spent hours trying to pull her porous sickness from her frail body but to no avail. But she wouldn't give up on our family, would she?

"Why?" I wipe salty tears from my mouth. "Why would she ask you to kill her?"

Zaden's light shines bright and pure, as clear as the full moon before snowfall. "She was in pain, Scarla. She didn't want to keep going."

"But... Leesa could have asked me. I worked in the underwing. I know all about herbs and poisons. I could've helped her die."

A warm brush of Zaden's magic caresses my cheek gently, giving me strength. "You couldn't have helped her. It would've torn you apart, and you never would have given up on her. That's why she begged me to do it."

I've witnessed my fair share of painful deaths, and I'm glad Leesa didn't suffer the same fate. But Zaden's right; I never could have taken her life from her, even if she'd pleaded on her knees.

Suddenly the Count is beside me, scooping up his fallen sword. "Welcome back, Jonshu." He runs a finger along the blade like an old friend or a lover. "Never send a mortal to do an angel's job."

Zaden shoves me hard, and I stumble to the cold rock floor while the sound of steel on steel rings through the cave.

Scarla

The two angels engage in combat, striking and parrying with dizzying speed. With my Gaze flicked on, they are a blur of color and light, their swords glowing as brightly as their celestial bodies.

Blinded, I blink away the Gaze until I see two men, both gigantic and muscled, moving faster than any human.

VanDyke lunges at Zaden and catches his arm, which drips blood immediately through a large gash. His speed is unflagging, but Zaden is losing blood quickly, red liquid against his dark green shirt, and I don't know how long he can keep it up.

The clang of swords meeting is a constant companion to the leaping and whirling of bodies.

I try to focus a trickle of Gaze—not so much that the angels blind me, but enough to detect any weaknesses. A core of light roots each angel to the ground. It is like the dull ribbon of light I noticed in the patrols, but thicker and more intense. And yes, there at the base of VanDyke's skull is a narrowing in the pipe of light. If I could pinch that in somehow, squeeze off that point, then VanDyke would fall.

I know it in my bones.

Zaden whirls around VanDyke and gets in a good lunge,

earning a trickle of blood from his opponent's cheek, but the wound is insignificant. Especially compared to Zaden's, which splatters blood all around the chamber every time he moves.

I glance over at Leo. He is transfixed by the fight, jaw slack and eyes staring. Can he even identify the bodies in the blur of movement?

Turning back to the fight, it's clear that Zaden is losing. Even my mortal eyes can detect a slowing in his pace, and I know that VanDyke will soon have him.

Energy surges through me at the thought of my angel lying cold on the floor, and I stare again at the weak points behind VanDyke's throat. I channel energy to that spot and squeeze as tight as I can.

At that precise moment, VanDyke stumbles, and it feels like a victory. Then Zaden kicks the other angel's sword from his loose fist, and Jonshu flies across the room, clattering against the far wall.

Zaden's eyes burn black, and he holds his sword to VanDyke's throat.

"Scarla is mine," he growls. Then he carves a large Z into VanDyke's cheek, kicks him in the chest, and stomps on his face.

Leo yelps, and Zaden's murderous gaze snaps toward him. The Margrave told me that nothing can stop him once the black rage overtakes him, and the full force of his anger is now directed at Leo. The Margrave stalks toward Leo, but I'm quicker. I throw myself in front of my old friend's body, blocking him from the Margrave's anger.

Black magic pulses from the Margrave, with purple veins snaking through it.

He is barely restraining himself. "Get out of my way, Scarla," he growls.

My knees shake, but I'm not going anywhere. I splay my arms wide, covering Leo's body with mine. "No."

If what Zaden said is true, I just committed suicide because his unstoppable rage will burn right through me.

I stand like a starfish before a stampeding bull, trying to stop this force of nature from executing its will. My arms are flung aside protectively, and I have no idea why I'm giving up my life to save Leo's. I just have the knowledge that I must stand here and accept my due.

I wait for the killing blow, for the murderous rage in my angel's eyes to strike me where I stand. His muscles bunch, and his fingers curl into a fist. I have no doubt he could punch into my chest and pull out my wildly beating heart.

That killing rage contorts his face, and my last thought is of pride; I'm pleased that I have held my stand to protect somebody I used to cherish.

His soulless eyes burn black, but miraculously, they lighten into gray, then gradually to green.

I pant, mirroring the pounding of my heart with my breath. I stopped my angel's killing rage.

With nowhere else for my churning emotions to go, I lower my arms and throw myself against Zaden's chest. His lips are on mine in an instant, and I melt into the kiss, pouring myself into him through his mouth, his tongue, his sweet taste.

His arms circle my waist, and my hands fly to his biceps, squeezing them and holding onto them for salvation, taking strength from his power. I can barely get my fingers around half of their girth, and I feel them writhe and contract beneath my touch, sensing the raw power within them.

Zaden releases me from the kiss, and I step back, panting.

His eyes are piercing and his forehead is scrunched. He studies me like he's trying to understand the stars. "What are you doing? This man betrayed you, and you're protecting him?"

I can't understand it myself, but I don't want Leo to die. He's my oldest friend in the world, and his ideals are in the right place, even if his heart isn't.

"Don't kill him," is all I say.

A rustle behind me has me whirling. Leo gets to his feet, stumbling over his boots, and grasps my hand. "Thank you, Scar."

I shake free of his grip, spitting my words. "You'll never have Gaze, Farmer." Leo's face falls at my harsh tone, and I'm glad.

Zaden looks back at the other angel, still lying on the floor with his nose broken and jaw shattered.

"Don't kill him either." I tug on Zaden's hand, pulling him toward the door, and he relents, following my wake. I've had enough of violence and death.

Guards and obstacles melt aside as Zaden and I follow the winding corridors and then down the stairs and out the main cavern.

"Will they forget they ever saw you?"

He pauses a beat, considering my question. "People forget everything they can't make sense of. Or they create myths about it. I usually fall into one of those two categories." He winks. "But I can help their memory loss along with a little glamor."

Outside, night has fallen, and stars twinkle above us in the deep blue. It isn't yet snowfall, and the fresh air is as sweet as any I've ever breathed.

"I'm not sure I can walk all the way back to the castle. Can we borrow a horse?" I don't know if all angels can conjure horses on demand or if that was just VanDyke's dealings with the Undercity Council. But I hope they can.

Zaden puts an arm behind my back and another beneath my knees and swoops me into his arms. "We're not walking."

His magnificent wings spread out behind him, as dark as night and twice as beautiful. They seem to absorb every particle of light, standing out against the black sky as twin mirrors of eternity. I could lose myself in their majesty.

I take a sharp breath as he launches us into the air, his mighty wings beating against gravity and winning, pulsing us higher with every lurching movement.

Then we are soaring through the sky, swooping evenly and gracefully. Zaden's wings are outstretched beside us, massive and powerful. My belly falls out beneath me, and the wind rushes against my face. I feel as light as a breeze and just as free, flying between heaven and earth. Cold air flows down my throat and makes me feel more alive than ever.

If I took my last breath now, I'd die happy.

The tingle of Zaden's power surrounds me, encasing me. I am wild and free and protected from harm by my own personal guardian angel.

Stars accompany us across the sky, and a few lights twinkle down in the city below, oblivious to the glory of our flight.

"It's magical," I breathe.

I can feel Zaden's chuckle through his powerful chest, which vibrates against me. "It sure is."

Zaden

Soaring over the streets of Malanox has never felt so liberating.

I clutch my precious cargo, Scarla, to my chest, perhaps gripping a little too hard. I'm terrified of how close I came to losing Gaze.

Her copper hair whips my face, but I don't mind—it carries her blyberry scent, and I imagine a stream of it flying out behind us through the sky like a streak of paint.

Blood gushes from the wound on my arm, and I can feel myself becoming weaker. An injury from a celestial blade does not heal easily, even for an angel.

I clutch Scarla closer against my chest, digging my fingers into her soft flesh, fearing that my weakening arm might fail me and let her plummet from the sky.

I will never let that happen.

If she fell, I would lose my chance at returning to heaven. I clutch her closer to me and feel my heart beating against her hip.

The brightest lights in Malanox shine from my castle. The mortals are scurrying belowground at this time of the night.

But not my mortal. Not Scarla. She is no ordinary woman.

I shake my head. Perhaps my blood loss is disordering my thinking, making me emotional and weak. I need Scarla for her Gaze, nothing more.

I will land in the castle forecourt, but it has been decades since I carried a burden as heavy as a human, and decades more since I tried to land while injured. I concentrate, blocking out the growing pain in my arm, and beat my wings powerfully to stop our descent.

The landing isn't perfect, and Scarla tumbles across the cobblestones.

She leaps to her feet and turns to me, her face alight with joy. She has all the wonder of a child on solstice, her copper hair wild and her brown eyes large and glistening.

"Promise you'll take me flying again!"

She steps away from me, and my strength goes with her. I stumble, cradling my arm, and Scarla's face clouds in an instant.

"You're bleeding. You're hurt!" She looks at me a moment longer, then springs into action, yelling toward the castle at the top of her voice. "Guards! Bring porters for the Margrave immediately."

For a commoner who rallies against the hierarchy, this woman sure has a regal manner. I'll rid her of her pesky morals yet, and then she might make a tolerable companion for her brief lifespan.

A few minutes later, two guards emerge wearing sorcered suits and help me inside. When the doors swing close behind us with a thunk, the sorcered patrols leave us and are replaced by servants wearing my livery.

At the sight of them, Scarla stiffens beside me, and I remember how some of my servants attacked her. Anger simmers within me, and I welcome it because it blocks out the pain of my arm. It gives me a purpose. I will seek revenge on those who mutinied in my castle, and my fury will not be contained until every last one of them is slain.

Footsteps have me turn my head. Xerxes, the man I plucked from obscurity and placed in a position of privilege and power, strides toward me.

Xerxes' face is creased, those beady eyes twinkling somewhere between feigned concern and fear.

He doesn't know that I know.

"Margrave, I came as soon as I heard. We must get you to your bedroom quickly." He glances at Scarla. "I see you returned with the lady."

The simmering anger in my blood boils into outright rage, and I welcome my loss of control. My feelings for this mortal, Xerxes, have morphed from ambivalence to hatred.

I stand tall and draw Asmoshu from my scabbard with a ringing clang.

Scarla stares at her enemy through narrowed eyes, and I imagine she is channeling Gaze. But her burgeoning powers are no match for Asmoshu, my black-veined assassin.

Xerxes falters, steps backward, and puts out his hand in a placating gesture. "Margrave, my Lord, I –"

His pathetic pleadings are sliced away as Asmoshu carves him from shoulder to hip, intersecting right through his weasely little heart. He will never disobey again.

With the remnants of the killing rage still circulating through me, I stride to the foot of the stairs and start up them, but my energy soon flags.

Behind me, Scarla barks an order. "Follow him in case he falls. Make sure he gets to his chamber without incident."

Her queenly tone demands respect, and my servants leap to follow her command. Just as well, because I collapse at the top of the stairs and must be carried to my quarters.

Blood leaks from my body, and I can only hope it isn't a killing wound. An immortal blow.

My eyes flutter closed, and moments later, Scarla is seated beside me. Her expression is cold and angry—this woman has no end of surprises. "You killed Xerxes."

"Yes." Honestly, I thought she'd be happy about it.

"I wanted to kill him myself."

I smile weakly, and the effort costs me. I hate how small my voice is. "If you kill, your vestigial powers will change. You need to consider that carefully and only murder if it is the right strategy."

She laughs mirthlessly. "I don't consider murder a winning strategy."

I raise an eyebrow. "Oh no? It's just a sensible emotional response then?"

She frowns, knowing I've won the argument.

My eyes close again, and when they next open, the light in my room has changed, and my arm feels improved. Scarla is still here, perched on a chair beside me that must have been brought in by one of the servants.

"How do you feel?"

I pull myself to a seated position and relax against the bed head. "Much better. You're a good healer."

She shakes her head, refusing the compliment. "No. I'm not a healer at all. You were cold, so I warmed you up. If anything, I'm just a walking heat pad."

I laugh, and I'm pleased to see the corners of her mouth tug upward. She could have escaped while I was incapacitated, yet she didn't. "And how about the servants who are ill? Have you warmed them up too?"

She tilts her head, studying me closely. "You surprise me, Angel. Just when I think you're a heartless old bastard, you show some care for others."

She's misinterpreting my comment. I don't care if those servants live or die, but I'm interested to learn more about her healing skills. Still, I don't correct her. If she thinks well of me, she'll stay, and I'll inherit Gaze.

"The servants are all doing much better." Her eyes twinkle. "Molly is completely healed and resting in her own room. But she won't be back at work anytime soon," she adds sternly.

I don't care. I don't even know who Molly is. But Scarla's healing skills are fascinating indeed.

She carries on, oblivious to my lack of concern. "Since you have a newfound interest in the health of mortals, I'll take you to a market so you can see how kind mortals can be. The dusk or the dawn market, it doesn't matter which. But when we go, you'll notice poor people giving away food to the destitute, and unhappy people cheering up the distraught. Really, it's impossible to hate humans after you witness the kindness that they show one another at the market."

"You are not going to the market," I command. "It isn't safe. Count VanDyke and your little friend are both still alive, thanks to you. They will be after you again. I forbid you to go."

As soon as the words are out of my mouth, I can see they were the wrong thing to say. Like an impetuous child, Scarla hates being told what to do; forbidding her to go is as good as issuing her an invitation.

I need to reel this in. "Actually, you can go. As long as you promise to take me with you."

Her face relaxes, and she gives me a playful shove. "That is exactly what I said I wanted to do."

Her push leaves a heat mark against my arm, as though her skin is made of warm tea. I want her to touch me again.

My gaze roves over her gently curving jawline and her round full lips. Even the curve of her shoulder is sensual, and I wish her shirt would fall a little lower so I could see more skin.

She is watching me watching her, and her nipples harden as my gaze caresses them, tracing the curve of her full breasts.

Despite my injury, I am instantly hard and straining against my pants. I ache for this woman's touch, and she seems to read my mind. Her sweet lips curve into a teasing smile. She leans in close, and her breasts press against my chest, so soft and voluptuous that I ache for more, but she leans over me with just the gentlest of touches.

Her lips meet mine, moving sensually against me, but after a moment, she is gone.

I reach around the back of her head and pull her closer, but she sidesteps my mouth and puts her lips against my ear, her hot breath sending tingles down my neck.

"I will feel your cock inside me one day, Angel. But not now. You're not strong enough." She pulls away.

"I am!" Maker-be-damned, that mortal has won this battle. I need her body, and she has the strength to walk away. It should be the other way around.

She stands, and her nipples are sharp points beneath her soft shirt. I imagine my hands pressing into her hips and pulling her toward me, pressing her against my hard cock. But she just smiles and walks away.

From the doorway, she turns, a silhouette of sexuality. "Soon, Angel. Soon."

Scarla

Well, I must be the world's biggest idiot.

I just turned down an angel-induced orgasm, which would have shaken me to my knees. But Zaden is still too frail, and I don't think riding him like a cowgirl would help him.

There will be plenty of time for that.

Plus, he promised to accompany me to the market, which is excellent news. I want to prove to him that mortals aren't all scum. And prove to myself that he has a heart.

But, it dawns on me that the market might not be the best place to prove that. Sure, you see random acts of kindness there, but you also see random acts of shit-holery. If I take him there and he ends up with a worse opinion of humans, I will have failed myself utterly. Hell, I will have failed all of humankind.

I need to see the market through fresh eyes before dragging him along.

Dusk is a few hours away, so I spend the time preparing a disguise. Safety first, and all that. I ask Molly to cut my hair, and she obliges.

"I don't know why you're doing this, Scarla. You're a Maker-be-damned ox head if you ask me. Your hair is so long and pretty, and you're a fool to chop it off."

But she does it anyway, and before long, my copper hair has been tamed into a neat bob that just curves in around my ears. I top it off with a mop hat like the maids here wear, and I borrow one of Molly's dresses.

"You shouldn't be going against the Margrave's orders. You're a dunderhead; that's what you are."

I lean in and kiss Molly's cheek. "Thanks."

My disguise is complete. Barely anybody in the universe has seen me wearing a dress, and I'm famous for my wild coppery locks, so nobody will recognize me. I should be perfectly safe at the market.

Plus, Leo and the count must be terrified of Zaden after he pummeled them at their last encounter. Zaden even carved his initials on the count's cheek, which was... cheeky. And hopefully, it will make VanDyke think twice about going after me again.

Molly straightens my dress. "I'm coming with you, Scarla. You can't stop me."

"Okay," I say cheerily, secretly pleased for the company.

At dusk sharp, we head out of the castle gates. The guards don't even blink an eyelid at me coming and going; I have full run of the place thanks to my healing powers. Many of them have a sister or father or cousin who I've helped cure of the Sighing Sickness, and the rest of them are just following the Margrave's orders.

The sight of his livery still makes me sometimes shudder, bringing back memories of being hunted through Penngrove Forest like a beast, and I know that some of the servants are Xerxes men... Which makes them Count VanDyke's men. But I have every confidence that Zaden will take care of that once his strength returns.

In the meantime, I will keep my head low and keep myself safe.

We march across the castle forecourt, then across the dry ground and over the bridge. The streets of Hightown no longer intimidate me, and I walk them with ease, but Molly darts her head from side to side and seems to shrink beside me.

"Hold your head high, Moll. You're just as good as any of these assholes."

She squeezes my hand and stands a little straighter. We pass through Lowtown, and the poverty startles me. I always thought the Lowtowners were better off than us Undercity-siders, but I was wrong. They live in shacks, hovels, making their living from hand to mouth and working hard for it. At least in the Undercity, we have coal to trade and plenty to eat.

Lines are forming around the snowmelt wells, so we divert around them, keeping our heads low in case we run into somebody who might recognize me.

Before long, we're on the steeply cambered path to the Undercity.

Molly is as excited as a puppy meeting a chicken for the first time. I wouldn't be surprised if she started wiggling her butt and barking. "I've only been here once or twice. Do you think they'll have oatcakes with berry drizzle? I had one once when I was a girl, and it was delicious. I've asked the cook to make it, but it's never quite the same. Do you think they'll have them?"

I smile. "Yes. I think so." Change jingles in my pocket. I've never had change before or money of any description. Undercity-siders don't use money, except for trade, and I've never worked in a market. The community fund meets all of our needs.

The market is bustling, with vendors calling their wares and

Hightowners trying to out-bargain Undercity-siders—but failing. The rich folks might think they won the deal, but they are always, always wrong.

I clap my hands, excited to be home.

A familiar figure with a tall boy accompanying her bends over a stall, inspecting some bamboo bowls. "Raylee!" I call, ignoring Molly's gasp.

"Shush. We can't let anybody recognize you."

I'd already forgotten. "Sorry," I whisper.

But Raylee heard my call. She turns, and her face looks haggard, with more lines than I recall. Her boy, Lee, has grown another inch, and his hair is lanky and dull. Anger washes over me at the treatment of the Lowtowners, the lives they are forced to lead when others have so much.

I've hassled Raylee so many times about my sister that it only seems fitting that I share the information I have. She is a little wary of me, probably expecting another assault.

I pull her into a hug. "Raylee, I've found out what happened to Leesa."

"Really?"

"Yes. My sister was ill, and she died a peaceful death. At the time of her choosing."

Leesa's oldest friend nods, absorbing this information and, I think, understanding the implication. Her smile is like snowfall, transforming her face into a younger woman's.

"Thank you, Scarla." She scoops my hands into hers and kisses them. As she goes about her day, walking back to the house with her son trailing after, I watch her go.

A shriek has me turning, and suddenly Molly is nowhere to be seen. Movements near the ox-hide hangings of the Undercity draw the crowd's attention, and I wonder if Molly has gone in there. But why would she be shrieking?

A hand grips my upper arm, digging mercilessly into my flesh. "You are coming with me, Gaze bearer."

A second hand clamps over my mouth, and I kick and scream, but the hand is moist and smells medicinal. My struggling becomes weaker, and I can't help but breathe in whatever poison has been placed in front of my nose and mouth.

Surely somebody will intervene.

But they don't, and my flailing stops.

The world goes black.

When I wake, it is with a pounding headache and a crick in my neck that is so intense it is almost paralyzing. It takes several moments for me to assess the situation.

I was at the markets, and nobody knew I was going except Molly.

I was kidnapped. And nobody knows it except Molly.

She has probably been taken too.

It is dark, so I fumble around to make sense of my surroundings. It doesn't take long. I'm in a small cell with stone walls on three sides and metal bars on the fourth. The crick in my neck is from sleeping on the stone floor, and my headache is from whatever they poisoned me with.

I have no idea where I am.

And neither does Zaden.

* * *

Hi there! Thanks for reading Vestige. It was sooo fun to write—who doesn't love a sexy, flying hero?!

To keep in the know about new releases, follow me on Amazon.

I write steamy fantasy romance with bad men and badass women.

* * *

FREE BOOK

Sign up to my newsletter to receive a free novella, A Mortal of Caprice. It's never a good idea to catch the eye of the fae king.

A Mortal of Caprice is set in a magical fae realm, and still filled with badass women and sexy men. Only this time they're fae. Yum. It is the prequel to a steamy fae romance series.

* * *

If you enjoyed reading Vestige, I'd really appreciate you leaving a review. Reviews are like gold to us indie authors, truly.

You can also find me on the socials (@zaradusk).

* * *

Turn the page for a sneak peek at *Scar*, the second book in the Fallen Angels trilogy.

* * *

Chat soon!
xx Zara

Scar: Fallen Angels book 2

Nausea blooms in my belly, and I fear that I'm waking up with more alcohol in my veins than blood.

Man, I hope I had a killer night because I feel like crap. I don't remember where I went and can't even open my eyes. All I can manage is lying still and trying to recall where I am.

My pillow is as hard as Hades. I wiggle my head back and forth slightly to figure it out, but the only message filtering through my brain is that it's unyielding. Uncomfortable. My whole body is stiff with cold, and the points where my shoulder blades and ass meet the mattress are painful.

This bed sucks.

Nothing like the squish-into-a-cloud mattress that I sleep on at Malanox castle. I've grown so accustomed to the spongy bed and cushy life that I can't handle a night on a dodgy bed.

I must be back in the city under the mountain... but even grogum stalk mattresses shouldn't feel this crap. Man, I'm getting soft.

I draw a deep breath, trying to garner the energy to open my eyes.

Between fluttering lids, I make out stone all around me. I'm used to sleeping under tons of rock—I grew up in the Under-city, so claustrophobia doesn't affect me. But this is unlike any cavern I've seen before. A single sconce holds a torch of flaming blubber-soaked frost wood, showing individual paving stones lining the floor and the patch of wall I can see.

I sit bolt upright. This ain't the Undercity. There, every cavern was formed through natural processes or, some say, through the Maker's will. Large caverns and tiny crevices, interconnected by mazes of tunnels.

But this room is manmade, crafted by human sweat. Tool marks are etched into the stone where some poor bugger has carved the rock to his will. Green slime grows in the deepest crevices.

Crossing my legs, I blink several times, trying to figure it out. My brain is still foggy from whatever I drank last night. The air is dank and close, untouched by even the faintest breeze.

I brush away an imaginary strand of copper hair, then remember I cut it all off. My tousled locks are short and curve around my ears like a boy. Well, that was the idea, but my hair is as disobedient as the rest of me, and I can feel it sticking out in crazy directions.

Memories filter back. I chopped off my hair in disguise to go to the dawn market without risk of being discovered by my enemy.

Another wave of nausea has me tipping to the side, retching, but nothing comes out.

My amazing I-am-a-servant disguise didn't work. Obviously. A memory assaults me of a hand clamping over my mouth and a foul-smelling rag pressed against my nose.

I leap to my feet, adrenaline coursing through me, suddenly on high alert. I'm not suffering from a hangover, I'm feeling the after-effects of being drugged. Drugged and kidnapped. Shit.

I need to figure out where I am, confirm who captured me, and escape.

I'm sick of being kidnapped by males. First, the Margrave of Malanox took me to his castle, and now one of his asshole angel friends has done it again. Probably. Angel VanDyke is at the top of my suspect list.

Anger tiptoes warily down my spine, warring with my drug hangover. On balance, my rage wins out, and my feet begin moving, pacing out the perimeter of my cell.

My dungeon is quite big, and the corners furthest from the sconce's flickering flames disappear into darkness. I need to know everything about this place if I'm going to escape, so I count my steps, which echo dully.

I'm pleased that my captor hasn't stolen my precious ox-hide boots. These were given to me by my mother before she died and allow me to stand on frozen tundra or burning ashes without destroying the soles of my feet. They are my most valuable possession—I guess the asswipes who took me didn't notice them. Or they were under orders not to molest me.

I stop in my tracks and quickly pat myself down. I'm still wearing the servant garb I thought was such an excellent disguise. A light-brown, coarse-woven dress with a white apron around the waist.

Usually, I'd rather swallow a skitter beetle than wear a dress. Straitjackets for women, designed to keep us in our place. Every time I put one on, I feel helpless, vulnerable, and weaker than the weather. You know you're in trouble when even a strong wind can defeat you. Plus, the damn things are cumbersome—heavy, voluminous, and damn restrictive in a fight. I prefer my shirt and pants.

I resume pacing my cell to figure out its dimensions. Twenty paces by twenty-five, a perfect rectangle—unlike anything you would find in the Undercity. Yet another reminder that I am far from home.

It's hard for me to know where home is these days. My heart clenches when I think of my dad, sleeping and working in the Undercity, and I want to be by his side. After all, he's already been abandoned by my mother and sister, although he would classify it differently.

Death isn't abandonment. His words play through my mind. Even absent, he tries to calm me down.

My sense of familial duty ties me to my father and the Undercity. But I really want to be in Malanox Castle by Zaden's side.

My body squeezes at the thought of Zaden. I have no words to describe our relationship. Sexual, definitely, but it isn't that easy. Sure, he's the hottest male in the Maker-be-damned universe, as far as I can tell, but it's more complicated than just lust.

The emotional side of our relationship is fraught with difficulties. After all, he did kidnap me and threaten to keep me prisoner until I die. But, on the other hand, he rescued me from Leo, who I'd considered my best friend before his stinging betrayal.

In short, Zaden's an asshole, but he's an asshole with a heart.

I sigh. All I know is that I want to spend more time with him to figure it out.

Boots stomp from somewhere nearby, and I realize guards are approaching.

A section of rock slides forward seamlessly, so perfectly integrated with the wall that I hadn't even noticed it. I curse myself for not using my Gaze the instant my eyes fluttered open. It should have been my first instinct to use my skills to assess my situation. I've only had Gaze a few days, so I suppose my instincts still haven't caught up with my abilities.

Hells below, I have to do better.

The slab of rock slides soundlessly to one side side with none of the crunch you'd expect from two massive slabs of stone, revealing an opening that shines with the light of a thousand suns compared to my cell's gloom.

A guard blocks the doorway, his features lit by the flickering flames from my wall sconce, a broad nose and prominent eyebrows. His uniform is dark gray with a slash of indigo running down each sleeve from shoulder to cuff.

Indigo is VanDyke's color—I recall seeing his footmen wearing livery in that hue. That means he is the fucker who kidnapped me.

So much light pours through the open door that my senses are overwhelmed. It seems as though the guard glows as brightly as an angel, but that can't be right—it must be my eyes adjusting from the gloom.

I rise to my full height, which is on par with his, and lift my chin. I may be a prisoner, but I won't allow myself to be cowed by anybody.

"Have you come to release me?" I ask imperiously, figuring I might as well try to stamp some authority onto this crapfight.

The guard just grunts and steps aside, disappearing into the darkness. He wasn't glowing—it was the angel behind him.

Count VanDyke.

I blink several times, trying to clear my vision. My nausea is ebbing, but a headache seems determined to take its place. I find the well of power within my chest, the one that controls my vestigial abilities, and I cast a gauze across it, turning down the intensity of Gaze so I can see the angel without going blind.

I am one of the rare few people alive with Gaze, which is why all these shitheads keep kidnapping me. They want to control it for themselves.

Too bad I can barely control it myself. Especially in my drug haze—another gift from the dickwad before me.

Still, I can wield it enough to dim the angel's shine while I assess him. He's beautiful. White blonde curls frame his pale, chiseled face, with fine features and a hard jaw. He towers over me, looking absolutely pristine in a cream linen suit. If a cherub mated with a God, they would produce Count VanDyke.

His perfection is marred by a bandage covering his right cheek, although the broken nose and shattered jaw Zaden gave him have already healed. I guess angels heal fast from flesh wounds, but his sliced flesh from the celestial blade is still bleeding. Good.

I want to ask how he keeps his suit so clean in such a disgusting dungeon. Instead, I tilt my chin higher and channel poise and grace. "How kind of you to have me as a guest, Count." I aim for insouciance. I don't want him to know how rattled I am by being taken prisoner-again-by a power-hungry male.

I'm getting really sick of this bullshit. But the last thing I want to do is expose any weakness to my enemy.

He shifts his weight, and the fabric of his shirt pulls tight against his chest, exposing the hard body underneath. I force my regard to remain on his face, knowing he is trying to distract me. I refuse to give him the satisfaction.

In any case, I wouldn't fuck him even if he was my ticket into heaven.

His fine lips curve into a slight smile, and his dark blue eyes twinkle in reflected torchlight. "I am glad you're taking this little... detour... so well. I know you hadn't planned to visit my castle so soon."

His smarmy grin makes me regret the tone I set for this conversation, but I suppose it's too late to go for pissed-off energy now.

I choose the middle line. "Look, Count," I say, refusing to acknowledge his status as an angel. "I don't know what game you're playing, but I want no part of it. Release me now, and I will spare your life. Again." I gesture toward the bandage on his cheek.

His blue eyes harden at being reminded that he owes me his life. The last time I saw him, Count VanDyke lay on the floor of the Undercity at Zaden's mercy, and if it wasn't for me, Zaden would have struck down his angel enemy then and there.

Clearly, VanDyke doesn't appreciate the reminder. His nose wrinkles, and I figure this cell must stink, and me along with it. "Don't forget your place, mortal. Whatever meager powers you have, you inherited from angels. They are the merest trickle of an angel's power. No matter what you do in your entire puny life, you will never have the same magic I have. You will be dead in the blink of an eye, forgotten to history. So never presume to hold sway over me."

Good. I'm pissing him off, and I couldn't be happier about it. The edge in his voice shows that I've gotten under his skin, and I know exactly how to burrow even deeper.

"Oh goodness." I smile broadly, proving that he hasn't affected my mood. "Somebody has a little inferiority complex. Now, remind me." I put a finger to my mouth as though deep in thought. "Who has the power of Gaze, which everybody seems to want so badly?" I tap my toes on the stone floor, pleased at the bunching in his shoulders which speaks to his growing anger. "Oh, that's right. It's me. And you can't kill me for it because it doesn't work that way. You have to wait until I die of natural causes. Which makes me, dickwad, immune to anything and everything you can do to me."

I put my hands on my hips in triumph, delighted at the effect I'm having. If I'm going to be his prisoner, I'll damn well irritate him for the duration.

The angel pulls himself together and smiles. "Oh, I'm so glad you mentioned that you'll have to give me Gaze on your deathbed. Because that's exactly how long I intend to keep you here."

The smile on my face falters, and I shove it back into place.

The angel steps closer, and cleanliness wafts off him like a bath of pure hot water. It makes me realize how dirty I am and how filthy my cell is. It also makes me want to run my hands along his cream suit and leave a nasty streak of grime.

VanDyke changes tack, smiling again, but this time with hooded eyes and a slight cock of the head.

"Perhaps I can make your stay more enjoyable," he purrs with a predatory smirk.

Gaze blesses me with the ability to see the power of angels, and I watch a bright orange tendril growing from the Count's open palm and snaking around my waist. It encircles my body, awakening every nerve ending. His finger of magic creeps upward and gently brushes against my breast, tugging on the nipple slightly.

I can't help it, my body tingles in response, and heat pools between my legs.

I may be able to see his power, but I'm not immune to it.

Rather than stepping away, which would only show my discomfort, I smile sweetly and step closer until his wave of magic encircles both of us, and mere inches separate his chest from mine.

Skin tingling, I lean upward as though to kiss him, lowering my eyes to keep him unaware. But at the last moment, I drag my filthy hands down the lapels of his cream shirt, leaving a beautiful, satisfying trail of grime.

Count VanDyke snorts in disgust and steps away. "You might resist me today, mortal. But one day, you'll fall to my charms. He pauses in the doorway to look over his shoulder. "After all, you will be here for a long, long time."

* * *

As soon as VanDyke leaves and the door slides seamlessly back into place, I kick my ass into gear and assess the space.

I remove the blanket from my internal well of power and allow my Gaze to flare. I scan my surroundings, and sure enough, the doorway shows up as bright lines outlining the rectangular shape in the rock. There are no other doorways or windows and nothing of note on the floor or ceiling.

I am too full of energy to sit, so I pace, thinking hard, pushing my headache down. I will not stay quietly under VanDyke's thumb for the rest of my days. Two plans quickly form in my mind.

The long-term plan is to play nice, eventually gain his trust, hopefully score a more comfortable bedchamber, then escape when he's least expecting it. That could take months or even years, depending on how gullible VanDyke is and how good my acting skills are.

The second plan is to fight like a mountain lion and escape using violence as soon as the chance arises.

I like Plan Two.

Minutes dwindle into hours, and the only marking of time's passing is the burning down of the frost wood in my wall sconce. It's called frost wood, but of course, in the extreme temperatures of our world, there are very few forests left, and wood is far too precious to use for fuel. Instead, we use compressed bundles of grogum stalk soaked in blubber. It burns slowly, but even so, the length of fuel is becoming shorter, filling my cell with the stench of smoky fat, and eventually, it sputters out.

The final spark traces through the air and disappears, leaving me in utter blackness.

Panic bubbles in my chest at being alone and at the mercy of an angel who is prepared to leave me to suffer in the dark. I reach deep inside myself and allow my Gaze to reach its fullest, hoping the trickle of light from the rocks will keep me company in the gloom and ease away my fears.

I don't consider myself afraid of the dark. Certain twists and turns in the tunnels of the Undercity are unlit; the farther you wander from the main cavern, the longer the distance between wall torches. But, call me crazy, being drugged, kidnapped, thrown into a cell, and having no light, has put me in a bad frame of mind.

"You're fine, Scarla," I tell myself, seeking company in the sound of my own voice. "You've seen worse."

I flick through my memories, searching for evidence that's true, but, in fact, I've never been in a shittier situation than this. At least when Zaden kidnapped me, he kept me in high luxury. Here, I seem doomed to spend the rest of my days in filth.

Powering my Gaze produces light from the doorway, a dull orange glow that delineates the opening from the surrounding rock. I experiment and try to turn the Gaze up even higher, wondering if that will make the gloomy light shine more brightly. As it is, I can't see my hand in front of my face.

Supercharging Gaze tires me. I never considered before that it must use energy. I only have a sense that it resides in the pit of my belly, and that's where I access it from. But clearly, using it at high levels fatigues me.

When I first inherited Gaze from Fra Perkins, Zaden showed up shortly afterward. I had no control over the power level back then, and he shone as bright as a star. I suspected he was a Sun God walking the earth. I've since learned that all angels shine brightly, each in their own color.

Zaden shines vibrant white and purple like he sleeps in starlight. It's stunning, with a distinct pattern and hue that is at once calming and exhilarating.

I wish Zaden was here now. His arms would wrap around me and hold me tight, and I would feel safe.

Perhaps he will scoop in and rescue me, then I won't need to rely on Plan One or Plan Two. Sadly, I can't be sure I have the patience to execute my long-term plan, and I lack the fighting skills to manage the other. Which makes Zaden my best bet.

Either way, I need to get out of here. My heart beats hard for a few seconds, and I get the sense it aligns with the drumming of Zaden's, wherever he is.

"Shit, Scarla," I tell myself. Zaden doesn't even know where I am. How will he rescue me?

Even worse, when I left his castle, he was on his sickbed, still recovering from his last fight with VanDyke. Hopefully, that means VanDyke is weak too, which gives me some chance to escape under my own steam. But, besides the bandage on his cheek, he looked freaking perfect.

Sick of pacing, I sit with my butt against the wall and pull my knees close to my chest for warmth. I hope the patch of rock beneath my ass isn't covered in that green slime. I wiggle and, thankfully, don't slide. I think I'm in the clear.

With my vestigial Gaze at full power, another light suddenly shines through the rock, far above me. It has the quality of an angel's glow but is much dimmer, and I wonder if I'm seeing VanDyke through layers and layers of rock.

But why am I just detecting him now? Does that mean my Gaze is growing stronger? Or has another angel entered the castle?

My breath hitches as the image of Zaden forms in my mind. It vanishes as the cell door slides inward. I leap to my feet, inwardly kicking myself—I didn't hear the footsteps approach. I have to do better.

This time, no blinding glow is exposed behind the door, so I can see instantly that VanDyke isn't present. It's just a pair of guards wearing their gray uniforms with the slash of indigo down each sleeve.

The same guard from before—the one with the prominent eyebrows and general Neanderthal look about him—pulls me to my feet. "You're coming with us," he says, more grunt than words.

I bite back a sarcastic comment. I'll save my backchat for VanDyke. Instead, I go willingly.

Wherever they're taking me can't be worse than this.

Can it?

* * *

The guards lead me up a never-ending set of stone stairs that curls around a central pylon. At least the air is sweet because I'm sucking in lungfuls of it.

Seriously, if I don't emerge all the way up in heaven—or at least as high as the clouds—I want my money back.

"Is it much further?" My thighs ache with the unaccustomed exercise. I can walk horizontally as far as you want, but up and down? No, thanks.

The Neanderthal dude grunts, and the other makes no noise whatsoever.

"Where are we going?" I persist. These guys are more likely to give me honest answers than VanDyke, but they're not talking. Not even a grunt this time. Obviously they've been ordered not to speak to me. Or they're just pricks.

Finally, we emerge into a corridor in the castle proper—no grimy stone floors and poorly lit spaces here. A light gray rug bordered in indigo runs the length of the hallway, and my eyes widen as I pass statues of naked women carved from actual wood and carved busts of some old white dude who VanDyke must consider important.

The outrageous waste of wealth forms a ball of anger in my chest. This is even more lavish than Zaden's castle, and I gave him a real hard time.

It still bugs me. The amount of riches being thrown away here is disgusting when it could be used to make poor lives more bearable.

Intricately woven tapestries along the walls are interspersed with oil paintings depicting long-forgotten scenes of people picnicking outdoors in the midday heat.

337

Can you imagine? Actual people going outside while the sun is shining? Apart from angels and the odd freak like me, nobody can survive full sunlight. It will singe a person's eyebrows right off before boiling their brain in the cauldron of their skull.

I shake my head. Before long, I am deposited through a doorway, and the door slams shut behind me.

I throw an angry glance behind me, but it soon melts from my face at the glorious vision before me. This room is forged from stone but lovingly carved and cleaned. A stone bath sits in the center of the room, filled with steaming water, fragranced with petals and blooms.

A silver panel hanging from the wall is polished to such a high shine that I can see my reflection in it. I quickly glance away, not wanting to face how disgusting I look.

Two maids wearing cream skirts and indigo aprons stand on either side of the bath with their hands folded demurely.

Nobody else is present. This could be my chance to escape—although I'm sure those guards are right outside the door. But before I do anything rash, I need answers.

Seeing the maids has jogged the final missing memory from what happened yesterday. I wasn't alone at the market, I was accompanied by my maid, Molly.

Not just my maid, but maybe my best friend—my list of buddies is rapidly shortening, and Molly is definitely up near the top.

"Where's Molly?" I demand.

One maid, the softer of the two, with slanting eyes and delicate bones, glances nervously at the other. I figure she's the weak link, so I aim my next question at her.

"Molly is the maid who was captured with me, and I need to

know where she is. I need to know that she's all right. So tell me, please, where is she?"

The woman pales, her waxy skin turning almost translucent. Her black eyes dart toward her colleague again, but she doesn't answer my question.

I shrug. "Fair enough, I get it. You're intimidated by my beauty, my beautiful clothes, my general air of superiority. Don't worry about it." I'm wearing filthy rags, my hair sticks out in every direction, my breath is rotten, and I stink—I have never looked worse.

The pale maid's mouth twitches in the beginnings of a smile, and I can see I'm getting through to her.

"Please, just tell me that she's okay, and I promise I won't ask any more questions."

The maid stares at her shoes, resting her focus anywhere but on me.

I sigh. I'll have to think of another way to get the information I need. On the other hand, it's hard not to be enticed by the aromatic steam rising from this hot bath. "I assume this is for me?"

The servant nods. Opening up this trickle of communication feels like a small victory.

I untie my apron around my waist and let it drop to the floor. Instantly, both maids are at my side, helping me out of my clothes.

"I can do it myself." They ignore me, of course, and keep pawing at me until I relent and allow them to unbutton my dress and pull it over my head. They even unhook my bra and tug my panties down, which feels utterly ridiculous.

How do rich people enjoy this?

Honestly, I would so much rather do that myself. Now I'm

standing naked, filthy, and as awkward as fuck in front of two women who barely acknowledge my existence.

Hurriedly, I step into the bath, eager to hide beneath the layered petals on the surface.

Space in the Undercity is limited, and groups of families sleep together, so I'm accustomed to changing near others. But we are all masters at turning our backs and averting our eyes, so the intense focus of these two women is disconcerting.

Heat from the bath scalds my toe when I step in, but I don't let that slow me down. I practically dive under the bath's surface and submerge my entire body for an instant before coming up for air.

The nervous maid glances at her colleague, and I can tell what she's thinking.

Why doesn't the heat burn her?

Perhaps they've heard of my heat resistance, another vestigial power I inherited over the years—in which case, they'd be thinking something different.

So, the rumors are true.

Yes, the rumors are true. My imperviousness to temperature is my most useful skill. Loitering outside as the sun comes up has gotten me out of many a fight in my time. It's my trump card. Also handy when the sun goes down, and the world turns to ice.

I smirk a little, pleased to have confounded these maids.

Soaking in the tub feels magnificent, as though my reserve of happiness is being restored. Every second beneath the hot, fragrant water brings me more contentment. Plus, it signifies that the Count intends to let me live aboveground in a proper bedchamber, possibly with my own personal maids. Plan One is progressing nicely.

Without a word, the nervous maid rubs shampoo into my wet hair and massages my scalp. Now, I hate power imbalance and the whole master-and-slave deal as much as the next girl, but having somebody massage my head is pure heaven and enough to make my ideals fly out the window. I could definitely live like this.

The taller, more self-assured maid brings me a towel and holds it out, expecting me to rise from the bath and into its folds. Well, I decide not to. If she doesn't have the decency to engage me in conversation, I'll happily play dumb.

I ignore her, close my eyes, and sink deeper into the blissful liquid.

The maid clears her throat, and I count that as another victory. Finally, she's made a damn noise. I peer at her through half-open lids, shake my head slightly and resume my repose.

I feel maybe ten percent bad for my behavior—after all, these maids are just following orders. But on the other hand, they have it much better than most poor bastards living outside the castle walls, and they choose willingly to work for a rich asshole like Angel VanDyke.

So, mostly, I feel good.

Until the maid begins tipping buckets of cold water into my bath—that erases my joy real fast.

With as much dignity as I can muster, I rise and step out of the bath into the waiting towel. The taller, crankier servant walks away to find a hairbrush, and I whisper to the other. "Why am I getting this wash? Is something special happening?"

She glances around to make sure her friend won't overhear, then whispers. "You're going to see the angels."

* * *

To keep reading, get your copy of Scar: Fallen Angels Book 2.

* * *

To get my novella set in the fae realm of Caprice for FREE, sign up at https://dl.bookfunnel.com/jtbq9u1oeu or https://zaradusk.com.

Zara x

About the Author

Zara has a pretty sweet life – hubby, kids, and a kick-ass Dyson hairdryer. But that doesn't stop her from inventing new worlds and having steamy affairs with her book boyfriends. Angels and demons and fae, oh my!

Lucky Zara, she gets to spend hours with those sexy beasts every day. The rest of the time she's working in health, negotiating with her kids, and beating her husband to the remote.

But mostly it's angels.

Come along for the ride with Zara and her feisty heroines. You can provide the mulled wine.

You can connect with me on:

- https://zaradusk.com
- https://www.facebook.com/zaraduskauthor
- https://www.tiktok.com/@zaradusk

Subscribe to my newsletter:

- https://zaradusk.com

Also by Zara Dusk

Steamy fantasy romance with bad men and badass women.

Before he can return to heaven, she must kill
Here I am again in a freaking castle, kidnapped by a power-hungry Angel. Only this time, I've swapped out silk sheets and a killer view for a grimy dungeon with no doors. Yay me.

My sexy Angel, Zaden, has no clue where I am, so as much as I'd like to sit around waiting to be rescued, I need another plan. The violent guards and mute servants aren't about to help. And my best—and only—friend is a prisoner too.

I need to get stronger. Hone my vestigial magic and learn how to throw a punch. The world won't know what hit them when I reach full strength.

But first, I need to find the damn door.

He's fated for heaven, but she's doomed for hell

My sexy Angel and I are on a collision course with fate. While he marches towards the heavens in search of the elusive Ring of Roth, I am shackled to the infernal realm, cursed to an eternity of fire and brimstone.

But I won't go down without a fight. I must overthrow the cruel Angels who reign above us.

But with the new power thrumming through my body and recent betrayals burning in my memory, it's hard to remember my noble motives.

All I can focus on is revenge.

The stage is set. The pieces are in motion. The war for justice is about to begin. But no matter the outcome, I can't shake my fears for a future without Zaden. Eternity in hell is nothing compared to eternity without him.

Free prequel novella

https://dl.bookfunnel.com/jtbq9u1oeu

I'm a mortal in a fae realm filled with marvels, like weather that's influenced by the king's mood.

But life isn't all forested streets and magical forests. There's the fact that everybody here treats me like garbage because I'm not fae. The bratty kids I teach in Human Studies are the worst.

When a student is kidnapped, I must tell the fae king. Because of the realm's rules about doing your own dirty work, I have to front up to his terrifying court and spill the beans face to face. I'd rather tango with a tiger. Especially since the missing faeling is the king's nephew.

Judging by the dark clouds in the sky, the king is already in a foul mood. But when he sees me, it'll get a whole lot worse. The sky will probably split in two.